praise for

a lie for a lie

"An addictive thriller about friendship, love, ambition, and revenge, *A Lie for a Lie* has twists you won't see coming and explores what really happens when you get back at someone . . . and when getting what you wish for comes with a high price. I couldn't put it down!"

—**Sara Shepard,** #1 *New York Times* best-selling
author of *Pretty Little Liars*

"*A Lie for a Lie* is juicy, twisty fun that I absolutely could not put down. First-time novelist Jane Buckingham stepped up and hit a homer in her first at-bat, which kinda makes me want to ask @Revenge to go get her too!"

—**David Koepp,** screenwriter of *Jurassic Park* and *Spider-Man*

"*A Lie for a Lie* is a grippy thriller with twisted betrayals, juicy secrets, and deception that will leave you questioning everything you thought you knew. A must-read for fans of Karen McManus and Sara Shepard and anyone looking for a fun read!"

—**Julia DeVillers,** best-selling author of *Trading Faces*;
Liberty Porter, First Daughter; and *Take Two*

"This thriller is so pulse pounding, reading it should count as a cardio workout! If you're into gripping suspense, juicy secrets, and love-to-hate-them characters, dig in! The plot twists will keep you guessing until the very end."

—**Michele Promaulayko,** former editor in chief of *Cosmopolitan* magazine

"A compelling tale that skillfully navigates the complexities of high school life, intensified by the menace of social media. With a gripping narrative that keeps readers on the edge of their seats, Buckingham showcases her talent for crafting captivating stories."

—Alex Morel, author of *Survive*

a lie for a lie

a lie
for
a lie

an @revenge story

jane buckingham

GREENLEAF
BOOK GROUP PRESS

Published by Greenleaf Book Group Press

Austin, Texas
www.gbgpress.com

Copyright © 2024 Jane Buckingham

Distributed by Greenleaf Book Group

For ordering information or special discounts for bulk purchases, please contact Greenleaf Book Group at PO Box 91869, Austin, TX 78709, 512.891.6100.

Design and composition by Greenleaf Book
Cover design by Greenleaf Book Group
Cover image by Alexander Krivitskiy from Unsplash.com

Publisher's Cataloging-in-Publication data is available.

Print ISBN: 979-8-88645-218-1

eBook ISBN: 979-8-88645-219-8

To offset the number of trees consumed in the printing of our books, Greenleaf donates a portion of the proceeds from each printing to the Arbor Day Foundation. Greenleaf Book Group has replaced over 50,000 trees since 2007.

Printed in the United States of America on acid-free paper

24 25 26 27 28 29 30   10 9 8 7 6 5 4 3 2 1

First Edition

For Jack and Lilia, always.

Be kind, for everyone is fighting a hard battle.

—Socrates

It's a beautiful night to die.

We crowd inside the gym. The familiar smell of old tennis shoes and stale sweat follow us to our seats. The cheerleaders are already on the court, tossing a skinny girl in the air. Personally, every time I see a cheerleader fly, I wish the girls catching her would change their minds at the last minute.

SPLAT!

Sorry. Never said I was a nice person.

At seven on the dot, the lights dim, and that stupid techno song they always play before the game comes on — "Heads Will Roll." Fitting, I guess. The cheerleaders do some dance they hope will make it to TikTok. The announcer booms into the loud- speaker. I try to tune him out as soon as he starts blabbering about how these players have gone undefeated. Does he really think we should bow down to them? Last I checked they were just boys, not God's gift to Milford High. Yet we hold up cheesy signs to show our support. Some hold them for their boyfriends. Others for their lat- est boy crush. Those stupid signs turn my stomach. I always want to say, "Do you know who those people even are, deep down? Do you know what they're capable of?"

Smoke fills the stadium. We drum on the bleacher seats, screaming until our voices are hoarse. In a cloud of dry ice, our school's team parades through a bal- loon archway. The announcer names each player along with his stats. Most of the players duck their heads and rush to the sidelines, proud but also not quite sure what to do with all the attention.

But not the last guy. He walks through the archway as the applause roars and spreads out his arms to accept our undying affection. We give him what he wants. We cheer and scream. The announcer reads his list of impressive points. Leading scorer all year. Total powerhouse. Yawn. Our hero.

I check the time. Any minute now.

The other players strip off their warm-up gear and take their seats on the benches, but our star player remains in the center of the court like he's owed this. But as the overhead spotlights gleam against his forehead, a thin bead of sweat forms. It's my first clue. It's happening.

First, his arms droop just a little, like someone has pulled down on invisible strings in his armpits. A confused expression comes over his face as he drops to his knees. Still, most of us still think this is part of his routine. We still cheer.

But then he's on all fours. A few of the players on the sidelines look over, confused. The music throbs. We figure it's nothing serious. But then, the star player pukes up his guts on the shiny school logo at center court, right where the tip-off takes place.

A puddle spreads. It must smell pretty awful, because the player nearest to him makes a grossed-out face and moves away.

The coach runs over with towels. We rise, tip forward, our brows furrowed. Whispers travel down the seats. The coach leans over our star. He puts a hand on the boy's back and says something, tries to get him to stand. But the star's knees buckle. He drops to the floor again in an X and starts to flail. His muscles move uncontrollably. The assistant coach is there, too; he wheels around and shouts something to another player. "Get an ambulance! Shut off that music!"

The techno song stops mid-beat. Voices, shouts, screams fill the gymnasium. We're all on our feet, gawking, wondering what we can do. The coach can't get the star to stop seizing. His pained face is turning blue.

A trainer rushes in. Some medics. A woman runs onto the court, pushing people aside. It's the star's mother. We hear a perverse laugh in the stands—not mine, but hey, I can't be the only one who wanted this. And then, an interesting rumor I hadn't expected starts to swirl—he puked out his intestines. He'd vomited a lung. There's an organ lying there, literally, on the polished wood floor.

"It makes no sense," other people say. "He was fine minutes ago."

When they load the player onto the cot, he's eerily pale and lifeless. We grow hushed, fearful. A few girls burst into tears. His mother walks next to the medics as they wheel him out. I feel bad for her, I guess. I always feel bad for the families, even though it's probably partially her fault. Bad behavior, toxic masculinity—it's learned at home. When a seedling is rotting, all you have to do is look at the tree from which it came. Chances are, there's rot there, too.

Still, I feel a little bad. I have a pretty good feeling how this is all going to end.

How do I know? I put all of this into motion.

I'm the one who got revenge.

It's been real, Milford.

Try not to miss me.

And remember not to lie to me.

one

"Sabrina! This mall has thirty-eight stores, and not a single one sells a decent pair of jeans," my best friend, Emily, grumbles as we stand sideways on the up escalator, peering with doom at the line of neon stores on the mall's second level. "How hard can it be to find a decent pair that don't make me look like a nine-year-old boy?"

"You don't look anything like a nine-year-old boy," I say for the tenth time today and probably thousandth in our friendship. "You've got the body of a supermodel."

Emily sighs. "Nope, models have to be 5'8" and I'm still 5'5"," she says, pushing a lock of her long, frizzy, strawberry-blonde hair out of her face. Changing the subject, she continues, "Anyway, I don't have the slightest clue what to get for my brother." She looks at me coyly. "How about you? Found the perfect gift for O-K?"

I groan. "Do I have to?" I laugh at the nickname Emily and I had given Kaye when she and my dad first started dating two years ago. I know I should be glad that my dad found someone he's happy with. Kaye's pretty and a successful lawyer with plenty of money but . . . ugh. She tries so hard. She's always overdoing the "Don't worry I'm not looking to replace your mom," spiel and doesn't pass up a chance to say, "I know how important it is for you to have special alone time with your dad."

It all feels like she's trying a little too hard and performing for someone. I never quite know how to respond. So, all I ever find myself doing is shrugging, saying, "Okay," and booking it upstairs to my room. Emily and I sort of made a game of it, and now we count how many times and different ways I can say "Oh, Kaye" in a day without her catching on. So far, our record is sixteen.

"Yes . . . no . . . she's the same . . . Parker's home from *Paris* . . ." I roll my eyes.

That's the other thing. Kaye's daughter, Parker, is *also* too perfect. She was two years ahead of me at school and was the "it" girl that practically every boy in the school had a crush on. Parker is smart, popular, and went on to become a three-sport varsity captain after overcoming some childhood illness. She has a hot boyfriend. She just did some impressive language intensive in Paris. *Blah, blah, blah.* Thankfully my dad hasn't asked Kaye to move in yet—she and Parker still live across Milford. I highly doubt Parker remembers me from high school, and it's going to be so awkward when we do get around to having a big family dinner. My plan, of course, is to try and avoid Parker forever, or until Kaye and my dad break up, whichever comes first.

I look at my phone. Still nothing. "Ugh," I moan.

Emily looks over too. "Sabrina, you don't even know if they are sending them today." She knows exactly what's up. I've been moaning about it for hours. "Harvard's totally going to want you. Stop stressing."

Now I'm the one to roll my eyes. "You aren't supposed to tell a person not to stress. It's just as bad as saying *relax.* You're so lucky you didn't apply anywhere early."

"Have you been manifesting it like I told you to?" she asks, as seriously as if she were talking about learning SAT vocab words.

I smile my "not so much" smile. It's sometimes hard to believe two such opposites can be such best friends. I'm the serious, studious one. Practical to a fault, one might say. I'm kind of a parent's dream. I work hard, I don't drink or party, I have literally never even kissed a boy, and my favorite pastime is cleaning my room. Emily, on the other hand, can get As in most subjects without cracking a book but would rather study social media than science. She can recite every marriage, divorce, and product launch in the Kardashian's history, and she knows more TikTok dances than most choreographers. Almost every day after school since fifth grade we've hung out—me studying, Emily scrolling on her phone, and Brooke . . . well, Brooke was a long time ago.

"I think it's a little late for that," I say trying not to make her idea sound as ridiculous as it is. "The decisions are coming out today."

Emily looks like a kid who's just been told there's no Santa. Sometimes I wish I could be as optimistic and, well, unrealistic as Emily.

"You're probably right," she says thoughtfully, but ever the optimist and my greatest cheerleader, she perks up again. "BUT you've got an insane GPA, your scores are like better than anyone's, you run pretty much every club, *and* there's the stuff about your mom for the, you know, emotional points . . ."

I wince a little at her wording, but it's true. Schools like their students to go through a little strife. It shows *resilience*. But you just don't know when it comes to a school like Harvard. *No one* is a shoo-in there. And yes, applying for early action admission, which I've done, helps me, but less than 9 percent of those applicants get in. And only super-qualified kids bother to apply. I've checked the stats. The odds are against me.

"Plus," Emily says, breaking me from my thoughts, "I did your Tarot cards last night, and it said BIG things were ahead." She says this as if she'd gotten an encouraging call from the admissions officer, not a $6.99 deck she bought off Instagram.

"Okay, okay, sorry," I grumble, sliding my phone back in my pocket. I turn it on vibrate, so I can quickly check it in case an alert comes in. I start humming along to the annoying holiday songs that have been playing in the mall since the day after Halloween.

"I'm going to run to the bathroom," Emily says.

I nod and point toward Box Lunch, a kitschy store that sells anything from Slinkies to fake poop to Funko Pops of the *Friends* characters. My eyes keep going back to the fake poop. I'm tempted, but wonder if it would be a little too on-the-nose as a gift for Kaye. Before I can chuckle, worry settles in. I check my phone four more times. I know a watched inbox never pings . . . but I can't help it. I want this so, *so* bad. The only thing I might want more is for my mom to still be alive. But this—Harvard—I need this.

When she returns, Emily's expression shifts as she glances at the Pops

I'm looking at. She picks up one of the doe-eyed Sanderson Sister dolls and smirks. "I don't suppose they have a Kurt Cobain or Nirvana series?"

"How is Charlie these days?" I ask. "Still grunging it up?" Back before he left for boarding school Charlie, Emily's twin, had gone through a full-on '90s phase, complete with flannel shirts, refusing to shower, and blasting '90s alt-rock in his room. Emily would have to scream at him to keep their adjoining wall from shaking when he played it. Which was always.

Emily shrugs. "Well, he seems to shower regularly now, which is an improvement." I know the hurt in her voice is at Charlie, not me. Emily shoves her hands into her pockets. "When he's home, he pretty much just shuts himself into his room."

"Still?" I ask.

"Charlie's just so—I don't know—depressing. Plus, with Tiger Mom asking every second what my grades are, what internship I'm doing this summer, and nagging me to go outside and get some vitamin D while coming up with a cure for cancer, I kind of wish I had thought of leaving first."

I stare at Emily with a "don't even joke about that" look. I don't think I would have made it this long without Emily as my best friend, and I know she feels the same. A few years ago, she and Charlie spent a lot of time together, creating a united front against their helicopter parents. Even though they're twins, they couldn't be more different. Charlie is a computer nerd, more comfortable staring at his screen and talking to online buddies than he is in the real world. They say nerds are cool these days, but Charlie never got the memo.

Before the start of ninth grade, Charlie announced that he'd applied to boarding school upstate. His mom sent him without much complaint. I was shocked she let him go. She had always been strict, but when their dad left, she became even more intensely focused on her kids' achievements as some sort of bellwether of her own success. But Emily felt hurt, like Charlie deserted her too. To fill the space, she spent pretty much most of her time at my house.

"Oh well," she says, picking up on my thoughts. "At least *you'll* never leave me."

"And you'll never leave me!" I say, bumping her hip.

Emily and I are not "popular" girls. But we're not total losers either. I'm more serious, and she's the kind of quirky that not everyone gets. I have a hard time connecting with people, and Emily can try a little too hard. So, we've become each other's lifeline. I know Emily would love it if we suddenly hit the friend lottery and became popular, but the only thing that matters to me is Harvard. I'd rather reorganize my closet then hang out with a bunch of drunk kids who think mastering beer pong is an achievement. The one real party I went to, years ago, was a disaster. I figure there will be plenty of time for parties at college. Though I doubt I'll even go then.

Emily hates talking about college, since it's all her mom wants to talk about. But Emily doesn't have to worry too much. She's gifted at math and science, something she considers more of a curse than a gift, and she plays the flute like a wood nymph. We've talked about me going to Harvard and her going to MIT and then living together off campus after our sophomore year. I would say half of our school thinks we're a couple, but that would assume they've ever thought about us. Which I doubt.

Emily has become a little more adventurous lately—especially with boys. Sometimes I wonder if it's a reaction against her mom being so strict and always saying how awful men are. Emily flirts a lot more than me. She's started wearing tighter jeans and shorter skirts too. She may not be the full-figured Kardashian type, but she's got long, lean legs and big, pouty lips. Unfortunately, what could be sexy on someone else usually comes off as gangly and clownish on her.

When I glance over, Emily is staring at her phone.

"What?"

Emily shakes her head. "Nothing." But I can see the corners of her mouth quirking into a smile.

"A text?" I ask. "Maybe from . . . *Jeremy?*"

Redness creeps into her cheeks. Jeremy is Emily's friend from band. Well, she *says* he's a friend. I try to sound as lighthearted as possible as I say, "I *saw* you guys coming out of the orchestra room on Thursday afternoon looking a little . . . *disheveled.*"

Emily's eyes pop. "You did?"

I nod. "What about Bennett? Didn't you guys make out after homecoming?"

"That was *one* kiss." Emily puckers her mouth like she sucked on a lemon. "I don't know what I was thinking. Bennett was a total dud . . . but . . . I *really* like Jeremy. Even if he is kind of a loser."

I try not to roll my eyes. Emily moves from boys as quickly as she does her hobbies. And each time, the new guy's "the one." Not to be an armchair psychiatrist, but it's pretty clear she's looking to replace the love of her dad, who pretty much up and left with his assistant and now has twin toddlers: Emily and Charlie 2.0. Emily jokes about it, but I know it hurts her. Of course, I'm one to talk. I had the opposite reaction. Once I lost my mom, I never wanted to feel that kind of pain again, which is pretty easy if you never put yourself out there or let yourself feel anything.

"Why didn't you tell me about him?" I ask, kind of annoyed. We don't keep things from each other.

"Well," she pauses, and I can tell she seems worried she's upset me, "you've been so worried about Harvard . . . and . . . I guess I just didn't want you to think I . . ." She sighs. "I didn't want you to think I was going to leave you like Brooke did us."

I shrug, trying not to take it too personally. I guess if there's a leader in our relationship, it's me. Not that Emily blindly follows or anything; it's just that I'm the sensible one. The one the teachers love, the one who never makes a misstep. And if I'm honest, a lot *is* about me. My mother dying. My dad dating. Me desperate to go to Harvard. Me making us study. Me making us do community service. Me choosing what clubs to do. Yet I have to admit I'm a little jealous. I'd love some excitement in my life. But it scares me and I'm just not sure where it would fit. I'm glad for Emily.

"Well, if you *really* want to know . . ." she teases. Then, gushing about how she and Jeremy kissed in the music room, she adds: "It was really sweet."

"Em!" I smack her arm. "Tell me everything!"

Emily puts down the rainbow wig she had been trying on and looks down. "Well . . . something happened last week that you won't like." She glances around nervously, bottom lip in her mouth.

I lean in, eager yet cynical. I mean, we're talking about Emily. How bad could it be?

And then she said it: "We took gummies right before rehearsal. Like, just one."

"As in *weed* gummies?" I try to rein in my emotions. "Em! You could have gotten expelled!"

"See! I knew you'd be all judgy." Emily lowers her head. Sometimes I feel more like her older sister than her best friend. "But it was so harmless! Like I said, it was just one." She trails off and shrugs. "Are you mad?"

I can tell Emily is a little embarrassed, but also a little proud. And . . . *am* I mad? I feel betrayed because she's only telling me now. And worried about her being so reckless. And surprised at her because I never thought she'd do something like that. Kissing is one thing. But drugs? At school?

I sigh. "I just don't want you to get in trouble."

"It was just once. Charlie has them tucked away in his room. And Jeremy said it would relax us."

I scoff.

Emily gives me a strange look. "You're not the only one with stress."

I try not to laugh. The last time Emily stressed was when she thought her mom wasn't going to let her watch the *Wednesday* finale because it was a school night. "What gives, Em? Your mom driving you crazy again?"

Emily stops a moment. "What? No. I mean, she's awful as always."

My knee-jerk reaction is to envy Emily because she still has a mom, but I know that's not fair. Mrs. Simmons is pretty intense. She loves that Emily and I are friends, so she's always nice around me. If Emily misses a music lesson, Mrs. Simmons loses it. When Emily gave up competitive swimming in seventh grade, Mrs. Simmons enrolled her with a sports psychologist to talk her out of it.

I wait for Emily to share why she's feeling stressed this time, but her attention is now on a kiosk that sells blinged-out cell phone cases. That's Emily.

"Well, thank God no one saw you." I say, trying to seem light and cool. "So . . . was it fun? The gummies?"

Emily thinks about it for a moment. "I didn't really feel anything. Jeremy said he did, but I think he was exaggerating." She holds her hand out in front of her face and says in a stoner boy voice, "He was like, 'Whoa! I'm so stoned.'" She giggles, but then looks anxious. "I laughed at him. Maybe I shouldn't have. I hope he didn't think I was making fun of him. Though it *was* funny. Do you think I'm out of his league?"

I roll my eyes, and then we're laughing again. Well . . . I'm trying to laugh. Part of me feels uncomfortable. I know I should be happy that Emily's having fun. But gummies? At school? I've been on the student council since ninth grade and on the honor board since junior year. We do our best to be fair, but drugs at school are a quick path to getting expelled. And Emily knows it.

Just then, someone whips past us from the other direction. At first, all I see is a flash of red felt. Someone slams into my side. Whoever it is backs up, several shopping bags flying from her hands.

"What the—?" she shrieks, standing back.

She looks at me, and I look at her. My heart sinks. Long blonde hair. A glint of straight, white teeth. Oh, great. Brooke Mills. Our ex-best friend. The last person I want to see.

"Um," I say, my cheeks turning red. "Sorry. Let me help—"

"I've *got* it," Brooke loops the handles over her wrists and tilts up her chin.

"Just watch where you're going!" Her idiot boyfriend, Finn, smirks at me while clipping me on the shoulder.

Emily takes my arm and pulls me into the closest store. Squishamals is full of squishy plush toys shaped like animals, fruits, other foods, and holiday designs. Most of the people in the store are eight-year-old girls. Great, and now Brooke thinks we still go here.

I grab an avocado plushie and squeeze it hard. I'm not the kind of person who carelessly bumps into people. I look where I'm going. Always. And of course, the one time I don't, it had to be Brooke. And Finn.

"Come on." Emily heads in the direction of the escalator. I walk briskly to catch up, eager to leave the embarrassment from bumping into them behind me.

Just before we step onto the down escalator, I stop walking, causing Emily to bump right into me.

"Ow! Seriously?"

All I can do is point. Brooke and Finn aren't alone. Emily looks on as the couple rejoin their little clique. I don't know why I'm so surprised to see her there. Brooke always seems to travel in a pack, and the food court used to be one of her favorite hangouts. Guess it still is.

We move to the side to let others in, and I catch us both staring over the balcony at the group below. I look over at Emily; she seems entranced by them. Her face is twisted into a snarky smile. *Is she talking about us? I bet she is. Or maybe she doesn't think we're worth the effort.* I guess it doesn't matter. Either way I feel small.

The kids Brooke is with are part of our school's popular group—they call themselves "the OGs." Like it's some great club you get to be in. Who knows what it stands for. The *Obviously Greats?* The *Only Gorgeouses?* From what I can tell, all they do is go to parties, get drunk, cheat on one another—oh, and act as gatekeepers, narks, and bullies. When we were in eighth grade, Brooke, Emily, and I laughingly dubbed the group "the Obnoxiously Grotesque." Of course, that was before Brooke started dating Finn Walters and became one of them.

Brooke and Finn are the pair any high school would want as their homecoming royalty. Tall, chiseled, gregarious, and a total jerk—it doesn't get more OG than Finn Walters. Emily shakes her head. I can tell she's seen enough.

And then Brooke whispers in his ear, and then he swings her around and kisses her on the lips.

I make a little snuffling noise out of my nose. "Kill me if *I* ever do that in public." It's doubtful that will happen, of course. I'll probably never have a boyfriend.

"I can't believe they've been together three years," Emily muses. She bites a fingernail. "I bet they cheat on each other."

I raise my eyebrows in question. Does she know something? Emily always seems to be in on the gossip.

I look back over at the group. I know who most of them are, even if they have no clue who I am. Finn and Brooke, Grant and his girlfriend Charlotte, Lily and her girlfriend Emma, Sketch, Mike, Tobey, Tess, and her boyfriend Jake. A lot of the basketball players and some junior girls who all seem interchangeable with long, straight hair, crop tops, and baggy jeans. Out of the corner of my eye, I notice Emily looking at Charlotte kind of wistfully.

"What?" I ask, an edge in my voice.

"Nothing." Emily sounds sheepish. "Her hair is just so gorgeous. I wish I had hair like that instead of this." She holds up a frizzy curl.

"Pay thousands of dollars for extensions, and it too can be yours," I joke.

Emily laughs a little. "You're probably right."

But then the piped-in holiday music stops, with a bit of speaker feedback, and comes back on . . . but clearly different. Though the tune is "Jingle Bells," the words are wrong, and it's louder than usual. Slowly, we all start picking up on the words as the verses keep repeating . . .

> *Dashing through high school, in a secret love affair,*
> *Falling for two girls, but it's a risky dare.*
> *He's dating his true love, but with another at the lake,*
> *Trying to juggle both and hoping not to break.*
> *Oh, stupid boy, cheating boy, thinks that he's God's gift,*
> *But let's just see what happens now that we know Grant's a*
> *piece of . . .*

The song cuts out just before the expletive and starts again at the top. Then as quickly as it started the fake "Jingle Bells" disappears and is replaced by the regular holiday soundtrack.

All eyes are now on Grant and Charlotte. The look on Grant's face is enough to convince anyone watching that the song is on to something. Charlotte, her face a cross between disbelieving and horrified, realizes there's a group staring at her and takes her tray, which looks to have some sort of taco bowl and beverage, and dumps it on Grant's lap, before running off in tears, followed by Brooke and Tess.

"Daaaaaaammmmmm," Finn proclaims loudly, while the other guys are laughing at a humiliated and now fully covered-in-food Grant who is busy trying to clean himself up.

"Oh. My. GOD!" Emily looks almost awestruck. "That could be the best Revenge yet! Taking on the OGs? That's brave."

I bite my lip. @Revenge is our school's anonymous gossip account that has been circulating since the beginning of this year. At first, they would just post salacious tidbits about students at Milford High, but lately, @Revenge has upped its game. Rumor has it that if a student has an issue with someone and wants payback but doesn't want to get in trouble, they can DM @Revenge, and Revenge will carry out something for them. The "revenges" are all little pranks—and they often get a laugh or a groan, and they definitely embarrass their intended victim. The acts are usually pretty funny and well deserved. Elisa Suarez, who had used "period pains" as an excuse to NEVER do PE, wound up with a huge red stain on her bright white jeans one morning as she walked out of a full school assembly and kept screaming it was just ketchup. Ben Kong discovered during a calc final that all his pencils had been painted over with clear nail polish and wouldn't write after he had offered to take, then refused to share, the communal class notes with his study group.

From what I knew, the revenge wasn't guaranteed. Revenge must deem the reason for punishment worthy, and there's probably a long waiting list. No one knows who runs it, if it's one person or many. But they're kind of becoming a cult hero giving payback wherever it's due. I think it's sort of dumb and seems like a one-way ticket to the principal's office. I don't follow the account. I tend to stay away from trouble.

But Emily follows it. She's looking at her phone now. "Knew it. It *was* Revenge. There's a new post." She shows me the screen. On it is a series of black squares, all labeled with a single number in consecutive order. The first post is *1*, the second is *2*, and so on. The latest post bears the number *14*. "Revenge posts when there's a new prank. It's gotta be the fake song. The timing works." Emily bites her lip. "I wonder who Grant's cheating on Charlotte *with?*"

I point at the numbers in each of the squares. "Wait, there have been *fourteen* acts of revenge?" How does Revenge even have the time?" I turn away from the screen. "I don't know why you even follow this. The teachers have got to be on to it, right? What if they're tracking who's looking at it?"

"If that's the case, then half the school would get in trouble." Emily slips her phone back into her pocket. "Frankly, I think most people think Revenge is kind of a beast! I mean, calling out *Grant*! I heard this rumor that some of the staff at school are looking the other way about the account because, for the most part, Revenge is doing more good than harm."

"So . . . who ordered the prank?"

"Who knows? Looks like Charlotte for sure was in the dark. We'll never know. It's not like Revenge ever reveals their source." She looks at me excitedly. "A lot of people think it's Ryder Cross . . ."

I shrug. Ryder Cross is our school's biggest agent of anarchy. In middle school, the boys' bathroom caught fire, and although no one could prove Ryder did it, he bragged about it all the time. He wasn't a bully—more of a loner—but people walked on eggshells around him regardless because his moods were so unpredictable. He'd been suspended so many times I was surprised he hadn't been expelled. That was really all I knew about Ryder, though. It wasn't like we ran in the same academic circles.

A crowd has gathered around Grant. Whispering. Giggling. Wondering why, just like we were wondering. I half expect to see some girl, hiding in the shadows, snickering—and Ryder Cross, for that matter.

A security guard rushes into the atrium and starts breaking up the tight circle. "Okay, everyone. Nothing to see here."

We're watching from above, but seeing the security guard causes Emily and me to hurry along. There's a new energy buzzing, though; what we've seen is strange but kind of thrilling. "I wonder how they got into the sound system. It's wrong, but also kind of genius."

"Maybe Revenge is super techy," Emily muses.

My phone starts to vibrate. I fumble with it in my pocket, hurriedly whipping it out to look at the screen. And then, the world vaporizes around me. It's the email I've been waiting for. *Harvard University Admissions Board.*

"Oh my God, oh my God," I whisper, stopping short. "Emily!"

Emily looks at me. "The email?"

I nod. I look around me, making a mental note of exactly what I'm seeing. *I will always remember this. Standing in front of Hot Topic. The smell of hot pretzels in the air.* I will tell my children about this someday maybe. *My* grandchildren. I will tell this in a TED Talk, in a boardroom, standing in front of Congress: *This is where I was when I found out I was admitted to*

Harvard University—the dream I'd worked so hard for, the dream I never gave up on, the dream I just had to have. My mother's dream.

With a trembling finger, I press on the email. But the words swim in front of me, making no sense.

Sabrina, thank you for your interest in Harvard . . .

. . . record number of applicants . . .

. . . tough choices . . .

Deferred.

two

No. NO! NOOOOOOOO!

I can feel myself breaking into a sweat, my heart beating faster, the panic coming on. Deferred? This is red alert. I mean, RED ALERT. Without thinking, without saying a word, I run away from Emily in the middle of the mall.

"Sabrina?" she cries, chasing after me. "Sabrina! Stop! Wait!"

"I have to go," I blurt out. "I just . . . I can't . . ."

I rush off. Emily chases after me, but her clunky heels only take her so far. I keep running. And running. As fast and as far as my feet will take me.

Emily probably thinks I'm ditching her. I'm not ditching her—well, I *am*, but she's my ride, so it's not like I'm leaving her without a way to get home or anything. I just have to get out of here. I can't be around anyone. I can't breathe. I'm sweating. And I feel like I'm going to throw up. I've had panic attacks since my mom died . . . but this time, it feels more intense. Worse than ever. Like I'm having an actual heart attack.

The mall isn't far from my house, so I slow to a walk after I realize Emily's out of earshot. Crossing the parking lot, I turn off the ringer on my phone.

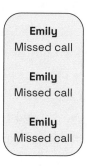

Emily
Missed call

Emily
Missed call

Emily
Missed call

I know she's worried. I'll explain everything once I wrap my mind around it. But right now, I feel too ashamed. Too miserable. Too empty.

At the edge of the parking lot, I look at Harvard's email again. *Deferred.* DEFERRED.

I touch my face with my hands to make sure it's still there. My cheeks feel like rubber. My eyes are squeezed closed so tightly they ache.

What did I do wrong? I did it all. Everything. All of it. I did everything right. What didn't I do?

I've never felt so rejected. So stupid. So *incompetent.* So lost. I picture some jerk in the admissions office taking one look at my application and saying, "What?" before tossing it in the trash. I can see him raising his brows at my audacity. *Why does* she *think she'd get in? Just because her mommy who wanted her to go there died? She's a dime a dozen!*

. . .

I'd first visited Harvard's campus the summer after sixth grade. My mom brought me. She told me she'd wanted to be a doctor since she was a kid. She wanted to join Doctors Without Borders and travel the world. She had gotten accepted into Harvard, but her parents couldn't afford it, so she went to University of Connecticut. That's where she met my dad. And when she got pregnant with me, she dropped out of med school. She and my dad stayed in Connecticut, and she became a nurse.

It wasn't that she wasn't happy, she told me during that trip. She loved me and my dad and our life. She just felt like she'd missed out by not going to Harvard and joining Doctors Without Borders. She told me the experiences you have in Doctors Without Borders are "the best" and something you can take with you anywhere in life. She called these experiences "calling cards" to use in any situation. These calling cards are unique in that they come from a part of a world people like us don't usually travel to. These cards are for a world where people dress up and meet other impressive people. A world where only good things happen. A world behind wrought iron gates that keep out the nasty people and problems beyond.

My mom died only a few months later. Our trip to Harvard was one of the last days I remember—really remember—with her. And I guess somehow, in my weird brain, I linked going to Harvard with being with my mom. Achieving what she hadn't. Breaking away from my family's bad luck. So, from then on, that was my future, the future I worked toward. It's taken a lot of backbreaking hard times. Hours and hours of homework. Sessions with tutors. Begging Dad for prep courses that cost way too much. Giving up parties and trips and dances.

I don't need people. They're too fickle and can go away at any minute. But Harvard. Going to Harvard would last forever. And I need it as much as air.

· · ·

The whipping wind stings my face. I wish I could cry, but I can't. I haven't been able to since my mom died. I always said I cried so much that day that I ran out of tears. But the *panic* is starting to creep back in. A heavy, insistent feeling that grows stronger with each breath.

I walk up the front steps of my house, just off our little town's main drag. The panic attack after running practically a mile leaves a sweat-soaked sweatshirt and wet hair, now basically dripping icicles. I've had these attacks ever since my mom died, and they've intensified as school (and life) have gotten harder. But today's felt different—panic mixed with the added gut punch of failure. I sometimes thought the attacks were a reminder not to let my guard down, to keep working, keep going. Today I realize they were just an early warning sign of what true defeat would feel like—a physical sign of all of my deficiencies.

The porch light is on, and the decorated Christmas tree glows through the front window. The scent of pine from the live wreath hanging on the front door is festive and familiar, but I feel no holiday joy. Instead, a pang of sorrow smacks me sideways: Before I left today, I thought I'd be returning triumphant, *a brand-new member of the Harvard class of 2028.*

And now?

Bells tied to the doorknob announce my arrival. Our dog, a scruffy mutt named Riley, leaps at my shins, yipping playfully. I gently nudge him away, not in the mood for his enthusiasm. I head for the stairs, trying to sneak up undetected.

But then there's a *POP* from the kitchen, and my father strides into the hall. He's beaming and holding a bottle of just-opened champagne. I watch as the fizzy liquid bubbles over the side of the bottle.

"Well?" He rushes toward me.

My gaze darts between him and the champagne bottle. Is that . . . for *me*? I'd told him the early decision emails were coming today. I also said I was feeling confident. I'd said it with *arrogance*. And once again, the gods had cursed me for it.

Some of the champagne starts gushing onto the wood floor. *Just tell him.* I can talk to my dad, can't I? But truth is I sort of can't. He just lets me be. Because I do the right thing. I work hard. I don't cause problems.

Someone steps up behind him. Kaye's hourglass figure is draped in a swishy, casual jumpsuit, probably from some designer brand I can't even pronounce, and she's wearing low, gray suede boots—an outfit more for an eighteen-year-old than a forty-eight-year-old. Her smile is wide—almost too big for her face. I clamp my lips shut. I can't give her the satisfaction of knowing that I've failed. I just *can't*.

Kaye smiles that sickly sweet smile. "Hope it's okay that I'm here! I'm just so excited for you!"

"What's that for?" I hear myself blurt.

My dad looks puzzled. "Are you kidding me? Early admission? Only the most important day of your young adult life. At least that's what you said this morning."

"Well, all I can tell you is today's not it."

All eyes turn to me. I hate lying. I mean, what's the point? Once you tell one lie, you have to come up with a second lie to cover up the first one. And if you forget what you said about the second lie, you have to create a third lie to explain away the other two. Eventually they all catch up to you, and you just get found out.

Dad never lets up. I force a smile and try to play it casual. "Well, I didn't get anything yet, so I guess I got the date wrong."

I watch as my dad sets the open champagne bottle on the counter. I hate seeing him like this. Kaye sets down the champagne flutes, confused.

"That's not like you to forget something this important, Sabrina."

Oh God, he knows. Keep calm. You're just paranoid. No way he knows. People get dates wrong all the time.

A bead of sweat runs down my forehead. Noticing the sweat on my brow, my dad studies me. The Big Lie is weighing on me. The one I haven't told yet. The one that still has my heart racing. The one that makes me jump when Kaye says, "Well, we shouldn't let all these bubbles go to waste. Why don't we have an early toast, to your early admission, Sabrina?"

My dad is still looking at me. He looks more concerned than suspicious. I let out a deep breath. He's not going to grill me. He bought it.

With my next lie teed up, I clutch my stomach for effect. "I'm not feeling that great. I think I'm just going to lie down for a bit. Think I ate something funky at the mall."

"Oh no!" Kaye raises her hands to her face in distress and steps away from me. "I hope it's not contagious. . . . Parker just got back, and I'd hate to ruin her vacation . . ." Her voice trails off but her subtext is clear. I am a pariah.

If only she knew.

"Can we get you anything?" my dad asks, breaking into my thoughts. "Pepto? Ginger ale?"

Well, since you're asking . . . I wouldn't mind a redo on this day. Or maybe even my life. Or if you prefer, you could ask Harvard to change their mind. That would be great. Or if that's too much trouble, just bring me a hole in the earth I can fall through. I'm not picky.

It takes energy to be sarcastic. And I was already using my dwindling reserves to stand up.

"No thanks, I'm good," I say shakily, doing my best to hold it together as I start up the stairs.

I walk into my room and close the door softly behind me. I set my purse down on my desk and let out another deep breath.

Deferred.

My eyes land on my once-prized Harvard pennant. The one we bought when we visited the campus with my mom that summer before she died. The one I looked at when doing homework. The one I touched for luck this morning on my way downstairs. The one I thought would hang over my desk in my dorm room. The one I would pass on to my own daughter someday.

Deferred.

Rage fills me to my fingertips. I lean forward and yank the pennant off the wall, sending pushpins flying across the room. I'll probably step on them days from now and puncture my feet. Stifling a scream, I open my desk drawer and grab my scissors. I start cutting up the pennant, and I keep going until the entire pennant is in pieces on my bedroom floor.

I try to tell myself it doesn't matter. But it feels like there's an elephant sitting on my chest and a walnut lodged in my throat. The sorrow hits me—and then the shame.

I sink to the floor and find myself absently picking up the pieces of my pennant and tossing them into the wicker trash can beneath my desk. Even with my voice screaming in my head, I still can't tolerate a mess.

You see? You aren't good enough. You shouldn't have even tried. You should have known better. You failed. Again.

• • •

An old memory surfaces, eager to pull me under to its murky depths. It's the one I try, over and over to push further down, since it always feels like a surprise attack.

It's always the same. I'm twelve years old. My dad's already at work. I'm downstairs, dressed, expecting to find my mom humming, making eggs or pancakes or some smiley face plate out of fruit. But all I find is an empty kitchen.

"Mom! Mom! Hurry up! We're going to be late!"

I start to wonder if maybe she overslept when I hear the blow-dryer blasting. Why did I always have to be the responsible one? But then I see her on the bathroom floor, fully dressed, like she's sleeping.

I call 911. They ask me if she is breathing. It was only then that I notice that her chest isn't moving. I break out into a sweat and start to shake. They tell me to sit tight. They are just minutes away. I call my dad. I call the school to tell them my mom was dead, and I wouldn't be in until the afternoon. Somehow, in my twelve-year-old brain, I think everything will be fine by lunchtime. I turn off the blow-dryer and put it back in the drawer. I put the caps on the jars and tubes of creams and tidy them up. Order. I need order. My mom can't be dead. This is all a mistake.

But it wasn't a mistake. I fidget during the funeral service. My dress is stiff. My shoes are too tight. The lady behind me is sucking on hard candy, and I want to tell her to be quiet, they're talking about my mom, but I try to stay still as I wring my hands in my lap. The gossip grows louder. I hear the whispers and try to tune them out, but they may as well be shouting.

"Maybe if they had found her sooner."

"Maybe if she hadn't fallen on such a hard surface," said another.

Maybe, I think, *maybe if I hadn't wasted time changing my stupid sweater I could have gone up there sooner. Maybe if I had heard the hair dryer going I would have gone in there before I went downstairs. If I had caught her in time maybe I could have saved her.*

Maybe.

Things took on a different shape after the experience. There was BMD and AMD. Before Mom Died and After Mom Died. I had always been more of an observer than a participant, but I became even more focused. Every conversation, every interaction, felt like a bad movie. I could recite the lines, but I couldn't feel them. So, I buried myself in acceptable activities. I was always studying, working. I was happiest in my house.

I remember opening the fridge a few weeks after Mom died only to find what looked like a chemistry experiment gone wrong. I can still remember the putrid smell of soured milk, moldy fruit, and beef filled with maggots.

I threw everything in the fridge into the trash and scrubbed every inch of the refrigerator until my hands were raw. I was hyperventilating and my hands were shaking. What I didn't realize is I was having my first panic attack.

Just breathe. Whatever this is, breathe.

Mom was gone. I was in charge. And now, if a panic attack came on, I would clean the grout in the tiles with a Q-tip, or scrub the fridge to make sure it sparkled, or reorder the clothes in my dad's closet so they were color-coded. Everyone applauded how grown-up I seemed, how strong I was, how helpful I was to my dad by taking on the cooking and cleaning and, well, everything else. If I had been someone else, I might have gotten into drugs, or worse, but my addictions were more acceptable.

I liked the quiet. I liked the lack of performance. I've lived in that silence since she died. Our house is always quiet. Me in my room. My dad at work or in his room. There is no laughter. No joy. My dad tries. I know he does, but he is heartbroken too. He loves me, but he just isn't *that* kind of dad. We feel more like roommates than father and daughter. I feel comfortable only with Emily (and Brooke back when we were all BFFs); they let me sit and do my work or organize their desks and medicine cabinets and not constantly ask how I was doing.

I run scenarios in my brain for every possible disaster. *What if my dad died? Or Emily died? What if I failed the bio test? What if we ran out of milk and I needed to make something for the bake sale?* I am always prepared. I always have a plan. I don't do something unless I know the outcome—or at least how to prevent a bad outcome. Yet somehow, somehow, I haven't let my brain prepare for this.

So. Shame. On. Me.

I take a few heaving breaths, then push myself up to sit. *Get a grip. You can't wallow like this.* I had diligently filled out other applications, each in its own well-marked folder with tabs indicating what still needed to be done. But everyone had been so sure I would get in. My dad, my guidance counselor, my tutor. *Not* getting in was too much to bear. So, I didn't do the essays. I didn't really think I would need to. I shouldn't have let my guard down. I should have known better. I should have known good things don't happen to me.

I glance at the Harvard University calendar again. December's photo is of the clock tower at sunset. I study today's date. December 21st. Got the date wrong. I wish.

I have less than two weeks to put together all of my applications for the regular deadlines. Less than two weeks to write convincing essays, to gather more recommendations and more copies of transcripts. Who am I going to get to write my letters of recommendation? It's not like I can ask Principal Morgan or my college advisor for another one. I'm too embarrassed to let them know I didn't get in. After bleeding Harvard's crimson and black for years now, who's going to believe I'd decided to honor colors from another school? If anyone even lets me in.

Don't think like that. I rise to my feet. Of course, another college will let me in. But it won't be Harvard. *I'm sorry, Momma. I failed. Again.*

three

I startle awake in a puddle of drool. My head is on my desk. My computer screen is dark, but my bedroom door is open, meaning my father must have come in here at some point last night. I look around frantically, praying he didn't notice what's left of the Harvard pennant in my trash. I did all my applications online, and my screen darkened hours ago, so I doubt he noticed anything. Meaning my secret is safe. For now.

My phone lets out an annoyingly empowered clip of Lizzo's "Good as Hell." *Emily.* I try to ignore the call. First one goes to voicemail. Then a text.

> I know ur there Bri Pick up!

She calls back with FaceTime. I take it, because I know she won't give up. I cringe when I see myself. I look even worse than I thought.

"*There* you are. I've been so worried!"

I rub my eyes. I don't even have to say anything, because she rushes on. "If this is what I think, that's just wrong, Sabrina. *Wrong.* Unfair. Was it . . ."

"Deferred," I say miserably, cutting her off before she can ask if I was flat-out rejected.

"Oh!" she sounds almost relieved. "I thought you got rejected!" *Thanks for the confidence, Emily.* "You'll *definitely* get in in the spring."

"Did your Tarot cards say that?" I scoff. And then I realize I am just being a bitch to my best friend. Quick to change the subject, I add, "Less than 10 percent of deferred applicants get in during the regular admission round."

"But *you* will," Emily says softly.

There's a long pause. It comforts me that Emily is just as stunned. She always believed I could do this.

"Are you still coming today?" she asks in a small voice. "I mean, you don't have to. I totally get it if you're not feeling up to it."

"Coming to what?"

"The drive at St. Paul's . . ."

I look over at the Harvard calendar on my wall. There in the Saturday square, in big red letters I see:

ST. PAUL'S CHARITY DRIVE

The last thing I want right now is to go out and be with people. It's hard for me on a good day. But now I feel like the shame is a smell on me, a film I can't wash off. Also, I got far less done on the applications last night than I'd hoped. I need to stay here and focus. But I'm not a flaker. I do what I say I'm going to do. I'm strong. That's what everyone tells me. Maybe it would be good to be around Emily. She'll help me through this.

• • •

A half hour later, Emily pulls into the driveway. I've been watching at the window, and I hurry out quickly, grateful that by the time I got up, my father and Kaye were already out.

I slump into the front seat of Emily's Jeep. She gives me a look that borders on pity, and I bristle, but then she leans over and gives me a huge hug. "I totally blame Mercury being in retrograde."

I stiffen in her arms. The hug was too much. Usually Em has me laughing with all her woo-woo talk, but I honestly can't deal with it right now.

"So, who got in instead of me?" I figure she'll know.

She looks away. "I haven't heard much. I know Harrison got rejected, and Anabel also got deferred."

This makes me feel a little bit better. Misery loves company. Maybe it means I'll have a better chance in the spring. After all, colleges only take a small number of students from the same school. Sure, you're competing with the rest of the world, but really your stiffest competition are your classmates applying along with you.

"Do you think Kaye and Parker will be here?" Kaye is on the committee too; it seems like every mom is on it. Well, except mine.

I shrug. "I hope not. She tried to get my dad to donate a bunch of my mom's stuff from the garage." Emily's mom wanted us to join the committee, and though Emily wasn't into it, I made her. Colleges like to see that. Sometimes I'm not sure whether I want to do something because I actually want to, or because I know I should.

Emily looks at me with wide eyes. "*No.*"

"Didn't happen." I reply. Kaye can have my dad, I *guess*, but she'll never get rid of my mom. *Ever.*

We pull up to where the charity drive is taking place. Rowena, the head of the nonprofit, stands in the parking lot, wearing a long trench coat and rain hat even though it's sunny. She's directing the traffic of people who are already here to donate their old clothes and other items to the cause. When she sees Emily and me, she beams and claps her hands.

"Girls, *so* glad you are here!" She looks for our assignments on the clipboard "Emily, you're inside sorting. Sabrina, you're out here taking the donations."

"Oh." I'm disappointed. Emily picks up on it and squeezes my arm. "I'll sneak back out when Inspector Gadget isn't looking," she whispers. And then she heads through the front doors, leaving me alone with my misery.

I pull my coat around me and look at the line of cars here to donate their items. Rowena points me in the direction of a tall boy. "Just grab boxes out of people's trunks and put them on the steps of the rec center. Someone will take them and bring them inside."

I trudge over. Someone's trunk is open, so I start lugging boxes and placing them on the ground. The car rolls forward. The woman in the driver's seat, I notice, is chatting with her middle-school-aged daughter, and they're both laughing. I feel a pang of sadness. How nice to be having a normal, happy Saturday. How nice to have a *mom*.

I move on to the next car. One of the boxes is so heavy my knees buckle under the weight.

"I got it," a boy's voice says behind me.

"It's fine," I insist.

"No, seriously. I've got it."

Almost dropping the box, I snap, "No, actually, *I've* got it."

He backs away, hands up. Clearly my tone was harsher than I meant. "Just trying to help. Sorry, Sabrina."

He knows my name. I turn and get a good look at him and almost lose my grip on the box again. Jake Cano, a senior, his soft brown eyes and curly hair mashed down by a ski cap. Another OG. Varsity basketball player.

Jake puts his hands on his hips and says, as if reading my mind, "We were in AP chem together last year. And economics. I sat in front of you."

Heat rises to my cheeks. Of course, I remember: a straight back sitting in a desk, long legs sticking into the aisle. I stare stupidly, not knowing what to say.

"You probably never noticed me," he teases when I don't reply. "You were always laser-focused. Which is probably why you always get hundreds, right?" And he sort of laugh-coughs like he's a little shy.

I run my tongue over my teeth and play his words back in my head. Is he making fun of me? It didn't really sound that way. But what then? And before I can even process that, it hits me again. All the studying, all the focus. It didn't matter. I wasn't laser-focused *enough*. I think of the Harvard admissions officer who reviewed my application. I see her as a stern, pinched-faced woman, gleefully stamping my application with *deferred*.

That walnut inside my throat swells. I can feel myself starting to break into a sweat. *No*, I tell myself. *No, no, no, not now.*

I turn away, willing myself to push down the feelings, but for all sorts of reasons, I can't. I need to sit down. Now I'm shaking, and my heart is beating so fast and loud I'm sure he can hear it.

Jake can sense I'm uncomfortable. "I didn't mean anything by the focused stuff. It was a compliment, seriously."

"It's okay. I get it." His kindness makes me feel worse.

"Sit here," he says quickly, ushering me away from the line of cars. "The other volunteers can handle this for a sec."

"You don't have to—"

"No big deal. Really."

He leads me to the stone steps outside the rec center, away from prying eyes. I don't know why I follow, but it feels nice that someone else is making the decisions—especially to steer me away from everyone watching.

"So," he says, after a minute or two of awkward silence. "People sure have a lot of junk in their trunk." As soon as he says it, he almost recoils at his own pun. Funny to see an OG a little off-kilter.

I bark out a laugh. "You don't have to babysit me. I'm fine." My heart rate is slowing a little, but I'm so hot, I have to take my coat off.

"I know," he says quietly, and kindly. But he doesn't get up to leave like I expect.

The scent of fabric softener and detergent wafts off Jake's clothes. His legs are so long that his knees jut up awkwardly. I notice his jeans have small, patchy holes, and he's wearing one of his socks inside out. Not that it matters. I suddenly remember that I've seen him walking arm in arm with a petite, perky junior named Tess Larsen. Being partnered is almost mandatory for an OG. Plus, a cute guy like him wouldn't be single.

"Just . . . bad news," I admit in a small voice. "But I'm okay. Really."

"Yeah, I get it." He nods quietly. "You don't have to be okay, though. No one has it all together. For real."

I look at him skeptically.

"Honestly," he says conspiratorially, "I'm sort of grateful. Makes me feel more normal."

"Glad I can be of service." Then I twist my mouth and ask, "Is every-thing . . . okay?" I mean, problems don't seem to reach the OGs.

"Just dumb life stuff." He stares at his palms. "A whole bunch of things piling up at once, I guess. I failed a bio test. I dented my dad's car." I can tell by his tone of voice that he's still bummed as he continues. "And there are scouts who still need players for next year coming to our next game, but Coach isn't starting me. So yeah, there's that."

"Basketball," I say, thinking. "You play . . ." But I can't think of a single position. Offense? Defense? Goalie?

"You don't need to pretend." He laughs. "I'm pretty sure you haven't been to a single game."

I open my mouth to protest, but then shrug. "Sorry. School social activities . . . kind of not my thing." Another thought comes quick: *How did he know I haven't been to a game?* Am I that much of a loser that even Jake Cano knows I never go out? There's no way he'd notice my absence *specifically.*

"I play center," Jake explains. "But mostly I just ride the bench since Finn is way better than me and gets all the glory. He's set to play for LSU. Full scholarship even though his family is loaded!" He looks away. "Anyway, I'm going to CU, which is fine, but these scouts are from some really good schools and have major scholarships. I just really think I could have gotten one."

"I'm sorry," I say. I mean it, and I do feel bad, but somehow, I still feel worse for me.

"Anyway." His tone is embarrassed, like he's revealed too much. "Told you it was dumb."

"It's not," I say quickly. "You work hard for something, and it sucks not to be rewarded. Heartbreaking, in fact."

He gives me a playful look. "You know a lot about breaking hearts?"

"Me?" I sputter. "Uh, that would be a no."

"You sure? For all you know, maybe you've broken the hearts of guys who sit in front of you in class. Guys you *never notice.*"

I stare at him. Jake's smile is warm. *Flirtatious?* Peppy, freckled Tess Larsen flutters into my mind again. They were one of those wholesome couples who always seemed to be smiling at each other, always holding hands.

It's an awkward silence, so I fill it. "Why are you here anyway? Doesn't seem your thing." Why is snarky my default tone?

"Even a dumb jock can be helpful sometimes," he says with a smirk and then adds, "My mom's on the committee. There were times when we didn't really have a lot, and St. Paul helped us out." He lowers his head as if he's second-guessing telling me all that. "Anyway. We should probably go back?"

"Sure."

He extends his hand so I can help him up. When our fingers touch, I try not to analyze. It's just skin on skin, one person helping another person to stand. That's all. He probably sees being nice to me as part of his charitable duties. Probably why he even told me all that; he knows we likely won't ever talk again.

We head back to the cars and start hauling more boxes from trunks. This time, Jake gives me a wide berth, even when the boxes are really heavy. I like that he trusts I can lift them, although at one point, he says, in a voice that's full of mirth, "Lift with the *legs*, remember?"

"Got it," I grunt as I heft the box from the trunk.

We get into a pattern: I pull out the boxes and then hand them to Jake, who walks them to the front steps and passes them off to Regan, another student helper, who takes them inside. It gives me more opportunities to touch Jake. I wish I'd thought to wear clothes a little nicer than my threadbare gray leggings and old ski coat. My hair is piled on my head. My shirt probably still has drool stains on it—and, God, this guy saw me sweating like a—well, whatever sweats a lot.

"Finish all your holiday shopping?" I ask. Stupid, I know, but I sort of just want to keep talking to him.

"Shopping? Not really," he admits as he puts more boxes on the steps. "I need to get to the mall. But I *hate* shopping. I think I'm allergic to it."

I think of the people I saw at the mall yesterday: Finn, Brooke, Grant. I assume Jake is friends with them. Was he there? I wonder if he heard about the song prank.

"Well, there's always this as an option," I say, pulling out a heinously ugly glass fish from the box.

"Yes, who wouldn't want a . . ." He studies it, laughing. "Bookend? Paperweight? Really heavy necklace?" He holds it up to his chest comically. I find myself genuinely laughing.

Then Emily appears by my side. "And here I was worried about you." She sounds almost annoyed. "Sorry it took me so long to come out. It's chaos in there." Her eyes dart from me to Jake, then back to me.

"I'm good." I glance furtively toward Jake. He has just dropped a particularly heavy plastic bin by the rec center's entrance. "Going fine, actually."

Emily blinks. "Well . . . great!" She pulls me a little to the side, looking
at Jake. "Oh my God, Sabrina! Jake? He is *so cute*. You should totally go for
him." I want to murder her; he can totally hear us.

"Oh my God, you're hilarious!" I laugh nervously as I move us farther
away and lower my voice, hoping she'll match mine. "How are things inside?"

But Emily keeps going, at least at a quieter level. "I heard he and Tess
broke up. Like literally a few days ago."

I can feel my cheeks turning red. I'd die if Jake heard this. Would I have
been so flirty if I'd known he was recently single? Now he's going to think I
was throwing myself at him.

When I look up again, Emily's smile dims, and she grows serious. "Hey,
so, I wanted to . . ." she starts, her voice cracking.

"Emily? Emily Simmons!"

We look up. A woman has rolled down the window of her car and is
hanging halfway out. She wears thick tortoiseshell glasses and has big teeth.
Jake has walked up to the back of her car and opened her trunk.

"It's Mrs. Armistead, dear! From your mother's office?"

"Oh. Hi . . ." Emily is always a little awkward with adults. "Nice to see
you," she says, turning her back on the woman.

"I heard the amazing news!"

Emily's cheeks drain of color. Her eyes dart, for a brief second, to me,
then back to the woman in the car.

"A Harvard girl?" the woman crows. "You must be over the moon! Your
mother is *so* proud."

Emily blinks. Even Jake stops from loading the boxes to look at us.

The woman waves her hand. "Anyway, huge congratulations!" She drives
away, her little electric car making an efficient *whirr*.

For a moment, the world is silent. Finally, I turn back to Emily with a
snort. "*That* was weird."

Emily looks like an animal frozen in a hunter's scope. Out of the corner
of my eye, I notice Jake is still watching.

"Em?" I repeat. My voice sounds strange to my ears. Choked. I try to laugh. "I mean, you didn't apply to Harvard . . ."

Emily's face is so pale. I've never seen her like this, not even when she had that terrible flu a few years back. I stare at her, a strange feeling washing over me.

"Emily?" My voice is sharp now.

Emily's bottom lip trembles. "I'm . . . I'm sorry Sabrina," she whispers, finally. She doesn't have to say the rest. Her expression tells the whole story.

All sound falls away. There's only a *wah-wah-wah* inside my brain. And then, it comes to me. Slow Sabrina. Always a little behind. Always taking a little longer to get the punchline. But now, the truth swirls around me, raw and sharp and painful.

Emily applied to Harvard early. And she got in.

Instead of me.

four

I stare at my best friend. It doesn't matter that I'm in the middle of a parking lot, around tons of other people. They're all blurs. All I see is Emily. All I see is the caught, guilty look on Emily's face.

"Tell me this is a joke," I whisper.

"I . . . I . . . it was my mom," she explodes. "You know how she is! She had me finish all my applications in September! She knew I didn't want to do early decision . . . that you were going to do it first . . . that you were applying early. But it's, you know . . . she knows it's the best chance. I swear I said it was *your* school. I *told* her. But she didn't listen. You know her, Sabrina! She *does* this! I had *no* idea she sent my application in early. Until a few weeks ago, when she told me she sent all of my stuff in, and. . . You'll definitely get in regular admission." She shuts her eyes. "I'm so sorry. Please don't hate me. *Please.*"

I stare at her. It's like she took a gong mallet to the side of my head. Everything is echoing.

"When were you going to tell me this?" I manage to ask. "I thought you wanted to go to MIT."

"I was going to tell you today. I swear. I was going to." Emily's eyes are suddenly pleading. "MIT . . . the kids there are just so . . . lame? In my wildest dreams, I never thought I would get in and not you. I figured it would be the other way around! Or we'd both get in . . . and then we'd get to be together and be roommates!"

Emily turns away. "I had no idea my mom was telling the world. I begged her not to. Not until I talked to you first. I'm *so mad* at her, Sabrina."

"So . . . you're going to accept?" I blurt it out before really thinking.

Emily's gaze meets mine for the first time since this bomb dropped. Her throat bobs as she swallows. "I . . . I . . . ?"

It's a trick question. If you get in early decision, you don't have to go. But no one declines. If you do, you lose any chance of your high school helping with someplace else. I know I'm supposed to say that of course she should. But I can't.

Emily's eyes water.

I'm flooded with guilt. "Emily . . ."

I don't know what to say. I don't know what I feel. Is she that controlled by her mom? Did she really not stick up for herself? Or was she just hiding behind her mom? Either way, how could she *do* this to me?

"I have to go," I snap, whirling around. I can feel the sweat, my heart racing. It's happening—again.

"Sabrina!" Emily calls after me. I feel her hand on my shoulder, but I shake her off.

"Leave me alone," I snap—with surprising venom.

Emily's eyes flash. She smiles in disbelief—and it's her smile that infuriates me more. "You'll get in! And we can be roommates? It will be okay."

I hear my voice rise. "It's not okay, Emily. It's *never* going to be okay. NEVER."

As I turn, I realize how many cars are lined up in the parking lot—*and* how many volunteers are watching. Jake, too. His brow is furrowed, but when I try and catch his eye, he turns away. *Great*. He's heard everything.

That walnut in my throat is back, except now it's the size of a boulder. And for the second time in twenty-four hours, I am fleeing a scene.

• • •

The holiday doesn't feel much like a holiday. I haven't finished my shopping by the time Christmas Eve rolls around. I'm so lacking in holiday cheer that I bike to 7-Eleven and buy my father a gift card for Olive Garden. I feel bad not putting more effort into his gift, and when I apologize, he waves me away, saying, "I love Olive Garden!" Which I know he doesn't, and that makes me feel worse.

It's the first holiday I'm truly surprised by a gift I receive—a used Subaru wagon, complete with a giant red bow on top. My father shows it off like he's in an old-fashioned game show. "I'm so proud of you, Sabrina. You've worked so hard. Mom would be proud, too." I still haven't told him the truth.

It's also the first holiday that, upon opening all my gifts, I don't immediately call Emily so we can compare our haul. Emily and I haven't spoken since the charity drive.

The silence hurts. I consider texting or calling Emily. We've gone from Snapchatting each other twenty times a day, texting endlessly, and FaceTiming constantly . . . to nothing. Complete silence. I don't know what I'm waiting for. An apology from her? It's so surprising that she hasn't—Emily usually apologizes for things she doesn't need to apologize for. I've always been the successful one in our friendship. The leader. The one on the right track. Until now.

I think of what I implied, too—that I didn't want her to accept Harvard's offer. So maybe it is me. I rehearse what I might say: that I'm happy for her, that it doesn't matter that she didn't stand up to her mom, that I totally forgive how it all went down. I want to feel that way. I do. I know I should. She's my best friend. She's smart and talented. I'm happy for her. Right? Oh, who am I kidding? I am a terrible person.

Jake Snapchatted me the day after the charity event, but I left it on Unopened. I couldn't open his message—surely it would be something pitying. I hate pity. I've been dealing with it for my whole life, and it makes me feel like even more of a loser.

On Christmas night, after I get through a long dinner with Dad, I head back to my room to work on more applications. I set my mind on the essays. I've heard back from a fresh batch of teachers and community organizers I'd worked with; they grumbled that I'm cutting things way too close and inconveniencing them over the break, but because it's *me*, they agreed to write a last-minute recommendation. I'm applying to almost twenty schools. And even with the Common App, where I only have to fill out basic application stuff once, I still have a bunch of essays that are unique to each school that I need to complete. And no school is a guarantee. In fact, I may not get into any of them. But I have to try.

It's now New Year's Eve. My eyes burn. My head feels full of sand. The computer screen wobbles, its square edges turning round. I've been up for what seems like one hundred hours straight, but I've finally reached the end of the applications. Let's *hope* my essays make sense. I'm finally at the stage where I've uploaded everything to the various schools' servers and paid the application fees. I sit back for a moment, rubbing my eyes.

My phone buzzes. When I turn it over, it isn't a text from Emily, as I thought (hoped?) it might be. It's a DM from an Instagram account I don't recognize.

> U ok?

I click on the account's profile picture. Images pop up, and I draw in a breath. Jake. My face goes hot. I hold my breath as the little dots in the DM window bounce up and down.

> Snapchatted u . . . I don't have ur number so I thought I'd try this! Ur not easy to find

My Instagram *is* hard to find. My name, Sabrina Richards, brings up lots of profiles. I only have a few photos posted, which I've carefully curated to be a thoughtful, pared-down, virginal representation of myself, an extension of my college application. (I mean, not that my actual life is much different. Certainly just as virginal.) Admissions officers look at people's social media pages these days. Some kids might have pictures of them from crazy parties or dead-drunk on spring break, but I wasn't about to risk my reputation. I post about causes I believe in, a few travel photos to show that I've seen a bit of the world, and a shot of me giving a student council speech. I'm a perfect, polished applicant.

Thinking of Jake searching for my profile—and then finding it, and then *looking* at it—fills me with embarrassment. My profile is ridiculously boring! It doesn't show any of *me* at all! My whole life suddenly feels like a sham—I'd worked so hard creating that Instagram page for Harvard to see, but Harvard wasn't even impressed.

I look at the DM again. *Am* I okay? Not really. Not at all. But I can't say that.

> Yeah fine thanks for asking

> Okay cool was worried

Worried? I try not to read too much into that. I wonder if what Emily told me about Tess and him breaking up is true. I wish, suddenly, I could call her and ask.

> All good worked it out

> U doing anything tonite?

I gawk at my screen. Now I *really* wish I could call Emily.

Jake doesn't give me time to answer. More little dots appear as he types some more.

> There's a party @ Sketch's U going?

Sketch, real name Christopher, is another basketball player. He's tall, loud, funny, and friendly. He's also got two parents that travel a ton for work. They're never home, so he's always throwing epic parties. There really isn't anything sketchy about him aside from some rumors that he doesn't actually *have* parents at all, which is why he never gets in trouble. Of course I know him. Everyone knows him. And of course, I'm not invited. I'm invisible to the OGs.

My knee-jerk reaction is a hard no. I don't do parties. What they signify, all the people who don't know I exist . . . and then the substances *at* parties, the behavior of people after *taking* those substances . . . all of it makes me itch from the inside. On instinct, I sit back down on my bed and pull the covers around me and ignore my phone. *This* is what I want to do. Burrow here. Stay where it's safe.

But Jake's face swims into my mind. His soft eyes. The dimple on his cheek. The way he'd guided me away from the crowd when I grew upset. Maybe letting loose just a little would be nice after how hard I worked. I've sent the applications to the other schools. The only thing I can do now is wait. What if he *has* broken up with Tess? What if this is some sort of . . . *date*? I've never been on a date before, though. I wouldn't know where to start.

I breathe out. Maybe I need to get out of this dark room; I feel sort of cooped up. Stretching, I rise to my feet and head to the kitchen for a glass of lemonade. I'm in such a daze that I don't even realize people are in my living room until my father calls my name.

"There you are," he says. "I thought you were sleeping."

I swivel and stare into the room. Kaye is with him. My gaze swivels to the third person. The young woman has Kaye's same glossy hair cut to her shoulders. She wears baggy jeans and cool high-top sneakers, and she has the high cheekbones and glowing skin of a French girl. Kaye's saying Parker's come back from Paris, via St. Barts, with her dad.

Parker leans forward, in a pseudo hug. "Hey, Sabrina!"

I stare at her. I am suddenly aware that I haven't showered in a few days. Parker, on the other hand, smells like—well—perfection. I can't take my eyes off her Starbucks iced coffee sweating water on my mom's wood coffee table. It's going to leave a ring. I move it to the glass end table next to her. I can tell they are all staring at me. But who drinks iced coffee in the middle of winter anyway?

Suddenly the light catches the edges of a diamond ring on Kaye's hand,

and for a moment I feel another panic attack coming on. She catches me staring at it and laughs, "Oh, don't worry, your dad didn't put a ring on it . . . yet." She winks. "It's a gift I got for myself. It shows my clients I am a *winner.*"

Have I mentioned how much I hate people who wink?

To break the tension, my dad holds up an envelope with a furtive smile. "Also. This came."

Even from across the room, I can see the Harvard logo in the upper left-hand corner. My heart lurches. It's a letter from Harvard. My *deferral* letter. Everyone is staring at it.

"Is that what I think it is?" Kaye chirps. But then her lips twitch. Everyone knows a thin letter is not a good sign.

"Wait!" I screech, suddenly lurching forward and ripping it from his hand. I press the envelope to my chest, my heart quaking. "Um . . . I . . ."

They're all staring at me. I can't do this in front of everyone. After what seems like hours, I turn to my dad. "There's something in the kitchen I need to show you. Right now."

My dad has sense enough to pick up on my urgency, and awkwardly, we walk out of the room. The kitchen isn't nearly far enough away from Kaye and Parker, but it'll have to do. I start to unload the dishwasher and wipe down the sink. It's a reflex. And then I hand him the envelope. "Open it."

He gives me a strange look, then slices open the letter with his fingernail. I can't look at his face as he unfolds the single sheet of paper. It's like I can feel his disappointment, though, coming off in waves.

"You can take the car back," I stammer, "since I didn't get in."

He sighs. "Sabrina. Honey. Of course, I don't want the car back. I'm proud of you for working hard. Not some stupid school. It's Harvard's loss. And there are plenty of other schools. I've always told you that. But . . . you knew? For how long? And why didn't you tell me?"

I squeeze my eyes shut. Isn't it obvious?

Dad seems to get this, too, because he gathers me in his arms then and holds me tight. All I feel is shame. And resentment, surprisingly. Dad was right all along. Harvard was beyond my reach.

"Please don't tell them," I mumble into his chest. "I'm so embarrassed."

I can feel him nod. "I won't. But they would understand. Everyone has a rejection and disappointment in their lives. Parker was talking about how hard it is to get into the Ivies."

Says the girl attending one, I think bitterly. It's humiliating. *Mortifying.*

To my relief, my dad doesn't make me go back into the living room to hang out. I'm sure he'd like nothing more for me and Parker to be best friends. But I can't do it. I retreat to my room instead, taking the back stairs so I don't have to see them again. With my door closed, I throw myself on the bed. I want to sleep. I'm so *angry*. At the Harvard admissions board. At Kaye's eagerness and Parker's perfect posture. At my father for reading me so wrong. For waving that Harvard envelope in my face in front of all of them. At Emily for taking the spot I should have had. For lying to me.

My phone buzzes again. It's another DM from Jake.

So?

The party. I shouldn't go.

But all at once, I feel defiant. I don't want to be the good girl. I don't want to do what my dad wants. What I thought my mom would want. I've avoided parties and all the perils of being a teen for this long and look where it's gotten me? I decide to message Jake back.

Sure.

How much worse could things get anyway?

five

Sketch's house isn't hard to find—it's at one of the highest points in town, with a huge front lawn, windows that seem to stretch to the moon, and a fountain with a peeing cherub statue in the circular driveway. The garage doors are open, showing off two identical white Range Rovers. Light blazes through every window downstairs, and bass booms through the cold winter air. I hear a sharp, nasty laugh from inside. Then a whoop. My new car keys feel heavy in my palm. Sabrina Richards, at a party, *asked* by a seriously cute boy.

I look down at myself. I have on jeans, sneakers, and a nondescript black sweater. It is the most basic outfit ever, and yet I'd changed my outfit at least six times to land on it. I wish I could have texted Emily for advice. She is forever showing me outfits on celebrities, influencers, and models. Outfits she says we'll wear when we live in New York City after college. I feel like the queen of the losers. The queen of the losers, I might add, who currently has no college prospects and was just tragically embarrassed in front of her father's girlfriend's perfect daughter.

Great. I can see Finn Walters and his posse by the doorway looking at something on his phone and laughing. I think about turning around and jumping back in my car.

"Sabrina!"

A figure breaks from the group: broad shoulders, hands in pockets, that fluffy hair. Had Jake been watching for me?

"Whoa," Jake says, jogging toward my car. "Happy holidays to *you*."

I follow his gaze. In my daze, I'd forgotten to take the remnants of the bow off the top of my new car. That's how little I'd driven it over the break.

I move to rip the pieces off. "Ugh."

"Nice gift." Jake taps the hood.

That envelope in my dad's hand flashes through my mind again. The way his shoulders had slumped—knowingly?—when I admitted I'd been deferred. But then I shift my thinking. I won't dwell. Not tonight. For once.

I look at Jake shyly. "Thanks for inviting me. I needed to get out of the house."

"Just don't hold it against me if they play really bad music. Sketch kind of has a thing for K-pop. We're thinking of holding an intervention."

I put my hands on my hips. "I actually think a lot of K-pop is fun."

"And here I thought you were only into classical."

Is he teasing? Flirting? I decide to flirt, too—or at least try. "Um. No. I took piano—for one year—and I was *awful*. I'm pretty sure I'm tone deaf."

"Sabrina Richards *bad* at something? Not playing concert halls since birth?"

I try not to let that sting. *Concert halls. Did Emily get into Harvard because of her music?* I try to concentrate on his grin instead.

Parked cars are jammed in the driveway, on the lawn, and all down the street. A lot of them are pretty pimped out. There's an array of brand-new Jeeps, late-model BMWs, a Volvo SUV, and a souped-up pickup, plus a lot of old beaters or gently used cars like mine.

We're at Sketch's door and passing the boy posse.

Finn looks at Jake and then me with a mixture of curiosity and disgust.

"Look, it's SERENA with the big . . ." he says, giving me a once over, his gaze lingering on my nonexistent chest, "brain."

I don't think Finn has ever acknowledged my existence—and ew, did he seriously just look at my chest?

"Sabrina, not Serena," I say evenly, and then, in my head, *SERENA, seriously? You stole my best friend* and *you're a total dick!*

Finn seems taken aback by my tone and laughs. "Be careful, buddy. The quiet ones are always the nastiest, if you know what I mean."

Before Jake can react, Finn turns and plucks a freshly poured drink from a partygoer. Then he glares at the guy, a scrawny freshman who seems flattered that Finn paid him a little bit of attention. "Yo, this smells like that piss EnergyFX."

The kid who handed it to him cringes. "Um. I don't *think* it is." EnergyFX was the sports drink created by some Milford High students a few years ago; it was supposed to be a "better, cleaner" sports drink that somehow became incredibly successful and is going to sell to some beverage company for millions. Even I knew that people loved it as a mixer with alcohol because supposedly whatever was in it helped reduce your hangover. Something about the electrolytes. To be honest, I'm with Finn. I don't think it tastes very good.

"Yeah, well if it breaks me out in hives, I'm coming after *you*, asswipe," Finn threatens. The poor kid cowers.

"Finn, babe, close the door," cries another voice. "You're letting in all the cold air!"

And now, up sweeps my old friend Brooke. Her long blonde hair swishes and glows. She wears a crop top ending just below her bra. It's like she doesn't even walk; she glides. Even Brooke's posture is different—straighter, haughtier, more confident. How is she not freezing? Her gaze drifts to me, and her eyes widen.

This was a terrible idea. I think I should go.

Brooke turns squarely to Finn. "Come inside, babe." She pulls her boyfriend into the house. "You, too." She looks at Jake. But not at me. The shade is not lost on me.

But Jake holds the door open for me to pass through anyway. All of a sudden, my stomach hurts.

"Um," I say in a weak voice. "I think I'm gonna head out, actually . . ."

Jake's eyebrows shoot up. "What? No!"

"I'm really not a party person." Like that wasn't pretty evident.

"I'm sorry, Finn can be . . ." He squeezes his eyes shut. "Please stay. It's taken me like a year to actually talk to you." His cheeks go red. "I can't believe I just told you that."

I stare at him dumbfounded. "Are you serious?"

He gives me a level stare. "Well, yeah. You're pretty intense. Not exactly . . .

approachable? But I always thought . . . I don't know. You seemed cool." He smiles shyly.

I feel sparkly inside. It's like the universe has given me a gift. But then, suddenly, I spy a figure through the doorway, glaring at me. It's Tess Larsen, Jake's ex. She's glaring at us—at *me*. Awkward. I shudder and turn back to Jake. When I look back, Tess is talking to some other kids now, a happy smile on her face. Maybe I imagined it.

"Are you and Tess . . . ?" I blurt.

"Me and . . ." Jake blinks. "I mean, we're not going out anymore, if that's what you're asking." He smiles. "Is that what you're asking?"

I have no idea what I'm asking. I have no idea how to navigate boys, *period.* But I look around, suddenly so tired of being on the outside. So tired of always doing the "right" thing. And then I shrug my shoulders. "Fine, I'll stay for a little. And maybe I'll even have a little of that." I point to the concoction in the trash can turned punch bowl.

Jake looks surprised. "Are you sure?"

"Why not?"

Jake turns to get us both cups. He hands one to me, saying, "Listen, I need to run to the bathroom. I'll be right back." He pulls me further into the foyer. "Don't go anywhere? Okay?"

"I'll try not to."

I watch as he goes, pushing myself against the wall to blend in. He passes by Tess, who wraps her arms around his neck and whispers something in his ear. He doesn't seem interested, but when he breaks free, she looks at me and winks. The party is packed, way more packed than the last party I'd been to with Brooke. I survey the crowd. Everyone seems to be having fun, dancing, and laughing. I see Tess again—this time in another corner, gesturing to a group of girls. They all turn to look at me. And it's not a welcoming look. Then I spy someone unexpected—Ryder Cross—pounding down a beer in the kitchen. After he finishes it, he lets out a colossal burp. Some girls wrinkle their noses.

I take a sip of what's in my cup. It's not terrible, exactly. I take another sip, and another. Someone bumps me, and my cup jostles, spilling liquid on the floor. No one cares. *This is someone's home. His parents are going to be furious.*

There's hardly any liquid in my cup anymore, so I head for a refill. A *whoop* sounds. I turn in time to see several party guests raising Solo cups in a toast. It's some seniors from last year and two people who were in Parker's class, Jason Magid and Grace Ramsey. That drink Finn was talking about, EnergyFX? Jason and Grace were the ones who created it. Of course, Jason and Grace's parents were both loaded. Like they say, it takes money to make money, I guess. I really hope Parker isn't coming. For the first time in what feels like months, I'm actually not miserable.

Then I realize there's a third person in their circle, too, someone else touching her plastic cup to theirs. As the circle shifts, I realize it's *Emily*.

My brain stalls. I thought she was skiing. Her father always takes them skiing this week. It's the one week a year she actually spends any time with him. And while she pretends she doesn't want to go, I know she waits for it all year.

For someone who spends most of her nights studying with me, Emily seems surprisingly comfortable in this environment. She's dabbing. She clearly doesn't need or miss me.

Jason pulls Emily closer and unveils something from behind his back. He whispers something to Emily, and Emily ducks down like she's about to be knighted. Instead, Jason pulls a sweatshirt over Emily's head. Emily pushes her arms through the sleeves and looks down at herself, grinning. Then she shows the other kids in the circle. On the front of the sweatshirt, in big block letters, is the logo of the school I've dreamed about for years. The same logo I'd ripped to shreds on the pennant in my bedroom. *Harvard University*. Because—right. Grace and Jason go to Harvard, too. And now, Emily is one of them.

The words stretch across Emily's chest, and she beams with pride. Worthiness. Success. Everything I'm not.

"Well. *That's* a plot twist."

Brooke's arms are crossed at her chest. Her surprised gaze swivels from Emily back to me. "Wasn't Harvard *your* dream?" Before I can respond, Finn grabs her arm and steers her away.

I throw back the rest of my drink, even though it's technically my second.

The *last* thing I need is Brooke's fake pity. The room feels like the temperature has risen twenty degrees. Not another panic attack. I have to get out of here. *Now.*

I push through the crowd towards the bathroom, hoping I'll find Jake. I see the door wide open, but no trace of him. I'm about to book it out the back door when I see Tess, leaning against the wall casually. She smirks, waves her hand, and mouths, "Bye-bye."

I push my way out the back door. I suck the frigid air into my lungs, but it doesn't feel like the oxygen is reaching my brain. I tuck myself around the corner, away from prying eyes.

This isn't fair, I think, and I let out a sob. *None of this is fair. I try so hard. I do what I'm supposed to. Why do I always lose? Why Emily? Why?*

But as a gust of wind from the open door smacks the side of my cheek, my self-pity turns to rage. I press my nails into the heels of my hands, so angry I can't see. I'm so angry that I tear off a branch of a shrub I'm passing and hurl it onto the lawn.

How dare she?

I notice that one of the vehicles, a white Kia sedan, has a huge red "A" spray painted on the driver's door. It looks fresh. I wonder if anyone else has seen it. I wonder what the owner of the car did. They'll feel angry, and maybe embarrassed, and maybe ashamed. Revenge *is* a hero in that way. People *should* be held accountable for the shitty things they do. For the ways they betray you. I wish everyone would know what Emily did. Then maybe they'd see things differently. I hear a nasty whisper at the back of my brain. I swish it away.

You're drunk. Go home.

"Sabrina!" Somehow Jake is suddenly beside me. Without a coat. I can see the goose bumps on his bare arms. "I thought you left!" It sounds like actual disappointment in his voice.

"Nope," I say, "but I don't think anyone would care if I did!"

"I would." He says simply. It's so nice that of course I have to ruin it.

"Do you think that's from that Revenge Insta account?" I say, calling his attention to the vandalized car.

Jake stares and gives a low whistle. "Oh, wow."

"Do you know whose car that is?" I ask.

He shakes his head. I'm a little relieved it's not someone in his universe.

"Do you think Ryder Cross did it?" I muse.

Jake sighs. "Don't know." I can tell he's ready to move off of my Nancy Drew line of questioning.

"Why has no one figured it out? Adults, I mean."

Jake shrugs. "It's not like Instagram is going to tell them. And anyone can make up a Gmail username and create an account."

"Do *you* follow them?"

Jake glances at me. "Do *you?*"

I shake my head.

"Smart girl," he says. "It's freezing out here."

"Sorry, I just needed some air," I smile, surprised at how seeing him has made me more comfortable. I toss my empty cup in the air. "But I could do with a refill."

Jake cocks his head like he's trying to stare at me from a new angle.

"You sure?" He asks. But my glare dares him to challenge me. "Okay, but I'm driving you home later."

"My hero," I say, smiling devilishly, handing him my car keys. We head back in, and I don't even care when I see Finn and Brooke in what looks like a serious conversation by the doorway.

I have officially stopped caring. I'm not sure if it feels good or bad, but one thing's for sure—it feels different.

And maybe different is exactly what I need.

six

I've never had such a horrible headache in my life.

When I open my eyes, I'm confused to see that I'm not in my bed but on my floor, halfway between my door and my desk. I'm in the same jeans and sweater I wore to the party, and my shoes are still on my feet. When I breathe in, I smell something . . . rancid. Like . . . licorice mixed with puke.

A poppy bass line rockets back to me. A slurred cheer rocking in my ears. Spinning lights. A Solo cup in my hand and a vile taste at the back of my throat. Jake, looming over me: "Sabrina, you okay?"

I shoot up, trying to sit. "Oh my God."

Everything spins. I clutch my head and drop back to the floor, dry heaving on the carpet. I'm hung over. This is bad. *Very* bad. I'd never been drunk before. I've barely had alcohol before. What was I thinking?

But then, it all comes back to me.

The room lurches as I try my hardest to crawl to my bed. It's only a few feet away, but it seems to take hours. I rip off my stained, wet clothes and realize I have chunks of God knows what in my hair. I feel too awful to even care. When I manage to get into bed and lie down, I moan, looking for something I can empty any remaining contents of my stomach into. The first thing I can find is my desk garbage can—I look and see puke covering the shreds of the Harvard pennant that's still lying at the bottom. Seems appropriate.

I try to remember the events of the evening. I go as far back as Jake finding me on the lawn last night before we went back into the party. I remember looking for Emily and not seeing her—and feeling kind of relieved but also disappointed. I remember having another drink, and Jake telling me I might have had enough. Clearly, I hadn't listened. One minute I'm in Sketch's noisy, high-ceilinged living room; the next I'm in the kitchen, talking to some girls I don't even know. Brooke's face swims in my mind, very close up. And Finn's. Was I yelling at him? I get a flash of standing outside in the cold, typing furiously on my phone, texting Emily, I think . . . I was so angry . . . but then Jake coming up behind me and putting a hand on my shoulder and putting me in the car. I also remember . . . yelling at someone? And then talking to someone else—Jake?—about . . . my mom. And . . . *Harvard?*

On shaky arms, I press myself up and look out the window to the street. My car is parked in the driveway. Panic hits me. Had I driven myself home? Wait. No, Jake did. How did he get back to his house?

I want to pull my head back into my shell. Now I understand why people have regrets after drinking. My memory feels wiped. But also, hovering there at the back of my mind like a dark shadow, is the terrible sense that something awful happened. I don't think it happened to me—I don't think anyone hurt me. It's something . . . else. Maybe something involving Brooke? Was I . . . yelling at her? Did I tell everyone I got deferred? And Emily? Did I scream at her, too?

Brooke. I close my eyes, thinking how close we used to be.

• • •

Brooke had brought the three of us together. She and Emily had been friends pretty much since birth. I met Brooke in fifth grade at the ice rink, during a brief stint I had taking lessons after watching *Ice Castles* one too many times. My passion didn't stick, but our friendship did.

Emily was a little hesitant about turning their duo into a trio, though I could tell she looked up to Brooke, who, because she had two worldly older sisters, seemed way more in the know than either of us. But when Emily's dad suddenly left during eighth grade, she and I bonded more—we'd both been through stuff. The way I saw it, a divorce wasn't as bad as a parent dying, but from Emily's point of view, at least my mom didn't *want* to leave.

Whereas her dad not only chose to, but also moved over two hours away and now seemed to care only about his new family. She said it didn't matter that much, that it wasn't like he had ever really been around much. But I know it hurt her that she barely saw him. Plus, she said, she'd rather be with us than at some stupid family thing anyway.

Still, Brooke, Emily, and I were together pretty much all the time. Our weekends were filled with sleepovers at one another's houses, making dance TikToks—well, that was Brooke and Emily, mostly, and I filmed. DMing celebrities' Insta accounts—one of Emily's favorite things to do—and watching and rewatching *Criminal Minds*—one of mine. Scrapbooking. More Emily's passion, as I pretty much don't have a creative bone in my body. We saw ourselves as different from other girls—more creative, smarter, more interesting. During sleepovers, sometimes we spoke to one another only in British accents. British slang became our secret code. We used it in school, at lunch, around other girls, and we felt envied. *Those friends are tight. They have their own language.*

We had our own activities—Emily had the flute. Brooke skated. I was— well, if it was an activity that *didn't* require social interaction, that's what I chose. I wrote short stories and essays. It wasn't like we spent every waking minute together—Brooke had skating friends, and Emily hung out with kids in her neighborhood sometimes, and me . . . well, I had my books and my introverted ways. But we were close.

Until we weren't.

It was the weekend before we started freshman year. We hadn't seen one another for a few weeks. My dad had taken me on a road trip up the coast, and Brooke's family spent every August in Maine. When we got together for our Saturday sleepover, we were so excited to see one another again.

The sleepover was at Emily's house, probably our least favorite place of the three of ours because her mom was so intense, but we rotated to be fair. When I got there, Emily's mom met me at the door, immediately full of questions.

"Hi, Sabrina, so glad you're here. I don't think Emily even finished *To Kill a Mockingbird*, let alone wrote the report!" Mrs. Simmons clucked her tongue. "I'd hate her to start the year with the teacher having a bad impression of her. I bet *you* finished ages ago."

"Um, yeah," I admitted. "I did it in July."

"Oh, Sabrina, you're always so on top of things. I wish Emily was more like you." Mrs. Simmons gushed. "Will you talk to her about it? Get her moving?"

"Sure."

It was flattering, kind of. Mrs. Simmons sometimes took care of me in a mom sort of way. She made sure I was signed up for the same school events that Emily was. She made sure I volunteered. When I was sick, she sent home freshly made green juice from her garden. She asked me like every other week if I needed help learning how to use a tampon. (Um, thanks, but no.) There was even a moment when Emily and I thought maybe she and my dad were flirting. Emily approved; I did not. But at the same time, as quid pro quo, Mrs. Simmons entrusted me with keeping Emily on the straight and narrow, which was ironic since Emily always seemed to have great grades without even trying. But somehow it was the effort more than the outcome that seemed to impress her mom.

I headed to Emily's room, down the long hall of her ranch home. I passed by Charlie's door—it was closed, but I could hear him shouting inside. My fist hovered by the door, and I almost knocked . . . but I held back. I didn't know what to say to Charlie those days. Since their dad left, he had gotten darker, moodier. He was always on his computer and playing video games. His room was a total disaster, and I had to physically restrain myself from picking up the half-eaten candy bars off the floor or tossing out the dead plants that he seemed to be growing on his desk. It wasn't like I was worried he would wind up some crazed shooter, but he wasn't the sweet Charlie we used to know. It was sad. I kept asking Emily if it was something we'd done to send him away—or maybe something happened at school? But Emily always shrugged it off.

"That's just Charlie," she would say, and quickly move on to another topic.

I heard Brooke and Emily talking in Emily's room. The moment I stepped through the door, Brooke grabbed my shoulders and started bouncing up and down.

"Maddie Crosby is having a party! We're going," she said definitively.

She whispered it, clearly aware that if Emily's mom heard, she'd put the kibosh on that plan immediately.

"Who's Maddie Crosby?" I asked, startled.

"Oh, Sabrina. How do you *not* know?" Emily said teasingly. "She's a junior? Friends with my sister? She lives a few streets away. Was on homecoming court?"

"I saw her at the mall today," Brooke added. "She said we should come. Everyone will be there."

By this point in our friendship, we had dropped the British accents. But hearing Brooke say this, it was like she'd acquired a new accent of her own— one I'd never heard. *Everyone will be there?* Who was everyone?

"Boys?" Emily asked excitedly.

"Of course." Brooke smiled. "All the hot ones." Then Brooke turned to me, eagle-eyed like she sometimes did. "So, Sabrina? What do you think?"

Brooke could be blunt. Even though she often teased, she did it while putting us on the spot. She was waiting for me to react somehow—none of us had ever really focused on our looks. I pretty much wore the same uniform of baggy jeans and a sweatshirt every day. Since Emily swam every morning and afternoon, she never bothered to do anything and always looked a little bit like a drowned rat. And Brooke? Well, this was the summer she turned pretty. She had truly transformed: boobs, long hair, no braces. Suddenly, we looked mismatched. Emily and I went together. But Brooke? She looked different.

"Um, what about our pact?" I asked, my voice cracking. Some girls our age had already been pushing the limits, sneaking drinks and hooking up with boys at bar mitzvahs. But the three of us had made a pact that we would not do anything with a guy until we had been dating for at least three months. And NO sex until senior prom. It was all about regret, self-respect, and consent. It felt empowering, but now Brooke was looking at me like I was a big loser.

"We're not in fifth grade," Brooke scoffed. "We're going to a party. Not losing our virginity! And even if something *does* happen . . . we can still have a little fun, right?"

Then she looked at Emily. "Unless you don't want to have fun either."

Emily lifted her chin. "Maybe some of us have already had some fun."

Brooke put her hands on her hips. "What kind of fun?" Emily always deferred to Brooke, so it was strange to hear her almost challenge Brooke, and clearly Brooke didn't like it. "Your pillow doesn't count, you know."

Emily batted her eyelashes. "It wasn't my pillow. But a lady doesn't kiss and tell."

Brooke and I both stared at Emily, waiting. It wasn't like Emily to fabricate things. So, did that mean it was true . . . and she hadn't told me? It all made me uncomfortable. Why were things changing? I wanted things to stay exactly as they'd always been.

"Let's find outfits," Brooke announced, clapping her hands.

"But . . ." I started, glancing toward the closed door in Emily's room, "your mom will ground you for life, Emily."

"We could just wait until she's asleep and sneak out," Emily ventured uncertainly. "The back door doesn't creak. She won't hear. And she doesn't set the alarm much anymore."

I stared at her. It sounded like she'd done this before or something.

"Come on, Sabrina. We don't have to stay long," Brooke insisted. "It's a high school party. Aren't you curious?"

I shook my head. "I'm staying here. We all should."

Brooke groaned. "Well, *I'm* going. Emily? You in?"

Emily looked from me to Brooke. I could tell she really wanted to go— and that she wasn't about to go against Brooke. I hated the idea of them going together and experiencing something without me. The summer before, my dad and I had gone to the beach for a week, and Emily and Brooke had hung out by themselves quite a bit. When I got home, they gave each other secret looks and had inside jokes I didn't know anything about.

Finally, I got it out of Emily: They'd played an epic game of Truth or Dare one night, resulting in prank calls, taking sips from Brooke's parents' vodka bottle, and walking to 7-Eleven and nearly shoplifting some Mentos before

Emily lost her nerve. The worst part was that Emily sounded kind of thrilled about all of it, like *this* was the kind of fun she wanted to be having. Had I been home, I probably would have put a stop to all of it. Suddenly, I felt shaky, like I was on the verge of losing two friends.

I sighed. "Fine. Whatever. Just for a little while, though." Brooke hugged me as if I had just told her we were going to Disney World.

We went into Emily's room and raided Emily's closet, trying to figure out what we'd wear. Brooke pulled out a low-cut top from the rack. "This would look amazing on you, Sabrina."

I'd never worn a shirt so revealing. I felt like a toddler playing dress up. My heart was pounding. I really, really didn't want to do this. But how could I back out?

Emily had us tiptoe quietly past Charlie's door, not that he would hear us with all the gunfire and sound effects coming from his screens. We snuck out the back door, careful not to let it slam and sure enough, we were out, scot-free. The walk felt like a maze through different streets. By the time we got to the house, the party was in full swing. The door stood wide open; there wasn't a sign of parents anywhere. Girls passed us wearing party beads, some wearing bras instead of shirts. People were dancing, kids were playing beer pong and doing shots, and the whole place reeked of sweat, booze, puke, and—something I couldn't put my finger on—a dirty bedroom smell.

My skin prickled. "We shouldn't be here."

"What?" Brooke asked, not hearing me over the deafening music.

"I want to go back!" I screamed. I pulled at Emily's sleeve. She was standing on her tiptoes like she was looking for someone. "Let's leave."

Emily's eyes widened in a pleading sort of way. "Maybe we could stay for fifteen? I mean, we just got here." Her gaze turned to Brooke. Brooke was dancing, twirling her body to the music, hardly paying any attention to us.

"Your mom will kill us if she finds out," I yelled over the sound.

In the doorway, guys were shoving each other, messing around. A few of them were in our grade, a few were older, and they were all extremely good-looking in that conventional, boring way. Emily was looking at them like they were a foreign species, and I could tell some were looking at her too. Their shoves turned into wrestling-type moves, and without any warning I suddenly had an entire drink poured on my chest. I reeled at how cold it was, and I could tell my face was becoming as red as my stained shirt now was.

"My bad!" One of the guys laughed, with his arms up. Then moved on, as if maybe he had stepped on my toe instead of drenching me in some red, boozy concoction.

"Come on," I said, grabbing Emily by the hand.

Emily pulled herself free. "Sabrina! We can't abandon Brooke!"

I hunched my shoulders. I was mad at that guy, mad at Emily, mad at Brooke. Mad at myself for coming. "Are you kidding me?" I pointed at my wet, destroyed outfit. "I can't walk around like this!"

Emily looked torn. Again, her gaze was on something through that doorway. Kids moved back and forth, holding red cups full of God knows what. A tall guy staggered by, laughing hard.

"I'll just make sure she's okay," Emily decided. "You go ahead, and I'll be right behind you." And then, as soon as she said it, she patted my wet shoulder and vanished into the crowd.

I couldn't believe it.

I stomped my way back to Emily's house, antsy and kind of heartbroken. I let myself through the non-creaky back door, and it was as if we never left. I crept down the hall, but as I passed Charlie's room, his door swung open, and Charlie stepped out, startling me. He was wearing his gamer headset and still talking to whoever was on the other side. His eyes widened. "Oh, I thought you were Emily sneaking back in."

"Sorry," I muttered. *Busted.*

My gaze drifted to Charlie's room. There were no lights on, but the room was lit up by three computer screens lined up on his huge desk. There were a bunch of overgrown and semi-dead plants, clothes in piles and candy wrappers and soda bottles scattered around. I jumped back, startled by the sound of an explosion, but quickly realized it had come from one of his computer monitors. Two had what looked like different multiplayer shooter games going; the other was pumping out some '90s tragic alt rock. The kid knew how to do anything on a computer, but this was how he spent his nights? Charlie bragged that he once hacked into NASA, but then Emily rolled her eyes and said it absolutely wasn't true and that she wished Charlie would get an actual life.

Charlie told whoever it was to hang on. "Where's my sister?"

"She's . . . um . . ." I clenched and unclenched my fists. "She's at a party." It was a betrayal, I knew, but I felt so mad.

"Oh." He nods. I can't tell if he's surprised or uninterested.

"At Maddie's," I said. "Some junior girl."

"I wasn't drinking," I added because I certainly smelled like I had been. He just stared at me. "But Brooke is, and Emily probably is." Because, again, I was a total tattletale bitch.

Charlie raised his eyebrows but didn't seem that surprised. He turned back to his room. "Well . . . like the name of the New Radicals song, 'You Get What You Give,'" he said and shut his door. I had no idea what that meant. Charlie sometimes said things that made him sound like an evil Yoda. Charlie-isms, we called them; it embarrassed Emily to no end.

I tried to distract myself by organizing Emily's desk and folding all the clothes we had tossed on the floor after trying them on. Emily wasn't a neat freak like me. She was more of a packrat, keeping every little picture, memento, or stupid thing, and she freaked out whenever I tried to really clean up her room. Finally, I sent a group text.

> When r u coming back??!!

I stared murderously at my phone. Finally, Brooke replied.

> U LEEEEEEEFT!!??!!!!!

Like she even cared.

Then Emily fired one off.

> COMING SOON, PROMISE!

Fifteen minutes passed. An hour. An hour and a half.

I heard a click outside and footsteps—Emily's mom? The woman was hyper-focused; if this wasn't the first time Emily had snuck out, how had her mom not clocked it? And if Mrs. Simmons came in here and saw only me, what was I going to say? It was one thing to narc on her to Charlie, but Emily would kill me if I told her mom. Mrs. Simmons might also kill *me*, because I hadn't been able to convince Emily to stay home. I couldn't believe Emily had put me in this position. But when I peeked out the door, it was just Charlie heading down the hall, probably going down to the kitchen for a snack.

Finally, at nearly 2:00 a.m., I heard voices. I flopped down on my bed, pretending to be asleep. Brooke and Emily banged around. Brooke kept burping.

"*Be quiet or you'll wake my mom,*" Emily snapped.

"I'm going to be sick," Brooke moaned.

"Well, don't do it *here*." Emily sounded pissed. *Really* pissed. "In fact, I think you should go."

"You're kicking me out in the middle of the night?"

"I told you not to drink so much."

So much? How about *not at all*?

"And I told you not to be such a little bitch," Brooke slurred.

Emily let out a little whimper. I widened my eyes. What had *happened*? Emily and Brooke didn't fight like this.

I watched as Brooke's shadowy form staggered to the guest bathroom. Within seconds, I heard the sounds of puking. Then I sensed Emily lying down next to me. I was almost going to say something—acknowledge Brooke's drunkenness, maybe—but then I heard strange noises coming from Emily's pillow. Was she . . . crying?

"Emily?" I sprung up in bed. "You okay?"

The sounds stopped. I wasn't sure if Emily was even breathing.

"Em?"

"I'm *fine*," Emily snapped. "Go back to sleep."

"Is everything okay?"

"Yes. No. I don't know."

"Is Brooke okay?"

"Who cares!"

My nerves started to prickle. "Did something happen at the party?"

"No, Sabrina. It's late, okay? Go to sleep."

I blinked in the rich, blue-black darkness. Brooke, meanwhile, continued to retch. It went on and on, though at some point I drifted off.

By the time I woke up the next morning, Brooke was gone, and Mrs. Simmons had left early for work.

Emily surveyed the bathroom, and she and I cleaned it thoroughly, making sure every inch of puke was gone.

"I can't believe her." Emily swore under her breath as she got down on her hands and knees and scrubbed the tile. Even I thought she was a little angrier than the situation called for.

"So . . . was it fun?" I dared to ask.

Emily didn't answer. Instead, she dumped a bunch of bleach into the toilet.

"I guess that's a no?"

Still no answer.

"You should have come home with me," I joked. Emily's jaw tightened. "Brooke was really drunk, huh?" I fished.

"It was dumb, okay?" Emily said, whirling around. "Embarrassing."

"Wait." I blinked. "Someone embarrassed you? *Brooke?*"

Emily threw the empty bottle of bleach into the trash can. But then, on second thought, she removed it and headed down the hall for the garage.

I followed her out. "What did Brooke do?"

"God, Sabrina, *stop*, okay?" Emily tossed the bottle into the trash bin in the garage. "She didn't do anything."

"But why won't you guys tell me! This is like that Truth or Dare weekend!"

Emily looked at me, brow furrowed. I couldn't tell what was going on in her head.

It was the opposite of what I expected. I thought they would have come home giddy and bubbling, full of stories of how amazing the party was. I'd also never seen Emily so rattled. Was it because Brooke was mad at her? But why was she taking it out on me?

"I need to do my summer reading," she said flatly. "Sorry, Sabrina, but I think you should go."

On the walk home, I texted Brooke.

What happened?

I stared at my phone. And waited. And waited. Nothing. Had she turned off her phone? Did she get in trouble and her parents took confiscated it? Did she lose it? By Sunday night, I had sent a series of unanswered texts.

On Monday at school, Brooke didn't meet us at Emily's locker like she usually did, but I showed up bright and early. Emily just gave me a watery smile. Just then, Brooke walked past—with a whole group of kids from the party. Maddie, the girl who had thrown the party, literally had her arm around Brooke as if they were best friends. There were a bunch of boys, too. Grant Dryer, a really good-looking tall boy who a lot of girls had messed around with in junior high, who I saw with a girl I didn't recognize at the party. Finn Walters. I hadn't seen him that night, but I assumed he'd been there. Finn lived in Emily's neighborhood. Though we'd been going to school with him forever, he'd grown into one of the cutest guys in our grade. Making varsity basketball as a freshman didn't hurt, either.

"What's *happening*?" I whispered. "Have you talked to her? She didn't text me back."

Emily slammed her locker door shut. "I have to go."

That whole day, I kept thinking Brooke would come over to talk to me at least. I mean, what had *I* done? Yet every time I saw her, I wanted to go to her, but she was literally surrounded by the OGs like they were the Secret Service. And then I started to realize something else—Brooke was with Finn.

First, I saw Finn and Brooke casually talking outside the lunchroom. Later that day, they were whispering by the flagpole near the gym. By the end of the day, they were leaning against a wall in the hallway, and Finn was *kissing* her. The one time I caught her eye, she looked at me for a second but then turned away. Like I hadn't been her best friend for three years. Like she'd just been *waiting* to cast me off.

I had to find Emily. It was a *huge* deal. The thing was, freshmen had to turn their phones in to the principal's office at the beginning of each school day and only got them back at the 3:00 p.m. dismissal, so it wasn't like I could text her. I didn't see Emily all day—or in the bus lines—so after school I biked over to her house, let myself in, and marched upstairs to her room. I heard music coming from Charlie's room, something fast and hard with lots of guitars—he hadn't gone off to boarding school yet. But Emily's room was quiet. When I pushed open the door, I found her lying on her bed, just staring at the ceiling.

"Okay, what did I do?" I demanded. "Why are you mad? Is it because I left the party early?" It was the only thing I could think of. "Look, I'm sorry I made you babysit Brooke alone. I should have stuck it out had I known she was going to puke. Did your mom find out? Is she mad?"

Emily looked at me for a long time and then finally got off the bed. "She didn't find out. It's fine."

I rolled my jaw. "*What* part of it is fine?"

"All of it."

"Including me?"

Emily shrugged. "*You* didn't do anything."

I took it as an invitation to sit down. "What's going on with Brooke? Guess who I saw her with today? *Finn.*"

Emily looked away, but she didn't look surprised.

"You knew?" I guessed. "Did this happen at the party?" *How did he even notice her?*

Emily's mouth made a tight line. "Guess it's because Brooke has boobs now. And, oh, she drinks. I tried to tell her Finn is bad news at the party, but it's like she was blinded by him."

"Bad news . . . like how?" I certainly didn't know personal details about Finn. Then again, Emily kept up with all the gossip, so maybe she'd heard something.

But Emily just shrugged. "Anyway, now that Brooke's going out with him, you can kiss our friendship with her goodbye."

I cocked my head. "You *think?*"

Suddenly, Emily looked kind of heartbroken. "She's been using us. Biding her time until someone better came along." She shifted positions, staring at the ceiling again. "At the party, she told me she thinks you're in love with her, and she didn't want the OGs thinking she hangs out with losers. She says we're embarrassing."

"*Brooke* said that?" I was stunned. There were tears in Emily's eyes. This must be why she was crying that night.

"You didn't notice? She blocked our numbers," Emily said, showing me all the undelivered messages on her phone.

I stared at my own phone. My messages to Brooke had not gone through. I was too worried about everything going on to even notice. Who had Brooke turned into? She did this for Finn? To be popular? Really?

At school, just like Emily predicted, on the days when our lunch schedules synced up, Brooke no longer sought us out. She chose the table with Finn and some of the other basketball players and their girlfriends. In the halls, she didn't even look in our direction. We all had honors Algebra II together, but she just stared straight ahead, eyes on the blackboard—well, when she wasn't giggling with Grant Dryer, who was also in the class. She started wearing makeup and tighter clothes. I kept thinking about what Emily said—we were dead weight. She really didn't want us around anymore. But we hadn't even *done* anything. I mean, I loved her, but I definitely wasn't *in love* with her. How were we suddenly so unlikeable?

It stung. I felt abandoned, left behind. It wasn't like losing my mom, but it still hurt. It was all so sudden, so surprising. How had I not prepared for this? Were there signs? Why didn't I see them? Well, at least I had Emily and that was really all I needed—and I would never let her go.

· · ·

I sit up and rub my eyes. My head pounds, but at least I'm not queasy anymore. My computer screen blinks. I muster up the energy to stumble over to my desk. My inbox is full. All of my college applications have been received. I breathe out. That's good, anyway. I guess all I can do now is wait. It feels like I'm settling for second best, but maybe I should look at this differently . I mean, Harvard isn't the only school. Maybe I could feel fulfilled elsewhere. Lots of people have to pivot, right? This could be some sort of learning experience.

Anyway, you don't deserve to go to Harvard. You're a bad person.

I'm startled by the mean little voice in my head. What brought *that* thought on? The alcohol? I've had enough health classes to know that drinking too much leads to anxious thoughts. Yet another reason I'll never be drinking again.

The doorbell rings.

I jump. All kinds of terrible thoughts enter my mind. *Kaye? A parent? Did I do something awful in my drunken state?* I wait for my father to answer, but no footsteps come. *My father.* Had he seen me last night when I got in? I squeeze my eyes shut. I desperately hope not.

Another ring. Maybe my dad is out, because no one is answering it. Sighing, I heft myself up and peer down the stairs. When I catch a glimpse of myself in the mirror on the landing, I see that my hair is springing up in every direction, and my skin is blotchy. A new thought hits me. What if it's Jake checking on me? I can't let him see me like this.

I peek through the little window to the right of the door. When I see who it is, I draw in a breath. Emily. And she's holding . . . a pie. I suddenly remember my nagging bad feeling about texting Emily something nasty. I quickly check my phone. Phew, there's nothing.

I blink. New Year's apple pies are this inside joke from a way-back-when sleepover—one New Year's Day, at like 2:00 a.m., we decided to make one from scratch, and we'd nearly burned down the kitchen. Last year, I brought one from this same bakery to Emily's door. This year was her turn.

". . . Sabrina." Her smile wobbles. "H-hey."

"Emily," I breathe.

Emily stands there, waiting. Realizing I should invite her in, I motion her inside. I can't tell if she's waiting for me to say more, and really, I'm not sure what I would say, but then she starts.

"You must hate me for taking your place at Harvard. It's all I've thought about."

Somehow that stings. I mean, I keep telling myself it wasn't a one-for-one trade, me not getting in because Emily did. "It wasn't your fault. Your mom—I get it." I shake my head as we walk into the kitchen. "I'm happy for you." I want to mean it. Maybe I do.

"And last night, at the party . . ." Emily rushes on as I grab some plates. "I . . . I saw you. And I know you saw me." I look away and open the drawer where we keep all the serving spoons and pull out a pie server.

"I had no idea Jason and Grace were going to do that with the sweatshirt. I don't even know why I went—Jason and I used to be in orchestra together, and he invited me . . . but I didn't know they wanted me to come because of getting into Harvard. And I definitely didn't think you were going to be there." She picks the pie server off of the counter and serves us each a generous piece of pie.

"I didn't know either," I mutter. I look at the pie and feel a lurch in my stomach.

"I was thinking you might not be feeling so hot, so I brought you this too, just in case." Emily pulls a plain bagel and some ginger ale out of her backpack.

I look at her gratefully. "Was it that obvious?" I ask, picking at the bagel, afraid to meet her gaze.

Emily looks up, as if measuring her answer. "Well, pretty sure Finn won't forget your name again."

I cover my eyes, waiting for more. I vaguely remember shouting at Finn.

"You definitely called him out, and to be honest, I think a lot of the crowd agreed with you." I can tell that's not all. "I didn't hear what you said to Brooke, but she did look pretty upset, AND she and Finn seemed to be fighting the rest of the night. But you actually left pretty early."

I feel like Emily is trying to make me feel better, but I just feel worse.

"Oh my God," she says, clearly trying to shift the subject, "AND Revenge struck! I didn't see it, but supposedly someone's car was totally vandalized."

I'm not sure whether to admit that I saw it, so I figure it's better to just keep quiet, and Emily, as always, doesn't seem to notice. "So what else happened? Tip any cows on your way home? Lose your virginity to Jakie?"

"Oh my God, Emily! NO!" Truth is I really can't remember what happened, but I did wake up fully clothed, and I really don't think Jake is the kind of guy to take advantage of a drunk girl.

I shrug. "Even if Jake DID like me, I'm pretty sure I ruined any chance last night. I mean, I don't even want to face him again. Maybe we should ask the Tarot?" I say, hoping this helps ease our tension.

"I'm over the Tarot. It's never right anyway," she says in that guileless, Emily way as if she found out unicorns didn't exist. "But you could double date with Finn and Brooke."

I can't tell if she's being genuine or sarcastic.

I groan. "No *thank* you. But more importantly, what about you and Jeremy? Was he at the party? Any more gummies?"

Emily scrunches up her nose. "Nope. I'm over him. Actually . . ." Then, as if she's had a huge revelation, "I kind of think I want to be bisexual."

I can't help laughing. Only Emily would just *decide* to be bisexual. Of course. It's so her. If we weren't on such thin ice, I'd try to guess which influencer had just come out. But instead, I tell her what I've been bottling up for two weeks: how I neglected to prepare any other applications, how I had to scramble at the last minute, but how I managed to get it all done. I also talk about my dad basically announcing my failure to Kaye and Parker.

Emily shakes her head. "Why are parents so *clueless*?"

"Now you know why I wanted to get out of the house to go to that party," I say, laughing.

"Sabrina Richards, crushing on an OG—*and* drinking?" Emily is genuinely shocked. "What ELSE do you need to tell me? Give it up!"

"Um," I cover my eyes. "I feel like hell."

Emily waves her hand. "Well, when you and Jake are a couple and you get super popular, don't block my phone number? O. Kaye?" She smiles.

"No chance," I assure her. Then we hug. I can tell we both want this back, but somehow it still doesn't feel quite real. More like we're pretending to be best friends. But maybe I'm being too sensitive. I've missed this. I am happy for her. I *am*. With a twinge, I think about that strange thought that came to me earlier—*you're a bad person*. I try and reach back into my murky memory of the night before one last time, feeling around for something that it could have been referring to.

But all I find is a dark, empty void, so I decide to let it go.

seven

That Monday, I drive my new car to school instead of having my dad drive me. He's cutting me some slack after that whole Harvard thing. There's a silver lining, I guess—he had absolutely no idea how wasted I was at the party. There's part of me that's sad about that. I know he loves me, but sometimes I feel like I take more care of him than he takes care of me. I know he wishes my mom was here to deal with all this stuff.

Because I never purchased a parking tag for the year—I never thought I'd be lucky enough to have a car—I have to park in "the dark ages" lot, which is at least a half-mile walk from school. I jog to the school doors, hands in my pockets, to meet Emily. But she isn't waiting where we usually meet. I wonder if she's running late.

I think a lot about what Jake had said about me being cold. And Emily saying I was judgmental. Maybe I'm a little set in my ways, but only because I have—or should say *had*—a plan, a goal, a reason to be so focused. I've always tried so hard to just keep control over my life. But maybe they were right. Where did it get me anyway?

I check my watch. Just a few minutes before the first bell. I pull out my phone and text Emily.

I glance at my watch. It's been five minutes. *Call me, Em.*

Going to class See u @ lunch

I need us to be okay.

A whoosh of warm air hits me as I step through a side door. Locker doors bang shut. People around me greet one another, asking how their winter breaks went. I notice quite a few girls are wearing the same style of brand-new-looking combat boots—they must have been on a lot of wish lists this year.

"Hey."

I look up and feel my insides wobble. It's like the physical opposite of a panic attack, but it unsettles me just the same. Jake leans against the locker next to mine, his arms crossed over his chest. He's looking at me—not angrily, exactly . . . more like concerned.

"Oh," I say. "Um, hello."

"So . . ."

There's a piece of hair sticking up at the crown of his head. I fight the urge to press it down. But all of the missing pieces of the night of the party needle me. *What had I done? How foolish had I acted?* I don't want to know.

"So," I say briskly.

"You feeling better?"

His voice isn't teasing—or mocking—it's concerned. Maybe that's worse. I let out a sigh. "You drove me home, right?"

"I did."

"How did *you* get home?"

"Walked back to my car."

My eyes widen. It isn't like Sketch lives close. It must be at least two miles from my house back to his. Jake shrugs. "I jogged it. Got some extra cardio in."

I squeeze my eyes shut. "I'm sorry that you had to do that."

Jake fidgets with his books. "I texted you. Didn't hear back."

I sneak a peek at him. "My . . . my dad took my phone for the weekend." That's not exactly true. I just was too embarrassed by my behavior to text back.

"Rough." Jake smiles. He seems relieved. "You know, you're not the first person to get too drunk at a party . . ."

I try to return his smile. "Well, pretty safe to say I will not be drinking or attending parties for a while."

"You know," Jake seems to think for a minute. "There are other things we can do that aren't parties. If you're interested."

My stomach does a flip. "Um, like what kinds of things?"

"Well, eating, for one."

I raise my eyebrows.

"And . . . snow sports." He gestures to the packed foot of it on the sides of the path. "Certainly, enough of it out there. Sledding, snowshoeing . . ."

"Snowshoeing?" I giggle. "Like those big paddles strapped to your feet?"

"I've got some." Jake puts his hands on his hips. "We should go. You could wear my sister's." A sly look crosses his face. "Nothing clears your mind like tramping through the snow with giant paddles on your feet."

"Um, maybe," I say shyly.

He smiles at me. The buzzing in my stomach hasn't stopped. I have a fleeting thought of Tess Larsen's nasty glares at the party that I'd temporarily forgotten in my drunken haze. I guess she and Jake haven't reunited. Maybe they really are broken up for good. Should I go for this? Go for *him?* Don't get me wrong, there's a huge part of me that wants to shut myself inside my locker. I can't get wrapped up in another person. It's too much effort. It's too messy and hard. But there's a yearning inside me, too. A loneliness.

Before I can even think, a crowd starts making noise at the end of the hall by the current events and awards board. Several people are whispering. Someone murmurs, "*That Instagram account.*"

I glance at Jake, and we both inch forward to see what's going on. Through the crowd of kids is the display of the winners of the English poetry contest. It was sort of an upset when Melissa Hadley had won with a really beautiful, sad poem about her family in the South. Who knew she had an inner poet in her? But where Melissa's poem used to be before winter break, there's now a new poem pasted on the front of the cabinet. It's printed on a piece of neon, lime green paper. You couldn't miss it. There are also copies strewn all across

the hall and on a small table next to the cabinet. I pick one off the ground
and begin to read.

In halls of learning, where knowledge lies,
A tale unfolds as trust subsides.
A student, burdened by sloth and despair,
Sought an escape from the scholar's affair.
The cheater smirks, feeling quite clever,
But now they've hurt others forever.
For those who worked with honest might,
Their efforts now dimmed by this unfair light.
A student cheats and others fall.
Their hard work worthless, discarded, small.
They spent long nights and early morns,
But now their grades are simply torn.
Their diligent hearts, their spirits shook,
Dreams now tarnished, like a once-sparkling brook.
Efforts abandoned, pride dismayed,
By the actions of one who sought an easier way.
The teacher's trust, now broken, frayed,
Their disappointment now portrayed.
The student's future, now shaken, unsure,
A once peaceful classroom now impure.
So, let us stand, united, strong,
Resilient in truth, against all that is wrong.
For the offender will stumble in life's grand test,
Where honor and knowledge forever rest.

The crowd is abuzz with mumblings of "Wait, so Melissa cheated?" and "I
bet it was ChatGPT!" and "I knew that she couldn't write for shit!"

As Melissa enters the hall, the buzz dies down. We all stare. But she's not
alone. Ms. Watkins, an English teacher, marches with her, heels clacking,
holding the same flier in her hands. As they disappear into her classroom, my
phone buzzes in my pocket. Other people's do the same.

@Revenge has made a new post.

I frown. Since when do *I* follow the Revenge account?

Curiously, I tap Instagram to load. A new black square shows up, this time with the number *16*. I can't quite remember the last count, but I think I've missed a few pranks between the incident at the mall and now. As I'm staring at the screen, it automatically refreshes, and another number appears: *17*.

"Huh," I mutter. "Does that mean there's *another* prank somewhere?"

"What's that?"

Jake peers over my screen. His brow furrows when he sees the row of squares. "I thought you said you didn't follow that."

"I-I don't," I mumble. "Maybe I've been hacked."

A different teacher steps into the hallway from a nearby classroom. "Okay, everyone. Let's get moving." He glances uneasily at the fliers now scattered all over the floor. A few more staff members round the corner, including the principal, and they all urge the students to move along.

Splitting with Jake, who is in a classroom on the other side of the hall, I follow the others back to homeroom. As I slide into my seat, everyone is talking about the fliers.

Craig Lowry, who is rarely seen without his scuffed-up skateboard, makes a face. "Someone should have reported her, then. Not gone to that psycho account with it."

Allison Samuels shakes her head. "Um, to who? Principal Morgan? Talk about shooting the messenger. All hail Revenge, I say."

"Okay, can we stop?" Calli rolls her eyes. "There's no way this Revenge person is responsible for everything."

"Or maybe you're just scared," Allison snarks. "Revenge still has another one to go. Maybe you're worried you're next."

• • •

After the bell rings at the end of first period, I gather my books and head to AP English. I'm still puzzling over how @Revenge is on my Instagram now. Is this some sort of weird cyber-spying happening? Like, just because I looked at Emily's Instagram where *she* follows @Revenge, it somehow loaded on my phone, too?

I see Emily standing outside my classroom door. Which is puzzling. I've got Emily's schedule memorized, and she has Latin II first period. That room is all the way across the school.

When she spies me, her face crumples. "Sabrina. It's awful. Come with me."

"What's wrong?" I gasp.

Emily leads me into the far corner of the bathroom. It's so close to the bell that no one is in here anyway. When she turns to me, it looks like she might cry.

"It's awful," she whispers. "I can't believe it. I think I might throw up."

"*What?*" I explode. "Tell me!" My heart is pounding. Something with her brother? Her mom?

Emily's shoulders shake. I'm not sure I've ever witnessed her like this, not even when she broke her ankle after tripping over a root trying a cartwheel in my backyard.

"P-Principal Morgan called me into his office," Emily blubbers. "And somehow . . . someone must have . . ." She looks up at me helplessly. "He knew about me and Jeremy in the music room. And . . ."—her voice drops ominously—"*the gummies.*"

My blood turns cold. "W-What?"

"He's already told Harvard, and they rescinded my acceptance! I-I have to do in-school suspension until the honor board meets! No free periods, no school events, Saturday community service. He's calling my mom now."

My stomach is tied in a knot. "Who . . . who told?"

"I have no idea . . . I just don't understand how he found out. We kept it so quiet!" she wails. "My whole life is ruined!"

"Oh, Emily," My heart shatters. "I'm so sorry." And I know I do mean this.

Emily looks up at me and tried to smile. "At least now you'll probably get in. I mean that's good, right?" Her breath catches.

I stare at her, dumbfounded. It's the worst silver lining I can imagine.

The bathroom door bangs open, and Mrs. Rowan, an aide who sometimes acts as the hall monitor, sticks her head in and gives us a sharp look. "Shouldn't you girls be in class?"

We duck our heads and move toward the door. Then Emily catches my arm. "Please don't tell anyone. Some of my teachers don't even know yet. It's so humiliating. My life is over!"

"It's going to be okay," I assure her. "We'll figure this out." But . . . *will* it? I actually don't know.

Emily looks at me with doom and hugs me tight. "I just can't believe this happened. Why was I so stupid?"

She turns and heads down the hall with her head bowed. There's a huge lump in my throat. My insides feel like they're being ripped apart. *How* did this happen?

As I head back to class, my phone buzzes at my hip. I pull it out, startled anyone is texting me during school hours. But it's not a text. It's a DM. I blink at the familiar yet unfamiliar handle, and my heart seizes at the personalized note.

> **@Revenge:** You're welcome.

I stare again down the hall where Emily has just disappeared. That nagging, spiky feeling I had over break is happening again. Why is Revenge texting *me*? How does Revenge even have access to my DMs?

And yet, when I scroll up, I find a whole conversation between Revenge . . . *and me.* When did *this* happen? At the very top of the DMs I read:

> You have requested to be friends with **@Revenge** . . .

and then

> **@Revenge** has accepted your friend request.

My mouth hangs open. *I* requested it. Am I losing my mind?

But then I look at the time and date stamp. It's four days ago. 11:45 p.m. *The night of the party.* The night I don't remember.

My stomach sinks like a stone.

I stare at the text bubbles. When I read them, my heart starts to race.

> I hope u can help me . . .
> . . . It's just so unfair . . .
> . . . Harvard's always been my dream . . .

I clap my hand over my mouth, terrified I might throw up. The memory comes to me with a bolt: *Standing outside, head spinning, teeth chattering, feeling . . . compelled. Righteous, even.* And then, writing:

> . . . can't believe Emily would . . .
> . . . in the orchestra room . . .
> . . . an entire gummy . . .
> . . . she was stoned . . . On campus!

I race to the bathroom before I puke.

eight

I don't know how I make it through school. I don't know how I'm able to do my homework. Every second, I fear I'm going to be found out. *How* could I be so stupid? *How* could I have done this to Emily? But also, how could I have known? Even if I was angry and wanted retribution, Revenge always posts silly, embarrassing pranks. Not something that would destroy someone's life. Until today. Why did Revenge do this to Emily? Why did Revenge do this to *me*?

That night, Dad tells me that Kaye and Parker are coming over for dinner. I just don't have it in me to make conversation. I convince my dad I'm sick with a stomach bug. A carryover from the bug I had this weekend, maybe. But a few minutes after six, I hear a knock.

"Honey?" It's my dad's voice that rings through, sweet and concerned. "Are you feeling any better?"

"Not really," I mutter as he walks in.

"Poor thing," he says, ruffling my hair. He sits on the side of my bed. "You sure you don't want to come down even for a minute? Kaye got you some chicken soup."

One of my eyebrow's arches. "I hate chicken soup." I know my tone is a little too harsh, and his shoulders drop.

"I don't know why you have to be like that," he says tightly. "I'm sorry about what happened with Harvard. The timing was terrible, and I shouldn't have shown you the envelope in front of Kaye and Parker . . . but Harvard isn't the only school out there."

I shut my eyes, annoyed that he's rehashing this.

"Kaye has some interesting ideas about some things you can add to your applications for those other schools. And some thoughts about other places you might want to apply. Good fits for you."

Oh, because she's a college counselor now? Plus, of course he's three steps behind. Like always. I pull the covers over my head and turn toward the wall. "I don't *feel* good, okay?" Now in so many *more* ways.

I can sense Dad standing above me, maybe trying to think about what to say or how to make it better. I know he loves me. I do. But without my mom, he just doesn't really know how to parent. I guess I'd hoped he would fill the void when she died. But he doesn't. He mostly just leaves me be. It's like he thinks somehow my mom is still doing the heavy lifting. Finally, he sighs.

"Okay," he mumbles begrudgingly. "Get some rest." I hear the latch catch as he closes my door.

Once I'm sure my dad is downstairs, I reach for my phone and scroll through my DMs.

> You're welcome.

• • •

I pick up my phone and navigate to Revenge's account, first looking at my crazed DMs and then Revenge's chilling message. Then, I scroll back through all the squares, looking for some kind of tell. Who *is* Revenge, anyway? Why can't we figure it out? Should I report Revenge? As furious as I am about what Revenge has done to Emily, I can't forget that Revenge has also punished total jerks. Clearly, to some people, Revenge keeps the peace and fights for justice.

But this? Yes, deep down, the hurt I feel for what Emily did is still there, but I didn't want this. I thought maybe Revenge would just embarrass her. Or expose Emily for what she'd done to *me*. Then again, if that's *all* I wanted, why had I included the thing about Emily and the weed? If I just wanted it to be about Emily and me, why didn't I leave it out? *You are a terrible person. You knew what you wanted. And that's what you got.*

I'm about to turn off my phone for the night when I notice something on my Instagram account I hadn't noticed before. There's a "1" on the message's icon, indicating I have a new DM. I frown. I swear I just checked my DMs. But when I click into my messages, my chat with Revenge is in bold. My stomach lurches. And when I look at the message, my heart drops to my knees.

> Be outside your gym locker @ 2:30 tomorrow
> or I tell your BFF who ruined her life.

nine

Bang.

The door to the gym locker room heaves open and knocks against the wall, letting out last period gym class. By the looks of it, it's freshmen only—upperclassmen can use their after-school sports as a P.E. credit or—for un-sporty people like me—they can opt for a credit in the history of modern dance.

A pack of sweaty boys spills out of the locker room. I watch as the girls exit their locker room looking a little more polished. Truth be told, everyone's just happy school's over.

But for me, the day has just begun.

It's 2:27 p.m. I've spent the last twelve hours running through every possible scenario, trying to guess, desperately, what Revenge was going to ask me to do. I lurk just to the left of a huge banner outside the gym for the varsity boys' basketball team. Above me are images of tree-tall boys all lined up, including Jake. Finn stands in the middle, the ball tucked casually at his hip. At the bottom of the banner is a list of the season's schedule, which includes a game later tonight. An *important* game, I remember Jake telling me. The game he'd been upset about because scouts were going to be there—and once again, the coach had passed him over.

I turn back to the locker room door. A few minutes have passed, and I'm fairly certain everyone is gone. My heart pounds. *I'm here. Now what?* And *what if someone sees me?* There aren't kids in the locker room, but there are other rooms being used close by for after-school activities. In fact, I can hear the orchestra warming up a few doors down. *Emily!* I kind of can't believe it. If I were her, I would have gone home to drown my sorrows, but she showed up at school today as usual, putting on a brave face. She even smiled at me, clearly having no idea what I'd done. The guilt is ripping me in half. I wonder if I could talk to Principal Morgan and try to convince him to go easier on Emily? She's never, ever done anything wrong. She shouldn't be penalized like this.

It's next on my list. But first, I have to handle Revenge. I don't want to do what Revenge asked. It's too dangerous. Then again, if I *don't*, Revenge will tell Emily—and everyone else. I'd lose her as a friend, and I'd probably lose college prospects and my dad's respect. Revenge has me right where they want me. Whatever Revenge needed done, I could only hope that it was quick, painless, and then I'd be free. Well, free to clean up Emily's mess, that is.

As if on cue, the moment the hand on the clock moves to 2:30, my phone buzzes with a DM. I glance around. *Where are you?* Revenge has got to be somewhere close, watching. All day, I'd looked for Ryder Cross in the halls. Could it be him? I didn't see Ryder anywhere, though that isn't unusual. It seems he comes to school whenever he likes.

And now, the hall is empty. The sidewalks outside the school are empty, too.

I click on the message.

> Grab the bottle on windowsill next to you.

I look around to see if anyone is watching me. No one is here. *Who are you?* My hands are shaking, but I look down at my phone and keep reading.

> Go to locker 18 in the boys' locker room.
> Pour the contents into Finn Walters's bottle.
> The locker room will be empty for 5 minutes
> before cleaners come. Go!

I peek at the windowsill in question. Sure enough, there's what looks like a sports drink bottle, but it has no label on it other than a star sticker on top. Had it *always* been there? And . . . *Finn*? I'm pranking *Finn*? I wish it was literally anyone else. *Anyone.* This can't be happening.

> Who asked for this? What did Finn do?

It's weird to think Revenge is talking with me, and even weirder to think that it could be Ryder Cross behind the screen. Ryder Cross and I have never said a word to one another.

Then I see:

> Not your problem. He's not a good person.

That could mean anything. It's a matter of opinion, too.

> Is this how it works? You don't even do any of your own dirty work? You just have like a revolving door of paybacks? People you're blackmailing?

> It's not blackmail.
> It's justice.

I want to leave. Like now. But I look around and think better of it. Revenge is probably watching me, enjoying every bit of this. I know I'm trapped. Revenge knows it too.

> What's in this drink?

> Relax. It's EnergyFX. It makes Finn break
> out in hives. It'll be fun to see such a
> dick scratching his balls all the way
> through the big game, don't you think?

I swallow hard. Something jolts inside me, then—a memory of Finn at the party just days before. The way he'd looked at that kid accusingly, asking if the drink he just stole from him had EnergyFX in it. He *had* said something about it giving him hives, actually.

> What did Finn do?

> A lie for a lie. That's all you need to know.
> Trust me, people will thank you.

Thank me? A memory comes to me, from not that long ago. It was after lunch at school, and I was heading to Physics II. I came around the corner and saw Finn blocking the way of some freshman boys. Even from where I stood, I could tell he was teasing them just by his imposing body language. There were looks of dread and shame on the other boys' faces, and it seemed like Finn was enjoying himself.

It wasn't the only time I'd seen Finn do this, either. He seemed to enjoy making people feel small. Even me, at the party, I realized, looking at me like he had no idea who I was despite the fact that we'd gone to school together since we were little.

I thought again about the other people Revenge had targeted. A lot of them had done bad things, and Revenge calling them out had halted the behavior. Maybe one of those guys who'd been bullied reached out to Revenge and called for this prank? So then, if I didn't carry out Revenge's wishes, what if Revenge passed on Finn and moved on to the next victim? Finn would keep picking on people.

People loved Revenge. People feared Revenge. It was like having The

Punisher at your school, fighting the good fight for the underdog. Whatever Finn did, I'm sure he deserves it. Besides, vigilantes are cool, right? I know I'm rationalizing, but thinking about it this way makes me feel a teensy bit better.

Out the window, several buses chug to the stoplight. Five minutes and counting. I grab the EnergyFX bottle. It feels full. I recognize the star sticker on the cap from somewhere—a mini mart?—but I can't think where. It's hard to tell, but it looks sealed. Hives aren't that bad. And if Jake gets to play, well, that wouldn't be the worst thing, would it?

> How am I going to get in his locker?
> Did u think of that?
> I don't have his combination.

I keep waiting for a response. Nothing. This is some sort of trap. I knew I shouldn't have come here. I'm going to—

> It's all taken care of. Hurry up!

Even though no one's around, I glance in all directions, just in case. This is some serious cray. My heart pounds as I open the locker room door. The door is so loud, but I try to do it quickly. If someone catches me, I'll just play dumb. *Oops! Walked into the boys' locker room by mistake! Don't mind me and my innocent sports drink!*

The locker room is empty and eerily quiet. The only noticeable sound is the drip, drip from one of the showers. I want to walk over and tighten the knob. I glance at my watch. Then the smell hits me. Ugh. Sweaty socks and body spray. What's not to love? A stray sock under a bench. Gross. To the right are the gym teachers' offices, but thankfully the doors are closed, and no one is inside.

I start down one aisle of lockers, then the next, searching for some sort of designated area for the basketball players. Finally, I find what I'm looking for—a section of lockers with a big banner that reads:

MILFORD HIGH VARSITY BASKETBALL

Just like Revenge said, they're all labeled with players' names and jersey numbers. Even though all the lockers have padlocks, most of them aren't even shut all the way. I can see inside most everyone's lockers—their shoes, their uniforms, jock straps, water bottles, balls, hoodies, and in one person's case, an expensive-looking pair of Beats headphones. I guess there's a sense of security since the area is roped off. And maybe the guys don't think anyone would mess with them, considering who they are. It's both entitled and naïve. I make a mental note that Revenge must have known about this strange little quirk. Maybe it's a clue about who Revenge is.

I duck under the rope to the square of lockers. My heart is pounding. I'm listening for footsteps. I hear the *tick* of the clock on the wall above me and look at my phone. Two minutes! *Oh God. What if they're early?* If anyone comes in here, I'm closed in and have nowhere to run.

My gaze lands on Jake's name on a locker in a corner. Unlike the others, his locker is closed and locked. But Finn's locker is wide open. I peer inside. There's only one bottle in there, a basic plastic number with bite marks in the sip top. It looks like it's been around for years, though maybe that's why Finn is superstitious about using it.

I slide the lucky bottle from the locker, half expecting alarms to blare. After I set it on the bench, I quickly twist the top to the EnergyFX bottle and work on pouring the contents inside. The whole thing takes just thirty seconds but feels like hours. There's more EnergyFX than can fit in Finn's bottle, and Revenge didn't say what to do with the extra liquid, so I replace the cap and toss the extra EnergyFX into the trash. It's not like anyone's going to raise an eyebrow at a random EnergyFX bottle. People drink EnergyFX all the time at our school.

Hurriedly, I place Finn's bottle back where I found it, trying my hardest not to bump his locker door or move it in any way. But then something catches my eye. On the inside of Finn's locker hangs a picture of a girl in red lingerie with black lace. It must be from ages ago because Brooke's boobs are way bigger now. It seems so un-Brooke to take a picture like that. And wear lingerie. Or at least the Brooke I knew. Maybe I never really knew her.

I consider leaning in to take a closer look, but the idea of looking at a naked picture of Brooke is just too weird, so I turn away.

Bang!

My spine straightens. It sounds like it came from the other side of the locker room. I press myself up against the lockers and listen for more. Footsteps. A breath. Someone's coming for me, knows what I'm up to.

It feels like eons go by. My legs are starting to cramp from the weird crouch I'm in pressed against the lockers. Finally, I stand up and peer around the corner. No one is there. Maybe I imagined it? I have a clear sight line to the door now, and I run for it. I've had enough of this locker room.

I push through the door and into the hallway again, suddenly in a cold sweat. I stare at the swinging locker room door as it eases closed. There's part of me that can't believe I did it. But there's also a part of me that's relieved. Maybe I've saved myself. Maybe this means Revenge will leave me alone. I make my way down the hall, and just as I turn the corner . . .

"Sabrina?"

I whip around, my heart leaping to my throat. Jake is sitting on the wall by the windows. He's blinking up at me as I flatten myself against the wall.

"I . . . I came to wish you luck for the game!" I can feel sweat trickling down my back.

He can probably tell I'm lying. No doubt my cheeks are red, my forehead is shiny, and I'm probably giving off some sort of scent of a liar. But after a beat, he smirks and gets to his feet. "I saw you were out this morning. Are you okay? Are you coming to the game?" Jake boyishly pulls in his bottom lip. "Not that I'll get to play much."

My mind zeroes in on that EnergyFX that's now in Finn's lucky bottle. Maybe, upon first swig, he'll be too embarrassed to step onto the court. How uncontrollable is this itching, anyway?

"I guess I could come," I say slowly.

Jake's eyes light up. "Really?"

"Sure. I guess." Best to keep an eye on how things work out on the Revenge front, actually. And now I have a good cover story for why I'm at the game in the first place. I was *asked* to go.

Jake looks pleased. "All right, then. I'll look for you."

I make up an excuse about homework and scuttle away, my cheeks blazing with a mix of excitement and dread. As I reach the parking lot, I realize something. I'm not ending this day with my life in shambles. I feel vindicated, almost, that maybe, just maybe, I've shut Finn out from the most important game of his life.

Maybe I've paid it forward and people will thank me after all.

ten

After seeing Jake, I book out of there and head home to make sure no one else has seen me lurking around. As soon I get home, I run upstairs to my room. No one is home, so I don't have to explain my urgency. I'm sure I have guilt written all over my face. I just couldn't bear it if anyone found out. I toss my purse on the bed and look in the mirror. Surprisingly, I look fine. Maybe a little stressed, but not guilty stressed. *Get a grip. It's going to be okay. It was just some stupid prank. Revenge will leave you alone now that they have what they want.*

Dad and Kaye are out tonight, and there is a note on the fridge. Leftovers. Not that I could eat right now anyway. Before I can set the note down, my phone buzzes.

It's Emily. I hate putting her off. I hate not having her to confide in. I know she thinks I'm still mad. If only she knew.

· · ·

I'm waiting at the light when my phone rings. *Emily, again!* And she wants to FaceTime? Oh God, I can't talk right now, but if I don't pick up, I will look like a bad friend. *Do you hear yourself right now? You are a bad friend. Pick up. She needs you.* Even though I'm not supposed to talk and drive, I have to take this. But I only take the audio call. Emily knows me better than anyone. She would know something was up just by the stress all over my face.

"Hey."

"Hey. You don't want to FaceTime?"

"Can't—I'm driving."

I decide to tell Emily I'm going to the game. I tell her about running into Jake and how I told him I was planning to come. I fail to mention that I said that out of panic. Yet another lie to keep the others company.

"You must *really* like him if you're going to a basketball game," Emily says. "It's not like *you* go to games, unless the band is performing."

Emily's voice is heavy, not her usual chipper self. Nice job. Destroying your best friend's life. Pranking the star basketball player. What was Harvard thinking? I'm a real catch.

Traffic for the game is thick and slow. I guess varsity boys' basketball is way bigger than I realized.

"I went to a few football games by choice, remember?" Emily informs me. "I *tried* to get you to come."

"I can't believe I'm even going to this," I groan. "And I can't believe you can't sit with me in the stands."

"I'm on house arrest. Only school and home—and playing warm-up songs with the band at crucial basketball games." Emily tries to make a joke, but she sounds miserable. "I'm definitely outta there the moment they take the court. Mom said I'm only able to go because the band *needs* me. Though I don't see the point, honestly. Why even stay in band when it's not going to get me anywhere?"

"What about Berklee College of Music?" I ask. When we were talking about colleges, she thought about going there just out of spite since being a musician was the last thing her mother wanted.

Emily's quiet for a moment. "Maybe."

I can hear the disappointment in her voice. It's like a knife to the heart. I have *profoundly* impacted Emily's future.

"I could go talk to Principal Morgan for you," I blurt out.

Emily's silent for a moment. "And say . . . what?"

"I don't know. That you're a good person. That you didn't mean anything. That . . . that you were talked into it, maybe! Did Jeremy talk you into it?"

"That's really sweet of you, Sabrina," Emily says in a soft voice, "but don't. Jeremy is in trouble, too. I think it might make things worse."

The light still hasn't changed. Then, a siren whoops by. I watch as the truck makes a precarious left turn; the siren fades away.

"Are you almost at school?" Emily asks. "Game's gonna start soon."

I clench the steering wheel. "Is this dumb? I don't even know anyone who's going. I'm going to look like an idiot. Maybe he asked a whole bunch of people to come. Maybe he was just being nice."

"Stop it. You're a senior. It's completely not weird that you're going to your school's basketball game. It's what you're *supposed* to do. Wave at me from the stands."

There are rustling noises on her end. "*Gotta go*," Emily whispers. "It's my mom on the other line." She quickly hangs up.

The light changes, and my lane starts to move. Every car is heading to the basketball game. After I hang up with Emily, I find a space at the back of the parking lot and slowly get out of my car. Most people who have come are in groups of three or four. I feel like I have a big sign over me that says *LOSER*. I'm astonished at my decision to even come to the game. This is huge for me. Like Emily said, I do like Jake . . . and I guess I do want to see him play.

But Jake's not the only reason. I want to see what happens to Finn. Part of me hopes he's colossally embarrassed. The tables will be turned for sure. Everyone will have a reason to tease *him*. But mostly I think I hope nothing happens. I don't like the guy, but I don't like being any part of @Revenge.

I follow the crowd into the gym. Everyone whips out their phones so the ticket-taker can scan the QR code proving they paid the ticket fee, but I, a basketball newbie who has no idea this is how the ticketing process works, wait at the kiosk to buy my ticket on the spot. I hate being out of my comfort zone. I hate not knowing what to do.

In the gym, chairs and benches are lined up on our team's sidelines, waiting for the players to arrive, but they're all empty. My gaze darts to a huge jug with an EnergyFX sticker on the side, and my chest tightens. I don't see any water bottles.

Someone elbows me from behind, and I jolt forward, feeling once again like I'm out of place. Eventually I start climbing the stands. Practically every seat is filled. The air is humid and stuffy. We're all packed in so tight you can tell who showered that day and who didn't. I look around. Everyone has a handmade sign. One catches my eye. It reads, *"He may be #18 but he's #1 in our hearts."* Another says, *"Our Boy's Got Balls."*

Ugh.

I continue my climb up the bleachers. There's a cheer from below—when I turn around, our school's cheerleaders have taken the court. A bunch of girls I recognize from Sketch's party in perky skirts and pom-poms chant and punctuate each line with a bright smile. Brooke and Tess are co-captains. *Great. I'm a literal Taylor Swift song.* A sophomore, Sophie McIntire, with a scraped-back bun, flies ten feet into the air and drops back down into a waiting crisscross of arms.

"You know every time I see a cheerleader fly, I kinda hope someone drops her."

I whip around. Where did *that* come from? But before I can tell who's speaking, the person behind me also climbing up the bleachers presses against me, and I continue to climb. I finally find a spot on the end of an aisle next to a few girls I vaguely know from the few years in middle school when I took chorus. They give me affable smiles, and I smile back and then bury my head in my phone, wishing I could text Emily, but she's probably warming up by now. I think about texting Jake, but that would look way too desperate. My heart starts to thump. *Has Finn drunk the stuff I gave him yet? How sensitive is he to it anyway? Maybe he won't react until later.* I try to push it out of my mind. After all, like Revenge said, it's not my problem. I didn't request it. I'm just the messenger.

After another ten minutes of cheerleaders dancing, I see Emily and scan the rest of the marching band. Jeremy is there, too, I guess because the band also needs his skills. I wonder how he's dealing with his own punishment. I don't know where he applied to college or if he'd gotten in anywhere yet. I can't believe I ruined *two* lives. The band finishes, and they sit down on the empty bench. Emily looks up at the stands—I assume for me—and I wave and try to catch her eye as she turns to head back out the gym doors, but I fail to catch her attention before my view of her is obstructed by the crowd. Just then, a popular techno song booms through the speakers. A disco ball I never noticed on the gym's ceiling starts to whirl.

"Helloooooooo, Milford High!" an announcer booms through a microphone.

The cheering swells. I guess this is kind of a big deal. Across the court, I see a small group of people in white and purple, the opposite team's colors. The colors seem pale in comparison to our school's vibrant crimson and gold, and the near-empty bleachers are kinda depressing. Now that I'm here, I feel even more awkward than I imagined. I consider leaving. Jake won't know I'm here, and who cares about Finn? The continued roar of the crowd unsettles me. I try to stand up, but it's like a magnetic pull is keeping me there.

"How are we *dooooo*ing today?" the announcer continues.

People bang a rhythm on the bleacher seats. A few rows down, I see Jeremy and a few of the other band members coming in to watch. Pretty ballsy of him to risk it if Principal Morgan said he and Emily couldn't stay. I consider wading through the crowd to give him a piece of my mind, but there are just too many people. I peer around for Ryder Cross, too. It seems weird that he'd be at a basketball game—I would guess he'd think that school sports, along with all other school activities, are extremely pathetic—but if he was Revenge, maybe he'd want to see his latest prank go down.

The banging continues. Courtside, I catch sight of Brooke on her feet, putting two fingers in her mouth and letting out a wolf whistle. Guilt washes over me again, and I have to do my best to quiet what seems like an impending panic attack. I've set up the prank that's going to colossally embarrass Brooke's boyfriend. Should I care? For all I know, Brooke must know full well that Finn is a jerk. Maybe staying popular is more important than the well-being of other students. It's not like I know her anymore. I think about calling Emily. She's probably in her car by now, but I feel like that would make it worse for her. And me.

The speakers crackle, and the techno music rises in pitch.

"Now, give it up for the Milford High Varsity Basketball team!" the announcer screams.

"Yeah!" the crowd screams back.

Smoke from dry ice fills the room. It swirls around the doorway that leads to the locker room. "With twenty-two assists, twenty-one points, here's your point guard, Brett Camillo!"

Brett jogs through the smoke to the center of the court. People raise posters and banners. Brett takes his place on the benches as the announcer runs through the next boy's stats—it's Sketch, the other guard. More cheers rise, though I hear someone near me cluck their tongue.

"These dudes act like they're God's gift to this school."

I look around. The voice sounds nearly in my ear, but when I do a full 360-degree turn, I don't see anyone who could have been speaking. But then, I hear the voice again.

"Do you even know who these guys *are*, announcer dude? And what they're capable of?"

Is the voice coming from my phone? But as I stare at it, no rogue video is playing.

The announcer lists the stats for the small forward, the shooting guard, and the power forward, and each boy runs through the plumes of smoke, straight to center court and then joins his team on the sidelines. I try to cheer extra loud when Jake comes out. Tess leans forward and gives him a big hug. Why do I feel territorial about him? I know I have no right to, but I don't like seeing his ex hug him like that. It must be hard to have to go to every game and almost never play. I have to agree with that grumbling voice I heard—we *are* really worshipping these players. I mean, it's great they play a sport, and rah-rah school spirit and all that, but do we cheer this much for any of the girls' teams?

Then, the lights dim even more. There's only one player left. It's taking the announcer a moment to get it together. My nerves feel sizzled. Are they scrambling in the locker room? Is Finn admitting defeat? Maybe the announcer is getting last-minute details that another player is stepping in for him.

Finally, the music grows louder. "And now, put your hands together for Milford High's Center . . . with seventy-two total points this year, twenty-eight assists, and fifty-two rebounds . . . number 18, *Finn Walters*!"

Finn appears through the smoke, and the whole gym erupts. Finn struts through the smoke, pounding on his chest and making pumping-up gestures to the crowd. Tess gives him a big hug, too. He breaks away, picks up Brooke and twirls her around. Such a showman. He looks . . . *fine*.

But then I notice something in Finn's hand. *His lucky bottle*. He's carrying it with him. The bottle is opaque, so I can't tell if he drank any.

Off on the sides, the other players are stripping off their warm-up gear. That includes the guys who aren't starting. I spy Jake pulling his sweatshirt over his head, his jersey rising up for a moment and revealing a taut strip of bare abs. My heart flips.

Finn makes a "more" gesture with his arms for the crowd, encouraging them to cheer louder. His smile is huge and assured, as if he's sure he's going to win this game all on his own. Off to the side, Brooke whistles through her teeth again and again. The spotlights gleam against Finn's forehead as he turns 360 degrees to take in the whole gym. It's only when he turns to face us again that I notice there's sweat on his brow. As in a *lot* of sweat. Maybe the itchiness is finally hitting him? And maybe he's trying to control the urge to scratch. That would make me sweat for sure.

His arms drop. I expect his right hand to creep to his crotch, but it just hangs at his side as if it's been severed. A confused expression crosses his face. Actually, it's confusion mixed with something else.

Fear.

I watch as Finn drops to his knees. The lucky water bottle releases from his hands and rolls onto the court.

"Yeah, kiss the ground, Finn!" someone near me bellows, but that isn't what he's doing.

Finn's on his hands and knees now, heaving. There's a palpable, obvious moment when the crowd starts to realize something is wrong. The cheers wane and then stop, replaced by a burble of worried murmurs. The music still drones on, but no one is clapping along with the beat. A few boys on the sidelines are on their feet now, and some have taken a few steps toward Finn to see if he's okay—including Jake.

Maybe it's a coincidence. Maybe it has nothing to do with the drink.

But then Finn's body convulses. Vomit spews from his mouth and covers the shiny gym floor. A collective *ugh* snaps through the bleachers. The basketball coach runs for Finn. He tries to help Finn up, but Finn can't stand. The murmurs in the crowd intensify. There are whispers, too, and gasps. The music finally stops, which only makes the situation seem even graver. We all watch as Finn's knees buckle, and he goes into some sort of seizure.

"Call 911!" Coach screams to an assistant behind him. A medic rushes forward to Finn. The players surround his body, which makes it difficult for me to see what's going on. Brooke has pushed to the court, too, along with a woman who must be Finn's mother—I don't know what other middle-aged woman would feel she has the right to shove through a bunch of high school boys.

My gaze darts to the lucky bottle—which, irony of ironies, has rolled all the way to the sidelines and is very, *very* visible.

"Is he going to be okay?" Voices swirl.

"It looks like he puked up an organ."

"That can happen, you know."

"He was fine just a minute ago."

The court seems to vibrate before my eyes. Our school's mascot, a tall kid wearing a horse costume, seems to have grown over nine feet tall. In the doorway, I see people who can't be here—my mother, Kaye, Emily. When I blink, they're gone again.

Suddenly, the place is swarming with EMTs. People rush in with a stretcher. A few minutes later, they've got Finn on the gurney and are wheeling him toward the exit. A medic is straddling Finn's body, squeezing some sort of tube into his mouth. They go by in a flash—they're sprinting, and I can't get a very good look. And then they're gone, the doors slamming closed. A good portion of the arena tries to go out with them, but only Finn's mother, Brooke, and a few others are allowed to follow before security steps in to keep the rest of us inside.

Principal Morgan appears in the middle of the court. He whispers to our school's boys' basketball coach, as well as the coach from Hartford's team, and then waves his arms to the crowd as if that's going to get our attention.

"Everyone," Morgan booms into the microphone. It screeches with feedback. "*PEOPLE!*" He screams again when no one quiets down.

"I'm sorry we all had to see that, but the medics assured me Finn is in good hands and is going to be fine! Of course, if you are concerned about what just happened, I encourage you to see one of the school counselors tomorrow. In the meantime, we know Finn would want his team to continue. So please stay, enjoy, and GO EAGLES!"

More murmurs. Some sighs of relief. Some people sound outraged. I can't get my heart rate down. I'm holding on to Principal Morgan's encouraging words. I know they said he was going to be fine, but he looked really bad.

I'm so lost in thought that I don't even notice that Jake is heading out to start the game until he's almost at the center of the court. Applause begins. Then people start to chant, "*Jake, Jake, Jake!*"

Jake keeps his shoulders square, and his brow is furrowed. I wonder how he's processing what happened to Finn. Jake wanted to play but not because of something like this. But as the players move into position, and Jake tips the ball toward his teammates, he starts to get into a groove. There's a lot I don't know about basketball, and I can't tell you the rules or the play patterns, and I don't even have a solid sense of the scoring system, but even I can tell that he's good.

My phone buzzes, and I look down, thinking it might be some sort of school-wide update about Finn. It's an update, all right. Just not the kind I was hoping for.

> **@Revenge** has made a new post.

I stare at the alert on my screen and click in to see what it was. A brand-new black square bearing the number *18* has appeared on Revenge's page, time-stamped a few minutes ago. Nausea roils in my gut. Around me, I can see other people reaching for their phones, too. Reading this. Seeing this. Drawing conclusions about what they've just witnessed. I want to get up, go outside, but I know that would look suspicious. So, it's only the minute the game ends, with Milford High defeating Hartford by a wide margin primarily due to Jake's performance, that I make a beeline for the exit.

I'm panicking, and I assume Revenge must be, too. It's one thing to cause someone to break out in hives, a whole other thing to *send them to the hospital*. My phone beeps again. This time, it's two new DM alerts. I feel like there's a huge spotlight on me because of who they're from. Shielding my phone, I read them . . . and then feel like I might throw up.

Nice work, Sabrina.

BTW, Principal Morgan was lying.
Seems everyone does.

eleven

The next twelve hours are a nightmare I can only think of in snippets. Flashes of moments, dark and light and dark again. The swarm of bodies I had to push through to leave the gym. The sweat pouring down my back. The dizziness and nausea and the feeling I might faint.

I stumble to my car, fumble for my keys, then peek over my shoulder for fear someone—Revenge—is following me, or at least watching. The night is dark and bleak. The lights of the gym glow. Another cheer rises up and then another. In the distance, I think I hear an ambulance, but I don't really know.

I jump into my car and slam the door. Then I crank the radio and scream into my hands. *What does Revenge mean Principal Morgan lied? What's wrong with Finn? And was this what Revenge knew would happen all along?*

· · ·

I can barely drive. I'm too shaky.

Refresh. No news from Brooke's socials.

Refresh. No news from the school's socials.

Refresh. No news anywhere.

Refresh. No news.

A text from Jake:

> Hey, where r u looked for u after the game?

I don't answer. I can't answer.

Refresh.

No news.

Refresh.

No news.

Refresh.

No news.

. . .

The bathroom tile at home is cool against my cheek. I have lain on this floor so many times during my panic attacks. Waiting to throw up. Waiting for it to pass. Waiting to die. My phone buzzes on the sink so many times that it vibrates itself right off the counter. I grab for it, thinking it's news, finally. But Emily's name flashes on the screen. When I answer, her voice is far away, like she's talking through water.

"What happened? Someone said Finn Walters collapsed!"

I must give her an answer, because there's a pause, and then she speaks again.

"OMG, is he okay?"

Do I say no? Do I believe Revenge?

There was a new square from Revenge. "Oh God. I can't look. Do you think he . . . ?" I hang up the phone before I let anything slip.

My secret has unfolded like a sweater that's suddenly released from its vacuum packaging. It takes up all the space inside me now. It presses at the insides of my skin to force its way out. I now weigh a thousand pounds because of it. No matter how much I vomit, the secret is still there. I had tried so hard to keep my life from ever spinning out of control. And I could never have predicted this.

Sabrina?
U still there?
R u ok?

Somehow I manage to look at my phone. I've missed three texts. But I can't answer back. Not now. We are still friends. This is the length I've gone to in order to maintain our friendship. I don't remember hanging up. But I do remember flopping back down on the tile floor and letting out a groan.

I don't deserve my bed. Only cold hardness. My heart is pounding so loud I think I just. Might. Die. And I wonder if maybe that would be better.

· · ·

The next thing I feel is my father, shaking me awake.

"Sabrina. *Sabrina.* You okay, honey?"

I'm still in the bathroom. I must have passed out on the floor. The overhead lights make my father's face look green. I feel like I'm in two places at once as I sit up: in my body, heavy with my secret, but also floating on the ceiling, disengaged—a ghost.

I mumble something about not being able to kick the awful stomach flu, but that I'll be okay.

But my father hesitates. He leans against the door jamb and shuts his eyes. It seems his skin has gone even greener than before.

"Honey, I have to tell you something."

His voice breaks. His eyes water. I know what he's going to say before his lips part, and he lets out a strange choking noise. I know it, and I try to close my ears, but the words come anyway.

"Someone from your class has had some sort of allergic reaction and collapsed. A boy. Finn Walters. I . . . I just got an email from the school."

I blink at him blearily. "Is he going to be okay? Can I see the email?" I ask, desperate for any news.

"Well . . . yes, I think so." He cocks his head. "You knew about this?"

I nod miserably. "Where is he now?"

"At the hospital." He lets out a breath. "Apparently, it happened at a basketball game."

I nod and he blows air from his cheeks. He hands me his phone. I scan through it for any positive news. It's pretty cut and dry. It says little about

Finn, more just that it might have been upsetting to students who were there and that the school counselors would be available 24/7. The school, as always, covering its ass.

He thinks I'm sad, mournful, shocked, scared. He doesn't know the monster that truly lurks inside me. But I'm too weak to admit what I've done. I have to let him believe what he believes.

All the while, my secret expands.

. . .

I pick up my phone and search for posts on Instagram.

Refresh.

Brooke posted on Instagram at 3:15 a.m. a broken heart image. Nothing else.

Refresh.

No news.

Finn's mother, who I found on Facebook, posted more details. A whole timeline, in fact, so I can now relive the tragedy I caused.

At 7:05 p.m., Finn collapsed on the basketball court. We all saw.

At 7:07 p.m., the team medic gave him an EpiPen with the belief he was in anaphylactic shock. We all saw.

At 7:14 p.m., they stabilized him and took him into the ambulance. He was in the ambulance when his heart arrested.

At 7:21 p.m., he got to the ER, and as they were transferring him into a room, his heart arrested again.

At 7:59 p.m., he was stable but put into a coma to prevent any further arresting, and they were awaiting further diagnosing.

She thanked everyone for their kind thoughts and prayers but asked to please not call or come by the house so the family could focus on helping Finn.

No talk of why. Only hysteria. Only deep, penetrating sadness. Only thoughts and prayers. Only pictures of Finn at his best when he was shining and healthy and alive.

I don't dare check @Revenge's Instagram account. I don't want any connection with them anymore. I unfollow.

But I know it isn't enough.

twelve

The next morning, my father is waiting for me at breakfast.
Normally he's gone by the time I come down.

"You don't have to go into school today if you don't want to," he says. "I know it's hard."

I shrug. "I should go." Staying home will be worse. Staying home, my thoughts will spiral and balloon. At least there I can try and focus on something else. Maybe find out more about how Finn is doing.

"Well, I'd rather you didn't drive, with you still not feeling well," he says.

Great, now is the moment he decides to play the doting father? But I can't argue.

"Sabrina," he says softly, his eyes on the table. "If this is bringing up any feelings . . . any memories . . . I know what you saw, with Mom—I know how hard that was."

I shudder. That's why he thinks I'm so shell-shocked—because I've gone right back to the place where I was when we lost her. He thinks I'm reliving it all over again. I guess that at least explains my reaction over someone he thinks I barely know.

"It's not that," I assure him. But maybe it is more than I know. Perhaps I'd known, deep down, that *something* was going to happen to him. This was my fault. Again.

I want to scream.

Somehow, I make it into school. My phone keeps buzzing. I fear it's Revenge, torturing me some more, but it's only Emily, calling me over and over. I don't answer. I fear my voice will give everything away. I just need to pull myself together.

In the halls, everyone is buzzing about Finn. It seems that every few steps I take, someone is bursting into tears or quietly singing or forming a prayer circle. Maybe if I hadn't been responsible for this, I would point out that half the people crying probably hated Finn for being a jerk to them. But I know I'm just trying to make myself feel better. He may have been a jerk, but he didn't deserve this. I wish I could cry, too, because at least I would blend in.

At the door to homeroom, my teacher is a traffic director. "No homeroom today. There's an assembly," she tells everyone who tries to come into the room. "Go to the auditorium."

I'm swept in the sea of students all heading for the auditorium. My phone buzzes again. It's Emily.

> Come sit w me I'm near the top

I halfheartedly look around, but I'm glad when I don't locate her. I'm safer around people who don't know me well, who aren't able to read my emotions.

I'm sitting mostly with people from my homeroom since my homeroom teacher sent us all here together. Hushed whispers swirl around me. I hear Finn's name again and again. *Heart attack*, people are saying. *Medicated coma. Breathing tube.* They've read his mom's post on Facebook, too.

Principal Morgan steps onstage, and the room goes quiet. He looks haggard and exhausted. I wonder if he's even slept. His mouth wobbles like he might sob at the slightest provocation. He'd be in good company. Right next to me, Marissa Tirelli, who I'm not sure even *knows* Finn, bursts into tears. Why is it people love to take part in other people's tragedies? Does it make them feel important?

"I'm sure you've all heard the difficult news," he says into the microphone, his voice catching. "Many of you were there last night. It's shocking. Traumatic. I highly encourage you all to lean on one another for support and friendship. If you're having trouble processing what's happened, we have an extra staff of counselors at the ready. You can leave class at any time. Their doors are always open. Always."

Murmurs. Soft whispers. I wonder how long the lines for the counselors will be. Snaking out the door, probably. I don't dare go. I don't trust myself with what I'll say.

Principal Morgan clears his throat. "However, there has been a recent development about the cause of Mr. Walters's . . . condition. I can't share the details, but there appears to be many concerns about what Mr. Walters ate or drank that day. So, we ask if you have any information regarding this, you contact me immediately."

Whispers spiral through the crowd. My heart feels like it's seizing. They know. *They already know.* And . . . this proves it, now. What I gave Finn, in that EnergyFX bottle—it must have made this happen. It was poison.

A hand shoots up. Someone calls out, "What does that mean?"

"He ate the cafeteria food?" another voice guffaws.

Someone coughs, but I can hear them push out "*Revenge?*"

Morgan waves his hands to shush us. "People, please! Let's not jump to conclusions. It's an ongoing investigation. However, I do want to bring to your attention something that may or may not have to do with this incident." He glares at the crowd. "The social media account targeting students from this school. This account purports to get revenge on students for any and all reasons. I'm sure many of you are familiar with it?"

I suck in my stomach. Around me, the crowd shifts, and squirms.

"Whoever is running this account has evaded our staff, as have those who have made the requests for revenge. But this is intolerable. *In fact, it is actually criminal.* The school has involved a private IT firm in conjunction with the police department to get to the bottom of this site—and we will, I promise you. And please know that the owner or owners of the account as well as everyone involved with requests for revenge—will all be brought to justice." He glares into the crowd. "*All of you.* Every last one."

I bite down hard on the inside of my cheek. My vision starts to tunnel.

Morgan holds up a finger. "If you know something, if you did something, come forward; tell us. Even if you put in a request, even if your revenge was carried out, you won't be as severely punished as you might if you choose to remain quiet and we find out later. Because we *will* find out."

A hand shoots up in the front, and though Morgan clocks it, he waves it away. "As far as Mr. Walters, we don't know if this was connected or not, and I'm certainly not going to start rumors, though I will say there's some evidence that whoever runs this site may have taken credit for Mr. Walter's accident. It's a dangerous coincidence, one that is stopping right now." He stares around the room again. "If you remain quiet, and we find out you were involved, it's not just a matter of being expelled. There will be criminal charges. There may well be *jail time*. Do you understand?"

The auditorium has gone silent. So silent, in fact, that I'm terrified everyone can hear my beating heart. IT professionals. Confessions. *Criminal charges*. Someone is going to talk. Someone must know who Revenge is. IT detectives can figure it out. That's their *job*. Or what if someone who confesses provides a vital lead? *What if someone links this back to me?*

If only I had just admitted what I'd done to Emily. It's bad, but it's not *criminal*. But now . . . there's no way I can say anything, to *anyone*. Even if I explain I had no idea what was in the EnergyFX bottle and thought it was just something that would embarrass Finn, not kill him. No one will buy it.

Jail. I . . . I . . . the guilt I'm feeling is bad enough. It's Revenge who deserves to go, not me. Only, what if they don't find Revenge? What if *I'm* the only linchpin that will help them crack the case? If Finn really was almost murdered—and I have to think he was—I can't sit on my hands, can I?

Can I?

Think, I will my sluggish brain. There must be a way to figure out exactly who Revenge is within the two-day window. There has to be a way to nail Revenge and make them accountable for this. I have to at least *try*. Or they'll be coming for *me*.

thirteen

Think, I tell myself as we stream out of the auditorium toward our first classes. The mood is somber. Everyone is whispering—about Finn? Speculation about Revenge? Someone in this crowd *is* Revenge—or they know who Revenge *is*. A person like that can't act in a vacuum. So many other pranks have been carried out. Don't all those people who asked for them feel the tiniest bit guilty? Or scared they'd get in trouble?

Then again, most of those pranks weren't nearly as bad. A locker full of tampons. A funny song. Outing someone who plagiarized. It was hazing, for sure, but not murder. Emily's and Finn's were the worst pranks for sure. Is *that* a clue about Revenge's identity? Because here's the thing—Revenge, when it comes down to it, is the judge. A person can give a terrible sob story about their peer, but it's up to Revenge to choose if and how they're punished. So, then: Why is Emily taking my spot at college worse than Grant cheating on his girlfriend—or a homophobic guy, for that matter, or a bully? And while I don't know what Finn did, how did he earn such a terrible punishment? And who asked for it?

Is this *personal?*

Not that it helps me with my suspects. There isn't much intersection between people who know Finn and people who know Emily. I wish I'd watched everyone more carefully at the party, but, well, I was too busy getting drunk. I think about the party again, though, remembering the painted Kia, which Revenge had also done. Ryder Cross was there, chugging that beer. He seems the obvious place to start.

• • •

Ryder's locker is near Emily's toward the back of the school. As I get closer, I see Emily waving to me to come over. She's clearly ready to burst over the recent events. Emily is all about the drama.

"This is insane!" she whispers when she sees me. "IT detectives? Revenge must be panicked!"

"Yeah, pretty crazy," I say dully.

Emily cocks her head at me. "I can't believe I missed it."

I raise my eyebrows, "Be glad you did. He looked really bad." And then, because I don't know how else to get through to her, and maybe because it's a little bit true, I also add, "It was kind of triggering. About my mom, all that . . ."

Emily's eyes soften. "Oh. Bri. Sorry. I should have realized. This must be really hard for you." She slings an arm around me. "He'll be okay, though. I have faith. Plus, I checked his astrology chart, and it said he had healing in his future."

Ugh. When will Emily realize all of that is ridiculous? Emily heads off to her science lab, and I scout around for Ryder, who normally stands out from the crowd with his half-shaved head, his broad, meaty face, his cheeks full of acne, and his affinity for slamming his locker door closed in sudden bursts of anger. When I get to where I think his locker is, the area is empty. I can't expect Ryder to be there just because I want him to be.

I slump against the cinderblock walls, wondering how I might track him down. Then I realize. Maybe I don't need to talk to Ryder at all. Maybe I just need a record of where he's been.

I try to come up with a script as I walk to the front office, where I know the secretary will have answers. I can't say Ryder and I are friends. No one would buy that. Maybe I could say I was tutoring him?

To my surprise, the office front desk is empty. I stand in the middle of the room for a moment, my ears humming in the silence. It's almost lunchtime, and probably the office is in crisis mode. Everyone in the principal's office knows me—and, frankly, loves me. I'm one of the "good ones." I'm often at the office to get information for the kids I tutor, or double-check on important dates, so no one would be suspicious if I was hanging around. Or even looking around. Right?

I hurry behind the desk and look at the files. There's a list of notes from teachers as well as absences for the day. What am I even looking for? If Ryder was in school the day of the basketball game, maybe. Revenge had to have been close by to plant that poisonous drink. I'm guessing student attendance is logged in the secretary's computer, which wakes up when I bump the mouse. It's password protected, though. Two assistants, Mrs. Archer and Mrs. Cabot, work this desk in two different shifts. I don't know them well enough to guess their passwords. I look down at the desk again, searching for any mention of Ryder Cross's name anywhere. For the trouble he causes the staff, you'd think there would be a big wanted poster of him up here or something.

What I find isn't about Ryder, though. What I find I don't even understand right away. It's a creamy file stuffed with a few papers. There's a sticker on the front that reads *Finn Walters*. I blink hard. Is this some sort of transcript? With the tip of my finger, I nudge the top paper inside the folder free. It looks to be some sort of printed medical results from a lab—I recognize the font and some of the test names from when my mom was sick. CONFIDENTIAL RUSH reads a stamp at the bottom. I stare at the list of tests that were done, and a familiar term catches my eye—*opiates*. So, this is a tox screen, then, from the hospital? I scan the results as fast as I can.

Click.

I jerk to standing. Down the hall, a door has opened, and several people are streaming out. I scan the paper again. Finn seems negative for everything except for traces of marijuana. But at the bottom, there's a urine screen, and something has come up with a positive value. I barely take in the words before I run around from the inside of the desk and careen out the door, ducking behind the wall so I can't be seen. I listen to murmurs as whoever it is walks through the office and into the lobby. When I peek around the corner again, the two secretaries, Mrs. Archer and Mrs. Cabot, have taken their seats back at their desks. Principal Morgan leans over the desk, speaking with

them. Will they notice that folder is askew? Then, I take stock of the two people who've come *out* of the office. It's a man and a woman, talking quietly.
On their jackets, in big letters, are the words *POLICE.*

I suck in a breath. I have to get out of here.

I whirl around and run down the hall. And as I round the corner, I
smack straight into someone. As I step back, dazed, I realize who it is, and
my heart drops.

Ryder Cross.

"Watch it," he grumbles, shouldering past me. And then, suddenly, I act
without thinking.

"Wait," I say, boldly grabbing his arm.

Ryder's eyes widen. He stares at my hand on his arm, and I do, too. I
quickly pull it away with a meek smile. Up close, Ryder smells like sweat and
cigarettes—actual cigarettes, not a vape pen. There's a sour look on his face
like he might explode. But I have to do this. I have to say something.

"I . . . I . . . know what you did," I say.

Ryder swings around. His brow furrows, and then he turns back to me. A
look of disgust spreads across his face. "Are you kidding me?" Then he moves
closer. "For a smart girl, you're really pretty dumb."

He's taller up close. There are flecks of hazel in his eyes. And he has his
backpack straps around both shoulders, like he's a little kid.

"I . . ." I start. But I'm not sure where to go with this. I haven't actually
considered what I'd say to Revenge when face-to-face.

"What's *Ricinus communis*?" I blurt. I want to google it, but I'm afraid
that would look suspicious.

"An STD?" he says, genuinely confused. "How the hell should I know?"

Then he walks off, bumping my side—hard—as he goes. I stumble back,
adrenaline coursing through me. Ryder continues on, walking right past the
police officers without stopping. Both officers glance at him. Their expres-
sions seem to indicate they know who he is. But they don't call after him.
They just let him walk out the doors. Why would they do that? Why aren't
they going after him? He has to be the number-one suspect. I'm not the only
one who's heard that gossip.

A noise behind me makes me turn. Mrs. Esry—my English teacher and one of the people I accosted to quickly write me another recommendation for my new round of college applications—has stopped short at the end of the corridor outside her classroom.

"Sabrina . . ." Clearly, she's just seen my strange interaction with Ryder Cross. "Is everything all right?"

I glance back toward Ryder, who is now walking across the school's front lawn to God knows where.

"Yeah . . ." Then I look at her again. "Are we allowed to just leave school today?"

"If you feel you need to." Mrs. Esry taps her lip, the corners of her mouth turning down with empathy. She's the kind of teacher who wears funky sweaters and brightly colored glasses, and she has a reputation for having a big heart for all students, not just the bright, well-mannered ones. "Ryder's had a pretty intense morning."

I feel desperate. "He seemed upset," I venture. "Did something happen? With the police?"

It takes Mrs. Esry a moment to finally answer my question. "Some people assume that because Ryder is a little . . . *alternative*, he is involved with that site Principal Morgan was talking about at assembly."

I blink at her, fully aware that *I'm* one of those people.

"Those officers pulled him in for questioning." She points at the man and woman in the jackets. "Don't get me wrong, Ryder's had his problems, but he didn't do what they accused him of. And they had no basis to question him beyond some gossip."

"You know he didn't do . . . ?" I try to ask as casually as possible. And there's no way I'm going to say *Revenge* or *Finn*.

She crosses her arms. "Because of Ryder's behavioral issues in school, his parents have willingly asked for someone on staff to monitor his online activity. It's a pilot program we're trying. They're worried about him. We all are. A young man, full of anger . . . the world is a scary place. We want to keep our school safe—and Ryder safe, too."

I make a face. I've never heard of this program. Is she talking about school violence? Shootings, even? It makes me squirm. Ryder is trouble, but I never thought he'd come to school with a gun. Do the teachers have some sort of blacklist?

"Does Ryder know you were monitoring him?" I ask. "Isn't that, like, an invasion of his privacy?"

"He knows, and he isn't thrilled, but it's the terms of his probation," Mrs. Esry says with a shrug. "And to be honest, it really helped him in this case. I wasn't here this morning when the police pulled him in, but I went in there the minute I found out. I know everything Ryder's looking at, everywhere he goes. Online, I mean—in real life, he's free to go anywhere. School, the park, parties, whatever. But I see what he sees and does on social media—internet searches, anything. I'm telling you this because Ryder has agreed to us sharing this information so he's not blamed for what happened."

"Couldn't he just make another account? Use another phone?" I know I sound too invested.

"Trust me, Sabrina, there is nothing Ryder does that we don't know. It's not him."

I turn back to the front lawn. Ryder has left. I wonder what he's thinking. I wonder what it's like to be profiled like that. Ryder earned the mistrust, but maybe the police should have only questioned him if they had more than just gossip. But I feel bad, too. I'd made the same assumptions. Fifteen minutes ago, I wouldn't have cared what Ryder thought of me, but now I feel bad I've hurt his feelings. Something else occurs to me, too—the police agents looked at Ryder dismissively because they'd *literally dismissed him*. They knew he wasn't Revenge. They knew he hadn't poisoned Finn.

Mrs. Esry heads back to her classroom. It's empty, I realize—she must not have a class this period. But then she turns around and gives me a pitying look. "How are you doing about . . . the deferral, by the way?"

It takes me a moment to respond. Harvard is so on the back burner of my concerns I can't even muster up a response right away.

"It's all right," I finally say. "I'm holding out hope for regular admission, I guess."

She smiles. "Good. And there are so many other possibilities for you. Harvard isn't the only school."

I nod, but I wish people would stop saying that. Then I consider asking her if she knows about Emily. But I've sort of had enough gossiping, and I wonder how it will make me look. Just like Ryder's stuff isn't my business, Emily's technically isn't mine, either.

Even though it's all my fault.

Mrs. Esry tells me to run along to class. I'm twenty minutes late already, but suddenly I'm so exhausted I don't want to go at all. If only I could be like Ryder and just leave. And I'm at square one again. I feel like a fool— of course, the staff knew the obvious Revenge suspect. Of course, they had already questioned him.

Once again, I wonder if I should just turn myself in. If I show the cops my messages from Revenge, maybe it'll help them find the true killer. And they'll understand I was put up to this, right? They'll let me off easier. They'll know that a girl like me would never do this. It's all there in the DMs, right away. Revenge forced me to do everything.

My phone beeps as I'm still thinking this through, slowly climbing the stairs to the second floor with the full intention of turning around and going back to the office and those police agents. When I see the message on the screen, my heart starts to race. Ballsy of Revenge to DM me. But maybe it's just what I need.

> Stop your snooping. Do you really want me to tell everyone you poisoned Finn? That you betrayed your best friend?

I'm about to write back when suddenly the message disappears. I reload but none of the messages from @Revenge are there. I go to the account. It's gone. *User not found.*

@Revenge is gone. My DMs are gone. All of them.

"Huh?" I whisper. I tap on Deleted Messages. They aren't there, either. They aren't *anywhere*.

My fingers loosen around my phone, and it clatters to the floor. But I don't pick it up right away. It can't help me anymore. It's like Revenge can read my mind, it seems. Those DMs were going to be my lifeline. My only way out. My word against Revenge's.

And Revenge knew that. So, they got rid of the evidence.

fourteen

I duck into the girls' bathroom on the second floor and stare fren-ziedly at my reflection. The corners of my mouth turn down. There are dark circles under my eyes. I look like a black-and-white version of myself. I look, I realize, like a mug shot—like someone arrested for murder.

I check my DMs again. Restart my phone, reinstall the app—*twice*—in hopes of getting my messages back. But they aren't there. I have nothing now. No proof that I was being blackmailed. Revenge holds all the cards. Any minute now, the cops might find out who Revenge *really* was . . . and then what? Will Revenge blame me for everything?

I can't let that happen. I need to find Revenge before anyone else does. But *how*? I slump against the sink, staring aimlessly at the posters various clubs have tacked up on the backs of the bathroom stalls. *Join the Ecology Club!* A poster about indoor track starting soon. An announcement for the upcoming drama production in the spring. My eyes glance at the logo at the bottom of the poster.

Wait a minute . . .

And then it comes to me.

But I have to wait a few periods to make my move. I've already missed half of AP physics, and even though the teachers are trying to be nice given all that happened, my teacher gives me a strange look when I finally stagger in, muttering an excuse. No one is really in fighting form today.

When my free period rolls around, however, I lurk in the hallway just outside the cafeteria near the drama club room. The bell has rung, but that doesn't seem to matter—half of the school, it seems, is standing around out-side, decompressing, and the teachers aren't doing a thing about it.

The drama room is empty. But what I'm looking for isn't in the drama room anyway—it's at the little table *outside*. It's unoccupied as well, but the sale sign is still up.

DRAMA FUNDRAISER!

Below the headline is a list of all of the sundries the drama club is sell-ing to raise money for sets and costumes for their production of *The Tempest*.

EnergyFX is on that list.

I knew there was something different about the bottle Revenge planted by the lockers. As I look through the open boxes behind the table, I get my answer. On the bottle's cap was a star sticker. I thought it was from a mini mart, but it's the label the drama club uses for items they sell in the hallways to raise money for the spring play.

It means that the bottle I used was purchased from the drama sale. *Here,* actually—so by a student, or maybe a teacher or someone on the staff. I notice something else on the poster: *No Cash. Student Bux Payment Only.*

I peek up and down the hall. It's empty. Stealthily, casually, I lift the flap of another box of items. T-shirts. Another box reveals movie theater candy. The candy costs five Student Bux—a rip-off, really, as the same box would cost about a dollar at Rite Aid. Then again, most students treat Student Bux like Monopoly money. Our parents add it to our accounts, and we use our student IDs to pay for everything from lunch to gym uniforms to drama club T-shirts. By that logic, there has to be some sort of tracker somewhere of all the student IDs that have been swiped in this sale.

I open another flap—*bingo*. There's an iPad just sitting on top of more T-shirts, practically waiting to be stolen. Even better, still plugged into the iPad, almost like an afterthought, is one of those Square Readers that can process credit card payments—or, in this case, Student Bux charges. This feels huge. It feels like I'm *close*.

I lift it up and wake up the screen. A four-digit passcode request appears.

I bite down hard on my lip. What could it be? The school's street address doesn't seem right. Nor would they use something simple like 1-2-3-4. I think of Sylvia Roth, the only girl I know from drama club who I've sometimes seen working at this sale. Sylvia is clever and witty; chances are, the other drama kids are, too. They'd be clever with their passcodes. The date *The Tempest* premiered in Elizabethan times. Not that I have any idea when that was. Shakespeare's birth year? Or maybe something else esoteric, or nonsensical. It could be anything.

Think, I push my brain. *How can I figure this out?* I peer along the side of the cardboard box, hoping for a miracle, but there are no numbers scrawled there. No sticky notes on the back of the iPad or an instruction sheet in any of the boxes. But this could be the difference between me getting in trouble alone and me getting the *real* person in trouble, the person who actually plotted a murder. What would the drama club set as their passcode? If only I had Emily with me. She's good at puzzles like this.

"Sabrina?"

I whirl around and nearly drop the iPad. Jake stands on the other side of the table, looking at me with confusion. I suck in a breath. I try to hide the iPad behind my back, but Jake has already seen it.

He cocks his head. "What are you doing?"

He stares at me. He's figured me out. I have no idea how, but that's the only answer. The guilt is probably all over my face. And Finn, despite Jake's frustration about playing basketball, was still his friend.

"What's going on?" He sounds wary. "You okay?"

"I'm fine," I shoot back. "Really."

"Are you sure?" He asks, more kindly than I deserved.

No, I want to shout. Then I set the iPad down. It's not like I'm going to be able to crack the code anyway. For what may be the first time, I feel like I can open up to Jake.

"Sorry. It's been a terrible twenty-four hours."

"I know. It's awful." Jake shuts his eyes. "Were you there? At the game? I wasn't sure you went . . ."

I nod, my gaze on the floor. "I wanted to call you . . . but then it happened,

and then you played, and I just . . . left early. Sorry. But I was kind of . . ."
The world swirls again. "It was a hard thing to see."

"Yeah." Jake's voice is choked. "Pretty awful." I think about how the game
continued after Finn was carried off the court. Sort of awful, now that we
know what happened. Cruel that the officials even let it go on . . . and that
Jake had to step in and take Finn's place.

"Are *you* okay?" I say softly.

His eyes go wide. "What?"

"About playing after Finn left. It wasn't like you knew how bad he was."

Jake is half turned away. He stares at his palms. "Right. Yeah. I just feel
really bad for him. I mean, it's not the way I wanted to get in front of the
scouts."

"I know. Of course."

When I look at him again, I can tell he's stressed. "I think RSU might
offer me a scholarship," he blurts out. "Which would be amazing. But I think
everyone thinks that *I* wanted this. And that maybe I had something to do
with it."

"*Seriously?*"

"Yeah, it's kind of crazy. I mean, him not playing was kind of lucky for
me. Not that I would have ever wanted that!"

In all my worrying about myself, I hadn't really thought about how it had
affected Jake.

"They called me into the office already. Asked if I had anything to confess.
They're threatening to kick me off the team."

I don't know what to say.

He glances at me pleadingly. "I didn't *do* anything."

"Of course you didn't." I feel sick. I'm *this close* to telling him that *I* was
the one who did this . . . but I'm too afraid. And besides, it wasn't me anyway. It was Revenge. I never would have wanted what happened to Finn to
happen. Not in a million years.

But I hate that he's being blamed. It isn't fair at all.

"I'll help you," I suddenly say. Jake's head snaps up. "Maybe we can figure out what actually happened—and who did this. This is a Revenge thing,
right? Maybe we can figure out who Revenge *is*."

Jake shakes his head. "Oh, Sabrina, no. I don't want to get you involved . . ."

"I want to be involved. Seriously. This Revenge thing is so messed up—and now *you're* getting penalized?"

I wonder if Revenge intended this all along. Maybe it's a clue.

"Please let me help you," I say. "I'm so under the radar, maybe I can find out some things. Maybe we can, together."

"That's really nice of you," Jake says warily. But then his expression breaks. "You really don't have to . . ."

"We can be a team," I say, grabbing his hand, giving him a meaningful look. Because, actually, I would *love* someone to work with on this. I would *love* a team. It would make me feel so much less alone . . . and scared . . . and lost. "Please?" I practically beg.

Jake looks at me for a moment, then nods and pulls me into a hug. "If you're sure?"

You're a liar, a voice whispers to me. Now I have so many reasons to make things right. But there's one thing for sure. I'm finding out who Revenge is.

And I'm taking them down. Before they get me first.

fifteen

Later that day, I'm packing up my locker when Emily jumps in front of me.

"Where have you been all afternoon?" she asks, as I catch my breath from her literal jump scare. "Want to come over? We can master sleuth who Revenge is and what happened to Finn. *And* who told on me, but that can be back burner for the moment."

"Oh." I finish packing up my backpack and slam the locker door. "I . . . can't. I have plans."

Emily cocks her head. "You do?"

"I'm, um, I'm meeting up with Jake," I admit. But I wave my hand as Emily's eyes light up. "To do homework." It's a lie, sort of. We're meeting to work on our Revenge hunt. I hate lying more to Emily, but what choice do I have?

But then something else occurs to me. "Wait, are you even *allowed* to hang out? Your mom isn't still mad about Harvard?"

Emily shrugs. "Oh she's still pissed, but after what happened with Finn, I think it gave her a little perspective. Of course, she still wishes I was more like you."

My heart lurches again. If she only knew how horrible I am. Then Emily's phone's FaceTime starts ringing. As she reaches for it, I see it's Charlie on the screen.

"What?" Emily answers, annoyed.

"Where did Mom put those brownies she made?" Charlie asks. I can tell he's in his room.

"Um, the kitchen?" Emily responds sarcastically.

"Thanks. Big help, Em," Charlie hangs up, annoyed.

I frown, realizing something. "Charlie's still home from break?"

"Yeah." She smiles at me in surprise. "Boarding school breaks are endless."

"He's been home this whole *time*? Have things been better with you guys?" I ask.

"I've barely seen him. He's just been in his room. It's basically like he isn't here except when he wants food. He's like a mole."

We're quiet for a few moments. Then I realize something else. "Hey, what's going on with Jeremy?"

Emily squints. "What do you mean?"

"Are you still hanging out? I saw him at the basketball game—how come he gets to stay?"

Emily's FaceTime starts to ring again. "Yeah, I haven't talked to him; he's kind of a loser." She waves to me, then answers her phone again. "*What, Charlie?*"

And I have to admit, I'm happy I'm not the one she's annoyed with.

. . .

My father texted saying he couldn't pick me up—something came up at work—but Parker, of all people, was coming to get me. Are you kidding me? I'd rather walk, and it's four miles. Maybe I can pretend I didn't see his text.

"Sabrina?"

When I whirl around, I see Parker in her Mini Cooper.

"Hi!" she says brightly. "Your dad asked me to give you a ride."

Ugh. It's like being eight years old and having a babysitter again.

"I don't mind the bus." Then I realize how weird it is to refuse a ride home with Parker when she drove all the way over here. "Actually, okay," I backtrack.

We sit quietly together as the carpool cars ease slowly forward. "Thanks for getting me. I hope it didn't mess up your day." I say, knowing I sound more annoyed than grateful.

"No prob. I was actually at the school, saying hi to some old teachers." She pulls her chic scarf tighter around her throat. "I heard you guys had quite the assembly today. What's up with this whole Revenge thing? Was Finn Walters really poisoned?"

"I really don't know that much about it." Parker is the *last* person I want to explore my theories with. But I bite down hard on my lip, thinking of the tox screen. *Ricinus communis.* I took a chance and looked it up. It's commonly known as the castor flower. It's found in flower gardens sometimes. This is Connecticut. People are crazy about their gardens. You just have to know what you're looking for. But then I figure maybe Parker has some knowledge I don't.

"Were you and Finn friends?" I ask her.

"Not really. I mean, he was two years younger than me. He did try to hit on me a couple of times, but no thank you," she says nonchalantly with the sort of ridicule that only a pretty girl can get away with. Like it's more his fault than hers.

"I guess you didn't like him, huh?" she says.

Immediately my stomach lurches—how did she know that?

"Yeah, I saw you yelling at him at Sketch's party."

Oh. God. Was EVERYONE there?

"Don't worry," she continues. "I didn't say anything to your dad or my mom." She pauses, then adds, "Did they check the cameras?"

"Cameras?" I feel my stomach flip. "What cameras?"

"These schools all have security cameras. Can't be too careful."

"I don't know . . ."

I wish I was with Jake. Or Emily. Normally Emily would be my confidante, and my hiding everything from her is making our strained relationship even more strained. I could have asked her to drive me home. But I obviously can't even begin to let her in on my detective hunting.

At least I have Jake. There's some comfort in not having to go through this alone. But it's not like I can tell him *why* we're working together. Does he really buy that I'm helping him out of the goodness of my heart? It's partially true, of course. But not all the way.

Jake and I met during study hall to strategize more. I also told him about *Ricinus communis*. How did Revenge know to use something like that as poison? (Though, when we dug into it a little more, we realized that the Russians used ricin to kill their enemies. And it was mentioned in plenty of spy novels.) The school has a gardening club—maybe we should parse through those names. Or there was a botany unit in chemistry. Or a true crime club that met after school . . .

I also shared a rumor—though to me, it was way more than a rumor—that Finn accidentally drank EnergyFX in his water bottle. Perhaps this was where the ricin was hiding. It's possible Revenge got EnergyFX from the drama sale—I don't know where else they sell the stuff these days. I didn't mention that I also knew the EnergyFX bottle poured into Finn's water bottle bore a drama sticker. Because, obviously, I couldn't. But Jake still seemed intrigued by my findings. In fact, he said it was some good sleuthing.

Problem was, we hadn't figured out how to bypass the iPad password screen yet to figure out who'd bought EnergyFX recently. We wanted to ask some of the drama students who worked the sale, but without giving away that we'd stolen their device. We were also afraid to make too many password guesses for fear of getting locked out. Jake was friendly with a kid named Stephen Calvino who worked the sale; he said he could try to sneak it into a conversation. But he couldn't make any promises. Who knew if it would even lead to anything?

"Sabrina? Hello?"

Parker said something I didn't catch. I ask her to repeat herself, but before she can, she slams on the brakes.

"Watch it!" she screams, blowing on the horn. Someone has walked right in front of the car.

The girl on the road freezes and stares at us, and for a moment, I barely recognize her. Brooke's hair is frizzy, there's mascara caked around her eyes, and she isn't wearing a coat even though it's below freezing outside. It's like she doesn't even know where she is. Eventually, she snaps out of her haze, enough to shrug and move out of the way.

Parker raises her eyebrows. "Wow. She looks catatonic."

Parker sounds so judgmental I find myself weirdly wanting to defend

Brooke. "I mean, can you blame her? She's Finn's girlfriend. It was bad enough to witness it high up on the stands, but Brooke was right near him. She must be devastated." I clock Parker's reaction, surprised by her skeptical smirk. "What?"

"Forget it. It's just gossip that's going around."

"What gossip?" I ask. Of course, she knows more gossip than me.

"Oh, just things. Like maybe she wasn't that into Finn?" She pauses.

"Brooke? She's devoted to him." It's weird to defend my enemy . . . to my *other* enemy.

Parker shrugs. "I probably have it wrong."

I stare at Parker, hating that I have to ask. "What did you hear, exactly?"

Parker leans in. It's clear she likes a good gossip sesh and any ear will do. "Supposedly she and Grant Dryer were seen that night. In his car." Her fingers squeeze the steering wheel. "You know. *Together.*"

I blink hard. That whole night, checking and checking and rechecking Brooke's social media accounts, waiting for her to update something, *anything*, about her boyfriend, figuring she was sitting in a waiting room, holding her breath, terrified . . .

Grant Dryer? I think about the scene at the mall the day I found out I was deferred from Harvard. *Could Grant have been cheating with BROOKE?* It never occurred to me anyone would ever cheat on Finn Walters.

Suddenly, something comes to me: a snippet from the party. It's hardly anything, just a blurry image. *Stumbling down a hallway, lost, looking for a bathroom. Walking into a bedroom instead. An out-of-focus Brooke stood with her fists pressed to her eyes and her shoulders tensed. Finn was right next to her, tensed too.*

"I can't believe you," he whispered.

Then he let out a groan and punched the wall.

It startled me, and I yelped. Brooke's head shot up. Her eyes widened as she saw me.

It goes blurry then.

My mind spins, trying to figure out what I remember seeing. And hearing? *I can't believe you.* Maybe he found out Brooke was cheating. And he tried to hurt her.

So, what would Grant think? It certainly could be motive for wanting revenge on someone. Motive for wanting someone *dead*, actually.

I blink hard, like I've suddenly woken up. Could Revenge be one of the OGs? Finn's friend?

Could Revenge be *Grant*? I have to play this cool. I shift my weight like the bomb Parker has just dropped isn't something that has cracked open my life but simply a juicy piece of gossip.

"Who'd you hear this from?" I ask, as cavalierly as I can muster.

"Just a friend. No one you know. And you're right—it's probably wrong. It seems so callous, right? She's right there when he collapses, and she goes off with a guy she's cheating with?" Parker says, thankfully pulling into my driveway.

It does seem callous, even for Brooke. My mind is whirring. I don't know if Grant fits all the criteria. He's on the basketball team, though, which means he'd know about a lucky water bottle and a penchant for sports bars. He'd know when the lockers would be empty. I have no idea how he could get his hands on the poison in question, but it seems like *anyone* can, so maybe it's a nonissue.

I spring from the car, barely managing a thank-you, and run through the front door, slamming it behind me. It's not until I'm up in my room that I wonder if Parker had come into the house.

sixteen

Later that day, I meet up with Jake at a hiking trail near my house. I needed to get out, and he suggested we meet up there. We're trying to pick apart that night at the game. I'm careful not to share too much but tell him I think it would be good to work our way backward from the incident to see if there might be something we've overlooked.

The thing is, Brooke and Finn must have made up before the game. From what I can tell, they looked pretty into each other.

I can't pretend I don't feel something for Jake. I'm softening a little in how I speak to him. It's just not easy for me to open myself up—to admit I care. I've lost my mom. I've lost Brooke. I've even lost the one thing I thought I could control, Harvard. And it all hurts too much.

We're sitting at the head of the trail—a secluded walking and running spot that gets very little traffic this time of year. Every so often, a die-hard runner crunches past, but for the most part, we're alone. I've already filled him in about the fight I witnessed at the party and the gossip I heard from Parker.

"Brooke was cheering her head off for Finn when he came on the court. It didn't seem like she was faking it."

Jake blinks dazedly. "Finn never let on that Brooke was cheating. And with Grant? Huh."

"Why *huh*?"

Jake leans back. "I don't know. They just seemed pretty happy. And she always seemed really into Finn. Plus, Grant and Finn are really good friends." His gaze flits to me for a moment. "You used to be friends with Brooke, didn't you?"

"How'd you know?"

One shoulder lifts. "I don't know. I remember you guys from junior high."

He did?

"We were nobodies."

"Everybody is somebody," Jake gives me a goofy smile. "Plus, you know what they say about the popular kids in high school."

I stare at him blankly. Clearly, I don't.

"If you peak in high school, you've peaked in life."

I smile.

"So, what happened with you and Brooke?" He persists.

I've never really talked about that with anyone but Emily, and as I say it, I realize how stupid it sounds. "We were friends, but then she started dating Finn. And she pretty much left me and Emily in the dust."

"Sounds like a Netflix movie my sister would watch." He laughs.

"Yeah, but those are always about the geeky girl who becomes popular. Not the losers she leaves behind," I say, not realizing how much it really did still sting.

"You really should stop saying you're a loser," Jake says seriously. "A lot of the so-called popular kids are the real losers. All they care about is themselves. Everyone's crazy competitive, talking about one another, jockeying for position. It's all they care about."

Jake continues since I'm almost too dumfounded to speak. "It seems like you and your friend Emily are real friends. Like good friends. Me, I'll be glad to get out of here."

I stare at Jake, surprised. I had always assumed life as an OG was all rainbows and unicorns. I wave my hands around, feeling suddenly emotional and all the more guilty for what I've done. So much hurt. So many lies. To Emily. To Finn. To Jake.

"You're really thinking Grant wanted Finn dead? *And* he's Revenge?"

Jake mulls it over. "I mean, maybe? Grant always seems bitter about stuff. Like, major chip on his shoulder. But man, I don't know. To do that to his best friend? And Grant got pranked, right? At the mall?"

"Maybe it's the ultimate cover-up? No one would suspect him," I muse.

"Only . . ." He shakes his head. "*Poisoning* Finn? That seems so extreme."

"Maybe he's really in love with Brooke?" Even I'm not sure I believe it. A puff of cold air spills from my lips as I breathe out. "Any luck on getting the code for the iPad?"

Jake shakes his head. "I tried to get some intel from Steve—the guy who worked the drama sale. But no luck. He says he never used the iPad; he was just in charge of watching the inventory. I tried one combo, but it didn't work."

"Maybe we should return it. And then, I don't know, hang around the sale or something and watch someone key in the code."

Jake smirks. "And what, steal it *again*? No, *that's* not suspicious."

My brain isn't firing on all cylinders. I consider the homework I'm eventually going to have to do, once the teachers decide that the Finn tragedy can't stand in the way of learning. How will I cope? Even if I do happen to get into a school I've applied to, I can't imagine I'll ever be able to think clearly again.

"Okay, I'll keep thinking about it tonight and if I can't figure anything out, I'll bring it in tomorrow. Do you want to talk to Grant, maybe? See what you can find out?"

"And maybe you could try and talk to Brooke," Jake suggests. "See what *you* can find out."

I sigh. "Definitely not excited about that. But . . . okay . . ." I force a smile and hold out my fist. "Wonder twin powers, activate."

Jake laughs. Then he reaches out his fist and bumps my hand. "Thank you again, Sabrina. Really. This means so much to me."

My mouth twitches. "I-It's no problem."

Neither of us says anything for a moment. Suddenly, things feel too intimate. I pull away and make a big deal of flicking a piece of lint off my sweater. Jake finally moves his fingers away, but his gaze is still on me, his eyes soft and caring. And then, suddenly, he pulls me in for a hug. I'm dazzled by the feel of his muscular chest against mine and his arms wrapping around my back. I breathe in his clean smell—mixed with that ubiquitous smell of school—and shut my eyes. I hope he can't hear my heart banging.

I try to relax in his embrace, but I'm too stressed to reciprocate. He lets go and pulls away.

"It's so awful," he murmurs. I can tell he's a little hurt. "But we're in this together, right?"

"Of course," I whisper back. "I'm not going to let you go down."

And hopefully, I won't go down in the process.

. . .

Maybe I still know Brooke better than I think, because when I consider where she might be after such a tragedy, there's only one place I come up with.

The outdoor ice rink is busy with skaters—hockey kids whizzing danger-ously past, figure skaters in the middle practicing their tricks, and wobbly first-timers clinging to the side wall, ankles buckling. Brooke wears a pink hat with a pompom on top. She's skating slowly, head down, feet crossing over when making a turn. When she was in elementary and junior high school, she took lots of lessons and skated in competitions, but once she got to high school and joined the OGs, she dropped the sport. But when we were friends, this was always what she liked to do. She used to joke with us that she was more comfortable on skates than she was in her sneakers. That she thought better while she was gliding. That she sort of . . . *lost herself.* It's a lit-tle sad seeing her skating alone now. I'm glad she's self-soothing, but at the same time, you'd think as Finn's girlfriend, she'd be surrounded by support. Does she really have no one to talk to?

I think about waiting for her to come off the ice, but I fear she'll breeze right past me. I push some cash across the rental window and lace up a pair of skates. It's been years since I've skated, and I'm nervous about the blades getting stuck in the ruts in the ice as I step out onto the surface. But I get used to it pretty quickly, dodging a group of younger kids as they skate pre-cariously past me. Then I hold on to the wall and wait for Brooke to come to me. That dazed look is still on her face, but when she sees me, she frowns—so she's not *completely* out of it, then.

She does a quick stop, throwing up tiny shards of ice. "Sabrina?"

"Hey."

Brooke shakes her head and turns and starts skating again, faster now. But she doesn't seem to mind when I fall in line next to her. We glide around the rink together in silence. Once we're halfway around, I say, "Remember how we used to come here all the time?"

Brooke just glares at me. I know that "thank you, Captain Obvious" look and wish I had thought of something different to say. But I press on, determined to find answers.

"And that time you raced the boys from St. Andrew's. You bet you could beat them, and they just laughed."

"Easy money," she says flatly. And for a moment, it's the old Brooke. We skate together in silence, side by side like we used to.

Ahead of us, a little kid falls, and her mom rushes forward to help her up. We skirt around them, and then I try to offer some comfort. "I'm really sorry about Finn."

Brooke glares at me. I immediately regret crossing that unspoken line, reserved only for close friends. "You realize I came here to get *away* from all that, right? So, if you've come to, like, *gawk* at me, or get some gossip, please just don't."

"I'm sorry. It's not . . ." I was so focused on getting answers it didn't occur to me that she'd *want* to be alone. "I just know how hard this must be."

Brooke looks at me almost kindly. She was there for me through everything with my mom. "Yeah, I guess you do." But as fast as her walls come down, they shoot back up.

"Where's Emily? Did you block her, too, because of Harvard?"

I'm stunned. Did she really forget? *She* blocked us. I stupidly spit out, "Revenge got her in trouble, and Harvard rescinded the acceptance."

"You're kidding!" Brooke looks genuinely shocked. I guess Emily has done a pretty good job of keeping it quiet. I figured Brooke would know. Now I feel like an idiot for telling her.

"Please, please, don't tell her I said anything!" I beg. How dumb could I be? Emily and I are already on thin ice.

Brooke raises her hands sarcastically. "Yeah, 'cause Emily and I talk all the time."

After a moment, she says, "Emily took your spot. So that's her karma. But I guess she likes taking things from people."

I want to say something, but I hold back. We skate in silence for a minute. It's weird. In some ways I feel like Brooke is exactly who she was, but in others, she's like this stranger I hardly know. But I'm here for a reason.

"I saw you and Finn fighting at that party."

Brooke's skate makes a sharp sound against the ice. "And?"

"I just—what were you fighting about?"

Brooke laughs meanly, now the popular girl I remember. "I'm shocked you remember anything from that night, Sabrina. You were pretty trashed."

"People are saying things about you," I blurt out. "Gossiping that you were cheating on Finn."

It's like pulling off a Band-Aid—and maybe a terrible risk. A series of emotions wash across Brooke's face: embarrassment, annoyance, anger. Then she scoffs. "About me and Grant, right?" Her eyes narrow. "You think I don't know?"

"I just . . . I thought . . ." But it hasn't occurred to me. "Wait, you've heard that?"

Brooke's eyes flash. "Please. My life is open season for everyone to evaluate, comment on, judge. Speculating about me is a sport. No one wants me and Finn to be happy. Finn's in a coma and . . ." The tip of Brooke's nose turns red. Tears well in her eyes. "He was *blue*, Sabrina."

"I'm sorry," I whisper. "Brooke, I'm so, so sorry." More than I could ever explain.

She opens her mouth to speak, reconsiders, but then takes another breath. "And no, I wasn't fooling around with Grant. *Finn* cheated. Not me."

I blink. "He . . . did?"

"Yeah. Over the summer. When I was away. That's what you saw us fighting about at the party. He was showing the guys naked pictures the girl had sent him. But Grant told me it was nothing. That Finn really loved me. That's why he and I were talking in my car. Finn was making fun of her that night at the party. He's not into her."

"Who was the girl?"

She looks disgusted that I've asked, but then shrugs. "It doesn't matter. It's all so dumb. But me and Grant? No thank you."

"So, you and Grant . . . you're not together?" I know I'm sounding like an idiot. It's just that nothing is as it seems.

"*No*! The idea that the night my boyfriend is lying in a hospital I'm off fooling around with someone? Jesus. I don't know who started that rumor, but it's crap."

"I'm sorry." It's all I can think to say.

"Are you, though?" Brooke's face is pinched. "Everyone wondered why Finn liked me of all people all those years ago. People said I had to be like this sex maniac or something, because I wasn't super athletic, or already popular, or even *that* pretty."

"People . . . weren't saying that . . ." I'm stunned.

"Yes, they were. I heard all of it. Suddenly, some people were desperate to talk to me and others, well, dumped me." She narrows her eyes at me. "And everyone was asking why the most popular kid in our grade would date this . . . *nobody*. But Finn liked me. Not because I was a sex maniac or a partyer—I know those were some of the rumors. We just got each other. He has a soft side. A silly side. He felt like—" she catches herself, "*feels* like everyone expects him to be this tough guy. You know, he's gone through a lot with his family. Stuff people don't really know—he hides it." She cuts me a glare. "We *all* have been through stuff, Sabrina. Not just you."

"I . . . I didn't know. I'm sorry."

"Yeah, well." Brooke shoves away from the wall where we've been standing, nearly colliding into a knot of passing skaters. "You do a lot of assuming about everyone, you know that? This person is nice because they're smart, this person is a bitch because they're popular, this person is dangerous because of the way he looks, whatever. Maybe it's time for you to start opening your eyes and stop assuming you know them because of their stereotype without ever even talking to them. Not everything is so black-and-white."

She skates off, then, choppy and fast, heading straight for the exit.

"Brooke!" I call out, and she turns, briefly, like she considers waiting. I'm breathless and try to catch up. But she keeps going.

I wait fifteen more minutes until I'm sure Brooke has returned her skates and left. The last thing I want to do is upset her even more. I think about what she's told me. *Should I believe that she and Grant aren't together? Is it strange that she was so forthcoming?* But the thing I think about most surprises me—*did I really have the past so wrong? Did Brooke feel as rejected by us as we did by her?*

I take off my skates, return them at the window, and head for my car. It's dark out now, past 6:00 p.m., and the temperature has dropped into the twenties. I start the ignition and blast the heat, holding my chilled fingers in front of the vents. My mind is full of thoughts about Brooke as I drive home. *What a terrible rumor someone started about her and Grant. It feels like something Revenge would do, actually.* And what about that Finn had cheated? It still gave Brooke a motive to hurt Finn, but I truly don't believe she had anything to do with it anymore—*or* wanted to set me up, for that matter. Is that a clue? Revenge hates Finn enough to order him to be poisoned. But maybe Revenge chose me deliberately to carry out the job. If I was to believe all those squares on Revenge's old account, eighteen other people had also made Revenge requests. Did Revenge choose me *specifically?*

I turn onto my street and decide to call Jake as soon as I get home to talk through all this. But when I go to turn into my driveway, my normal spot is occupied. It takes my brain a moment to catch up. Words stretch across the sedan's sides and back bumper.

Milford Police.

seventeen

I consider driving on. Pretending I don't live here. But just as my foot hovers over the gas pedal, ready to gun it, the front door opens, and my dad peeks out. I'm glad it's too dark for him to see my face through the windshield, as I can only imagine the terrified expression on my face. I have no choice but to pull up to the curb and park.

My dad remains at the door, holding it open to let me inside. When I clock his expression, I notice he doesn't seem to be looking at me like I'm a murderer. In fact, his expression is kind of gentle.

"Everything's okay," he says quickly, his gaze cutting to the squad car in the driveway. "They're just asking everyone at the school questions—about that boy."

I let out a tiny breath. *Just questions.* I still want to run, but my father leads me into the living room, and before I know it, I can hear him introducing me to two officers who are standing near our couch, hands clasped. They are the same ones I saw at school. One is a stocky woman with a tight bun and dark red lipstick. She steps forward first, so I figure she's the boss. Behind her is a tall guy whose name tag reads *Alvarez*; he has eyes that turn down at the corners and enormous biceps. And of course, standing back toward the kitchen is Kaye. Great.

"Sabrina, this is the police team helping to look into what happened to that student," my dad says.

"Hello, Sabrina," the woman says. "I'm Detective Andrea Carson. This is my partner, James Alvarez. We're really sorry to hear what happened at your school this week."

"Yes," is all I can squeak out. I haven't moved from my spot in the hall.

"You don't have to be scared," Carson says. "We're just trying to talk to a lot of the seniors, get a picture of who Finn Walters is and what might have happened." She smiles. "Principal Morgan says you're a smart girl—top of your class."

"That she is," my dad says proudly.

"Impressive." Carson leans against the couch. "You were at that game the other night?" I can't tell whether it's a statement or a question.

"I . . . was," I say haltingly, praying that my body doesn't break out into a cold sweat. My dad looks surprised.

"You go to a lot of games?" This one is a question. And I know I don't have a good answer.

"No," I say quietly.

It hangs in the air.

"It's not usual for a kid to just . . . collapse like that, you know?" The detective continues. Again, question or statement?

"Have they figured out what made him collapse?" Kaye asks from the corner.

Carson glances at her and then looks at me, long and hard. *Does she know that I know?* Then she shrugs and looks at Kaye. "I can't disclose what's going on. But the doctors do think it was an outside agent that made him arrest rather than some unknown heart condition."

Kaye crosses her arms. "You mean like something chemical? Drugs?"

"I can't really elaborate," Carson says. She looks at me. "So, do you know of anyone who had an issue with Finn?"

"Me?" I point dumbly at my chest.

"I'm not sure Sabrina and Finn run in the same circles," my father pipes up.

"Well," the male detective says, "the school isn't *that* big." He picks up a framed photo of me, Dad, and my mom from the table.

"He . . . he dates a friend of mine." One, that's not true. Brooke's not really my friend. Two, even I know that sounds like a dodge.

The female detective raises her eyebrow and makes a note on her pad but thankfully moves on. "You know anybody else on the basketball team, Sabrina?"

"I mean, some of them have been in my classes, I guess. Study halls."

"What about"—Alvarez checks a notebook—"Jake Cano?"

I blink. I can feel Carson watching me. "Someone says they've seen you two together a lot lately," she says.

Someone? Who?

"Jake's really nice," is all I can offer. "We did this charity drive together recently."

"Nice that he got to play in the game the scouts were here for when Mr. Walters took that fall," Alvarez says in a snarky voice.

My head whips up. "Jake's wrecked about having to do that. He wouldn't have wanted—" I can't finish the sentence.

"*Someone* must have," Alvarez continues. "Maybe someone else on the team? Or someone who didn't like him?"

I shake my head, helplessly.

His beady eyes pin me. "I hear he could be . . ." He pauses, trying to figure out how to say it. "Well, not always Mr. Nice Guy."

"He's . . ." I really don't know how to respond, so I just say, "He's . . . okay."

Carson stares at me with her penetrating eyes, and I can she tell decides not to pursue that line. "Were you aware he had some severe allergies?" she asks. Is it a trick question?

"No," I lie, then realizing that's stupid, I add, "I mean, yes. Sort of. I know he was allergic to EnergyFX," I say, hoping that's enough.

"Oh?" Detective Carson says, clearly wanting me to continue.

"I heard it gave him hives," I offer.

"EnergyFX?" Kaye straightens up. "*That's* what poisoned him?"

Now all our heads swivel to Kaye, including the cops.

"Not exactly," Carson says. "Though when we tested Mr. Walters's water bottle, it's obvious the liquid inside—mostly undrunk—was EnergyFX. I guess my question is why would Finn fill his sports bottle up with something he's allergic to?"

Kaye clucks her tongue. "This is going to be terrible PR for the EnergyFX brand. I wonder if they'll lose the sale."

I stare at her strangely. It almost sounds like she's happy.

But the detectives have moved on. Alvarez is looking at me again. "What are your thoughts on the Instagram site that gets revenge on people?"

I duck my head in shame. "Our principal mentioned it at the assembly . . ."

"You think there's truth to that person being involved?" Carson asks. "Strange timing, with that Instagram post . . ."

I lick my lips. "I don't know."

"Have you seen the account?"

I stare at the fibers in the rug, ashamed. "I've looked at it, yeah."

"You have, Sabrina?" My father clearly can't hold in his astonishment anymore.

"It's not just me. And the account doesn't actually say anything. It just had these . . . squares. With numbers."

"That represent a revenge that's been carried out, correct?" Alvarez asks.

"I guess, but . . ."

"But no details on what the revenge was, or who it was against, or anything like that, right?" Carson jumps in.

When I nod, she nods thoughtfully. "So, it's all speculation. That's the allure of it. The account is taking credit for stuff, but it could be all smoke and mirrors whether this one person actually did those things or not."

"I mean, bad things *have* been happening to people," I say. "These . . . pranks, I guess. But that's all they were—just dumb stuff, mostly."

Alvarez frowns and looks at his notebook again. "But they got a bit darker lately. Vandalizing someone's car . . ."

Carson looks up at me. "Do you think revenge is ever justifiable?" she asks. "I've heard that this Revenge account sometimes goes after bullies. Racists. Bad teachers . . ."

"I don't think it's a good idea," I say quickly. "Ever."

"Detectives, with all due respect," Kaye jumps in, before I can even breathe. "I'm not sure why you're harassing a young girl who is clearly traumatized by what she witnessed and badgering her about a school *prank* site.

So, unless you are saying she is a suspect and needs a lawyer, which I am, this conversation is finished."

My mouth literally drops open. O . . . KAYE? I genuinely want to hug her.

Detective Carson looks almost amused, and Alvarez puts away his notebook.

"Nope. All good. We'll check back if we have any more questions."

And with that, they let themselves out the door.

eighteen

I'm not sure who is more surprised by Kaye's coming to my defense, me or my dad.

"Wow," Kaye says, as if wiping her hands of the situation. "That was totally uncalled for! If they contact you again, Sabrina, do *not* speak to them unless I am with you."

"Is she in trouble?" My dad is panicked. "Why would she be a suspect?"

"No, that's just the police way of doing things," Kaye says, calming him down. "They could make Mother Teresa feel like a murderer. That's how they get people to give up information."

My dad looks placated but still concerned. "Sabrina, is there anything else you know that you should tell us? Or them?"

For a brief second, I think about coming clean. Telling them both. Maybe I misjudged Kaye. Maybe she could help me explain all of this.

But before I can, Kaye continues. "I can't believe EnergyFX is involved."

Yep. She sounds not just interested but happy.

"EnergyFX," my father repeats. He looks at Kaye. "Isn't that the drink Parker was involved in?"

"Parker?" I ask. *How was she involved?*

"Yes." Kaye seems keenly interested in a piece of string stuck to her sweater. "I mean, she came up with the idea! Which they totally stole from her."

My brain is circling EnergyFX, too. *Why would Revenge deliver the poison through that particular drink?* EnergyFX has a particular taste because of the cane sugar it's made with—it isn't the same flavor profile as most other sports drinks out there. Chances are, Finn would have taken a sip or two but stopped when he realized what it was. I'd seen him carrying his bottle onto the court, but I hadn't seen him drinking from it. But the cops are right: Wouldn't it make more sense to put the poison in a beverage Finn *loved*, so he'd drink more of it?

Then again, ricin is incredibly potent—maybe Revenge only wanted him to get a tiny amount, and diluting it in EnergyFX would ensure he didn't drink too much. Is it a clue, too, that two students at my school *created* EnergyFX? Like maybe they're involved in this revenge somehow? Or targets? Kaye's musings flit through my brain again: *That's going to be terrible PR.* And Parker? She had been at school. She's the one who told me the rumor about Grant and Brooke.

"Why didn't you tell me about this . . . account?" my dad asks.

I almost want to laugh. Was my dad serious? I eye Kaye and then dare to say, "Dad, you barely know how to log on to Facebook."

I feel my dad bristle, but then his shoulders sag, and he sighs. "Well, please keep me posted, and as Kaye said don't talk to anyone about this—especially the police."

I head quickly up the stairs and find myself straightening my duvet. The detective's words circle in my brain as I redo my bed's already perfect corner squares I had done this morning. I don't like how they mentioned Jake as a suspect. It's too close to the truth for all the wrong reasons. What about the suggestion that people knew Finn was a bully?

My phone rings, startling me. Emily's name flashes on the screen, and I groan quietly. I'm not in the mood to talk right now. I silence the call, but Emily just FaceTimes me again. Sighing, I answer.

"Hey."

"Hey, Sabrina." Emily sounds concerned. "Everything okay?"

"Yeah. Why?"

"I texted you a bunch, and you didn't respond."

"I was kind of fighting with my dad," I say quickly. It's not really a lie. There's a silence.

"Was he mad you were with Jake?"

Jake? I shut my eyes. I'd completely forgotten that I told Emily I was busy with Jake. Now I feel like she really has caught me in a lie.

"No—I mean yeah," I backtrack. "He just doesn't like it when I keep things from him."

There's another pointed silence. We both know I keep a lot from my dad. Like my panic attacks. My lack of friends. My fears.

Emily lets out a breath. "Is everything okay, *really?*"

"Sure. Of course."

"Because . . . I don't know. You've seemed kind of . . . *off.*"

I don't dare breathe. I look away so she can't see my expression. "I'm fine."

"Is it about Harvard?" She swallows hard. "You're still mad? You can tell me . . ."

I let her words sink in. *That's* what she thinks this is? I realize how evasive I must seem to Emily. How stressful that must be. I look back at her and gush, "Oh, Em, I'm *not.* Not at all. I promise. You don't have to worry about that. It's just life stuff," I babble. "Kaye and schools. And the Finn thing, of course."

"I just wish you would talk to me," Emily says. "Tell me what's going on. I feel like you're . . . I don't know, holding back. You know you can tell me anything, right?"

I want to squeeze my eyes shut and disappear. I want to confide in Emily like I used to. I don't want our friendship hanging in the balance like this. And part of me knows she would forgive me, but can I be brave enough? Will Emily understand that I made a terrible mistake? I can't bear to lose her.

We say a few more things, and the mood levels out. Once we hang up, we're laughing again. But a new cloud hovers over me. I think of the mountain of secrets I'm keeping from Emily now. I need to sort this out. I need to get free from Revenge. I need to get out from under all these lies . . . soon. Otherwise, the friendship I worked so hard to keep will go down the drain.

· · ·

Plink. Plink. Plink.

I shoot up in bed. The room is dark and fuzzy at the edges. I turn on my phone flashlight, but I can't figure out where the sound is coming from. I peer through my half-open door into the hall. My father is sleeping across the landing. The last thing I want is to wake him up.

Plink.

Finally, I realize where it's coming from: my window. I rush over. A shadowy figure is standing on my lawn. My heart lurches, but when he steps into the light, I realize . . . it's Jake.

I heft the window open, letting in the frigid air. "Jake?"

"Can you come down for a sec?" Jake yell-whispers. "I've been texting, but you aren't responding."

Crap. I look at my phone and realize Jake had texted. *And* FaceTimed. But I had already fallen asleep.

"I heard the police were at your house. Someone saw them parked here."

I shut the window and listen to my silent house. No noises come from my father's room. Quietly, I tiptoe to the first floor, praying our dog won't wake up and attack me with wiggles and yips. I pull my parka from the closet and slip out the front door before bothering to button it. Jake is waiting on the porch. I consider asking him in, but I'm already on thin ice.

"Did you talk to Grant?" I ask. "Because from what Brooke told me, it doesn't sound like they were doing anything."

"Yeah," Jake says. "He sort of gave me that idea, too. He'd already heard that gossip." I tell him Brooke had, too. "Grant's really upset about Finn. He wants to figure out what's going on with Revenge, too. He took screenshots of some of Revenge's posts."

My eyes widen. "The numbered squares?"

"Yep. I guess he's been trying to figure out who Revenge was since he got pranked."

Jake pulls out his phone. "Yeah, he says he still has no clue who it is. But he sent me a bunch of the screen shots, and sometimes, there are comments below the squares."

I'm shocked. When I'd looked through the squares after Revenge did that to Emily, it seemed like the comments were closed. And if the teachers were investigating Revenge before all this went down . . . it seems like a risky thing to do.

"Did Grant show the police this?" I ask, praying there's nothing that links me to any of it.

Jake pulls in his bottom lip. "I don't want to sell the guy out, but he distributes a lot of performance enhancers to the team. *I* don't use them . . . but a lot of other guys do . . . I don't know. I think he's worried that if he hands over his phone, they'll see everything *else* he's up to."

"Did Finn take Grant's steroids?" I ask. Grant is feeling like a strong suspect again.

Jake doesn't answer, but I can tell from the look on his face that's a yes. I stick that fact in the back of my mind as Jake continues.

"Get this: The police questioned Grant, too, and told him they're getting a warrant to recover all the deleted activity from the Revenge account."

Jake seems relieved, and I try to mimic his enthusiasm. Frankly, I'm a little nervous given that I haven't been entirely honest with the police so far. Jake notices I'm shivering and scoots closer. Then he does something that makes me shiver for a completely different reason. He takes off his jacket and places it around my shoulders. We're sitting so close on the step that our legs are almost touching. I can see Jake's breath as he exhales, and I can't help but imagine tiny molecules that were once inside of him are drifting into my nostrils to become part of me. I think about the blazing way the detectives stared at me earlier today, especially when they mentioned Jake's name. He might have more to lose than I do. If the cops want to pin this on someone, Jake might be the obvious answer.

He calls up his photos with screenshots. Jake is right—the comments used to be open. And now I understand why people felt they could comment—it seems that all the commenters are fake accounts, throwaways people created for the pure purpose of speaking to Revenge. It takes me a moment to really focus on the text on the screen. Someone with the handle *punkdrgon411* commented:

> We all know Nell is a racist witch.
> She pretends she's all PC, but I
> heard her saying she thinks
> people who aren't white smell.

Revenge responded:

> You're welcome.

I shiver when I read the cold response. That's what Revenge said in my DM, too.

I look at the comment again. "Nell Ryan?"

Jake nods and says probably. Nell was a junior I didn't know, but I remember the stench. Someone had put a small dead fish in one of the pockets of her backpack. But since she didn't know it was there and kept carrying it around, it began to smell so bad that everyone assumed the smell was Nell. No one would sit or stand near her even long after it was gone, and she has yet to shake the nickname Smelly Nelly.

"It's not as if Revenge is giving anything away, though," I say with disappointment, pointing again to the screen. "All they say is 'ur welcome.'"

We move on to the next screenshot. The square bears the number 3, and someone with the handle *mercyqfirestorm6* comments that Mr. Washington, an AP bio teacher, is a perv who gave hot girls who flirted with him in his class As and everyone else lower grades.

"Seriously?" I ask. I took AP bio last year, but I had another teacher.

Jake shrugs. "Mr. Washington took a leave of absence starting in November. I have him for study hall. He hasn't come back. I heard that someone tipped the administration off that he had porn mags in his desk."

I take a minute to process what Jake just said—*Mr. Washington? Really?*—before I point to the next screenshot. "But look." Revenge commented again . . . but only with "Got your back." "Revenge doesn't give any personal details away. The only thing that seems consistent is they always post in the middle of the night."

I note the time of the reply—3:00 a.m. "Well, that's proof that Revenge isn't me," I say with a laugh. "I can barely stay up past midnight." Even being outside now, well after 1:00 a.m., is giving me a pounding headache.

Jake shakes his head playfully at my attempt at humor as he scrolls through more of the screenshots. The structure of each is the same: a numbered square with some gossip about what the person did. I'm beginning to see why the detectives can't figure out anything—there's not a ton to go on. A lot of the requests are personal, but not *that* personal. More about general wrongdoing, like cheating on a test or being a crappy teacher. If the detectives did uncover my request, they'd know instantly it's from me. Revenge continues to reply in the middle of the night, often a week after the request was placed. Sometimes they vary their response with things like, "U bet," and "Consider it done."

There's only one instance, in numbered square *4*, where Revenge is even remotely conversational.

"Look at this," I whisper, pointing to a comment by a *pybck_365* talking about how a junior named Derrick Hannigan is a bully and a coward. "He has a Finsta that he uses to troll people. Here he calls out Annabelle Grad for being a 'fat cow' and below that, he commented with the eggplant and mouth emoji on a bunch of gay guys' posts. He's bad news."

Revenge's response glows before my eyes.

> Got your back. Been there, Man.

I look at Jake. "Has Revenge been bullied, too?"

Jake rubs his jaw. "That could be a good motivator. The powerless doing something to feel empowered. Going after the bullies and everyone else."

"I feel like only a guy would say 'man,'" I hypothesize. "So, a guy who has been bullied might . . . but that leaves tons of people."

"But look, Revenge says 'been there.' Does this mean they're no longer being bullied?" Jake stares hard at his phone like it might change what it says.

I see Jake's point, though that wouldn't narrow down the field much. I sit back and rub my eyes. "Maybe . . ." I try to suppress a yawn, but it escapes before I can stop it.

"Sorry, Sabrina. I guess I woke you up for nothing."

"Not nothing," I say, because I was happy I got to see him. "I think we're getting close."

Jake nods, and then I remember something and blurt it out before I can edit myself. "Brooke told me Finn had been getting pics from some girl. Do you know anything about that?" My cheeks burn. It's extremely embarrassing mentioning naked pictures.

He shakes his head. "Finn and I weren't that close."

I decide to change the subject and move on to the next theory about EnergyFX and Finn's sensitivity to it. "If Revenge wanted to hurt Finn, why put the poison in EnergyFX? I mean, he might have smelled it and decided not to drink it, wouldn't he?"

Jake stands straighter. "Are you *sure* that's how Finn was poisoned? I thought it was just a rumor."

Every muscle in my body tenses. Of course *I'm* sure, but I can't keep all the lies I've told straight. "I mean, I'm not sure about *anything*, really."

Jake thinks a moment. "So, you're thinking EnergyFX might be a clue somehow? Or like some sort of message against Grace and Jason?"

"I don't know." I shrug. "Maybe it's nothing."

Jake lets out a breath, and for a few moments we're quiet. I listen to him breathe. Next to me. On the front steps.

"At least it's a beautiful night," he says.

I stare up at the sky. It really is beautiful. I wonder if he means it or if he's just saying something to break the silence. And then I speak. "I've never seen so many stars." Truth is, I've never taken the time to look at them. I've only studied them in a book—for a test.

"Stay up late enough, and they're always there."

I smirk at him. "You don't strike me as a guy who would know all the constellations."

"I was a Cub Scout for three years. I learned all kinds of stuff," Jake says proudly. He points to the sky. "Up there, the Big Dipper."

"Please, that's an easy one." I say, scanning the sky, trying to remember another constellation I studied. This was Emily's realm, not mine. "Can you find . . . Orion?"

He moves closer to me and points, his arm grazing my shoulder. "Easy. Is that a personal favorite?" he asks, nudging my shoulder.

I'm suddenly aware of how close Jake's face is to mine. I'm afraid to turn toward him, though. Afraid for what might happen . . . or what might *not*. But then, Jake turns toward me. My heart starts to thump. It's so loud I wonder if Jake hears it, too. I can't believe I said Orion. *Everyone* knows Orion.

"Sabrina," he starts.

I dare to look at him. His close, pink lips. The freckles on his nose. His wool hat, pulled down over his eyebrows. He leans closer to me, and closer, and closer, and suddenly his lips are on mine, soft and warm and buzzing. It's over fast, *too* fast—I hardly register it's happened at all. But when he pulls away, he's smiling shyly.

"Sorry, was that okay?"

My mouth hangs open. I can't speak. All I can do is nod. Jake laughs softly. I want to grab his hands and pull him toward me and kiss him again, kiss him a whole *bunch* of times, because for those few seconds our lips touched, I wasn't thinking about the trouble I was in, or how scared I felt, or how desperate things seemed. I just felt . . . happy.

But I don't because something catches my eye on his phone screen, which is lying between us on the steps. The screenshots are still up. Jake has scrolled to the very last of the bunch, which says more or less the same thing as the others—a vague request, and then Revenge's answer. But suddenly I realize that Revenge's answer is peculiar . . . and familiar.

> You get what you give.

I blink at the phrase. It's not one I hear very often. I don't even know what it means, exactly. Yet I *have* heard it—but from who? I root around in my brain, trying to figure it out. Even the spelling seems familiar, like I've seen that before, too. And then I realize: a door slightly ajar, a peek inside a room so packed with shelves of collectibles there's hardly any more space. A scrawled, handwritten poster above a shelf that reads *You Get What You Give*. Little plants under a sun lamp. A whole little garden indoors. But . . . a garden of *what*?

Pieces snap into place. I know someone who says that phrase. Down to the spelling. Down to the usage. And those *plants*. Could any of them be poison?

I'm thinking of Emily's twin brother, Charlie.

nineteen

I toss and turn all night. I didn't say anything to Jake about Charlie. I don't even know if my thoughts make sense. And yet, that phrase, you get what you give . . . it haunts me. So does the memory of those plants in Charlie's old room. I wish I knew what he grew in there. But Charlie's great with computers, apps—he'd know how to hide an account and evade suspicion. He'd also know, as Revenge, how to make our DMs disappear. And I still don't know how EnergyFX connects—did Charlie know Grace and Jason? But maybe it doesn't connect at all.

And Charlie *was* at boarding school, so how could he have done all the pranks? Maybe that's why Revenge gets the last person he helped to do the next one. According to Emily, Charlie hasn't gone back yet. That would have given him ample time to get revenge on Finn.

But am I really thinking *Charlie* is Revenge? Why would Charlie hate Finn? Was *he* bullied? He's exactly the kind of person Finn would target. Maybe stuff was happening I didn't even know about—stuff even Emily didn't know. Maybe *this* was why Charlie abruptly chose to go to boarding school instead of ninth grade at Milford High with the rest of us. To get away from Finn and the OGs.

Was that *possible*?

The following day is Saturday. Emily has community service cleaning the bathrooms at school as part of her punishment. To make things worse, it's also the accepted students at Harvard day for the tri-state area. I text her asking when she'll be done.

Ugh, who knows my life is literally in the toilet!!!

If I didn't feel so bad, I would laugh. I definitely don't want to question Charlie while Emily's around, so if I'm going to do this, the time is now.

My nerves are jittery as I drive over. I consider calling Jake to get him involved, but if Charlie *is* Revenge, and Jake and I march in together, he'll know what's up. And then . . . who knows . . . Revenge holds all the cards, including all of my DMs and all the ways I'm culpable. Charlie could release all that information to the world if he felt spooked. I have to tread carefully.

I park at Emily's curb, realizing it's been a while since I've been here. Luckily, Emily's mom's car isn't in the driveway, which gives me hope I'll be able to avoid her, too. When I ring the doorbell, no footsteps sound for a while. I wonder if they're *all* out. But then, the door flings open. I blink at the person on the other side. It's Charlie . . . but not. His shoulders are broader, and it looks like he's grown at least four inches. His hair has grown out, too, and his face looks more chiseled. And are those serious *biceps*?

"*Charlie?*" I blurt out.

"Hey, Sabrina." He pushes a hand through his messy hair. "Uh, Emily's out all day with my mom."

"Oh, really?" I feign surprise. *How did Emily get away without telling him she's on school janitorial duty as part of her punishment?* "Well, I just wanted to drop off some notes I borrowed." I wave a notebook. It's a lame excuse, but Charlie doesn't seem to care. Still, the way he's hopping from foot to foot, I can tell he's eager for me to leave. Not yet though.

"So, how are you?" I ask. "I haven't seen you in forever." I can't help looking at his arms again. "Did you start playing a sport?"

"Nah, just going to the weight room." Charlie leans against the door frame. "Releases stress. Plus, lifting weights—it's not like you have to be coordinated to do that."

I smile at him, and he smiles back.

"Well, you look great."

Ugh. That sounded way weirder than I meant it to.

Charlie shrugs. There's a long pause. I clear my throat. It's strange to be acting so friendly right now with the person who might possibly be Revenge. I try to keep at the front of my mind that for the most part, Revenge has done *good* things, calling out people who are jerks—I can see Charlie doing all of that. But I also have to remember that if Charlie *is* Revenge, he knows all about me . . . and what I've done, both to Finn *and* his sister . . . and also that he's the one behind Finn's poisoning. I need to know if that's true.

"Do you mind if I wait for Emily?" I ask looking at my watch. "I'm thinking she'll be back pretty soon."

"Uh . . ." Charlie looks at me, confused. "I mean, you *can* . . . but it said on the calendar they'd be gone all day at some Harvard thing."

Harvard thing? I almost, almost, tell him that's impossible. But then I remember how Emily says she and Charlie have barely talked. Is it possible she hasn't even told him this? It's sad, actually. They were so close once, and Emily couldn't share something so awful.

"Do you mind if I drop this in Em's room?" I say, waving the notebook. Charlie sighs. "Sure."

I start down the hall. It's a convenient excuse because Emily and I are always returning or borrowing something from the other. I head into Emily's room and leave the door cracked. I put the notebook on her desk and start doing what I always do—putting order to the chaos. Some people wouldn't like their friends touching their stuff, but Em always begs me to clean up her room. It's just not her thing, and her mom always gets on her for it.

I move her pens all back into the holder, pile the schoolbooks in one area. I scoop up her scrapbooking supplies strewn on the floor, all the brightly colored paper, stickers, and ribbons and put them in the box I had created for her a year ago for just this reason. I toss a few candy wrappers in the trash, and then I stop. There, in the center of her bulletin board is her Harvard acceptance letter. And a banner up on her wall almost mirroring where mine had been. My heart drops, and again I feel the anger I had felt toward Emily—the very rage that caused me to reach out to Revenge. The jealousy I felt until, well, until she had it rescinded.

But then I start to wonder, *Why would Emily want it there still, glaring at*

*her? All that she could have had and what I took away? Maybe she's still holding
out hope?*

Am I?

The sound of Charlie heading down the hall toward the kitchen snaps me
from my daze. I have no time to waste. I head out of Emily's room and notice
Charlie's bedroom door is open. I tiptoe toward it, my heart banging. His
bed is perfectly made; all the trash that used to line the floors is gone. Things
may not be my level of organized, but Charlie has cleaned up his act. But he's
still got all three different video games going on, playing on three different
screens, and all of his Grunge posters, Nirvana, New Radicals: *You get what
you give*. My stomach twists.

I scan his desk for the other evidence. I mean, I don't even know what I'm
expecting to see, but there's nothing, only some scattered notebooks, pens,
and USB cords.

"Uh . . . ?"

I spin around. Charlie stands in the doorway, one eyebrow raised.

"Uh, hi!" I say, flustered. "Sorry . . . I was just . . . what happened to all
your plants?"

"Plants?"

"Yeah, your room used to look like a rain forest!" I try to make it sound
like a joke. *Remember, he could be Revenge,* I remind myself. *Don't tip your
hand.*

"Oh. Those were my mom's." Charlie doesn't seem that bothered by the
question. "She didn't go out much after my dad, and I think the gardening
phase was right before the DIY phase, which I think was before the home-
made jelly phase. That was a disaster." He chuckles.

And then something terrible happens. My phone beeps in my hand, at
the same time as his computer screens blare in a loud and jarring screech.
On the screen, clearly visible to both of us, reads: *Google Alert, Finn Walters.*
There's a new news hit about him.

I have no idea how to react. Laugh nervously? Play it off like it's no big
deal?

Charlie steps toward me. He's got a strange look on his face. He's gotten a lot taller I realize again—and he looks so much stronger looking than he used to be. We're the only people in this house, as far as I can tell. Why hadn't I told Jake I was coming? Why hadn't I come with backup?

"Couldn't happen to a nicer guy, huh?" he says, gesturing to Finn's name on my phone. His tone is anything but kind.

I swallow down a gulp. "Sorry . . . what?" I try to sound light. Unaffected.

He waves his hand. "I just think it's crazy, 'cause that guy is a dick." He looks at me nervously. "But now everyone's making it like he was some saint."

I try to process what he's just said. "You didn't like Finn?" My mind is spinning. *Would Revenge be so forthcoming? Is this a trap?*

Charlie lets out a breath. "Did anyone actually like Finn?"

I have so many questions, but I can't even think what to ask. But then Charlie just keeps . . . *going*.

"You know I saw him—over the break—at that party New Year's Eve? I waved at you, but . . . I think you were kind of wasted, so not sure you saw me."

"Sketch's party?" I blink. "You were there?"

"I tagged along with Emily. She wanted me to come, but it's *not* my scene. I mean, I went to boarding school to get away from all those people."

I try to think. I swear I hadn't seen him there. Then again, it's not like I'd seen much of anything in my drunken state. The idea of Charlie seeing me drunk is somehow especially embarrassing.

"I saw Finn, and I had this idea that I was going to go over and, like, talk to him." Charlie's voice cracks. "Someone needs to stand up to that guy. I hung outside, waiting, and I saw Finn. But he was arguing with someone. A girl."

"Brooke?"

"No. Someone else. It was on the side of the house."

"Who?"

Charlie shakes his head. "I didn't know her."

"What did she look like? Tall, short? Hair color? What was she wearing?" *Is this the girl Finn was cheating with?*

"It was dark, Sabrina. I didn't really see."

"Not anything?"

He looks at me strangely like he's wondering why I care so much. "I saw the car she drove, I guess. Finn didn't get in it with her. And then, Finn walked past me and saw that I'd seen them together. He gave me this 'keep your mouth shut' kind of look. Like he owned the place. I felt just like that scrawny kid who couldn't stand up to him years ago." Charlie looks disappointed in himself.

I think about all of this for a minute. "What kind of car was it?"

Charlie waves his hand. "A beater. White Kia, I think? The only reason I noticed it at all was because there was a big red A painted on the door."

I blink hard. *Revenge.* This all has to go together. But *how?* Was I standing in front of Revenge right now? Why wasn't Charlie coming after me if he was? offering me all of this information . . . it doesn't make sense.

I clear my throat, daring to ask him something. Anything. "What were you going to talk to Finn about, anyway? Him bullying you?"

He frowns. "Bullying me?"

"You said 'clear the air.' I just meant . . ."

His video games are still going in the background, I realize, but Charlie is no longer manning the controls. "*Who* said I was being bullied?" He was angry.

Words are jammed in my throat. The thing is, I don't think anyone told me. I just assumed. And now I'm standing here, looking like an idiot, and Charlie doesn't look hurt—he looks offended. And maybe, I think, not like someone who'd be Revenge. I'd overstayed my welcome. Not that I was that welcome to begin with.

"Sorry. I . . . I . . . uh . . . made a mistake," I say softly. "I'd better go."

Charlie just stares at me. I keep waiting for him to say something, but he remains quiet. So, I back out of his room and head down the hall I know so well and out the door into the safety of my car. My head is still spinning from the strange conversation. But at least I have something new to look for. At least Charlie was useful in that regard.

That Kia. And the person who drives it.

. . .

"One decaf latte," I say to the barista at the Starbucks drive-thru window. "And make sure it's decaf. *Please*," I add. I've learned the hard way that caffeine and panic attacks don't work well together.

After I collect the latte, I sit in the Starbucks parking lot and stare blankly at the passing cars on the road. Maybe what Charlie told me isn't anything. But maybe it's everything. *A white Kia with a big A on it*. I could kick myself—I'm such an idiot. *The Scarlet Letter*. An adulterer.

The girl Finn had cheated with. Those naked pics Brooke mentioned and Grant talked about. Was that why Revenge marked her car? That certainly could give someone good motive to hurt Finn, too.

I rub my eyes. I need to tell Jake about this. He said he didn't know who the car belonged to, but maybe we could drive around and look for it together. But as I'm about to call him, a FaceTime call from Emily comes in.

"Hey," I answer. "What's up?"

"If you thought the girls' bathrooms were gross, NEVER go in the boys." Emily sounds miserable. "Just cleaned all of them and calling to say hi. Wanna come over later?"

"I stopped by your house, actually!" I confess shakily. "Dropped off some cookies!"

I don't want Emily catching me in a lie. Hopefully Charlie won't say I was asking for her. And Emily will think he ate the cookies. "I talked to Charlie for a second. He looks so much . . . more mature!"

"Ew," Emily's voice is distant. "But yeah. He's grown like six inches. What did you even talk to him about?"

"Nothing, really." What was I going to say—that I thought he tried to kill Finn and was Revenge?

"So . . . ?" Emily asks.

"Nothing!" I repeat, too strongly.

"I meant so do you want to come over?" Emily must think I've totally lost it.

My lies are getting to be way too overwhelming. All of a sudden, I can't handle it anymore.

"Em . . ." I choke out. "I, um, need to talk to you about some things."

"Okay?" Emily sounds worried.

I can hear my heart swishing in my ears. Am I really going to say this? But it would give me so much power. It would give Revenge less ammunition. Maybe the truth will set me free.

"I, um . . ." I start.

"Sabrina, hang on," Emily interrupts. I hear muffled voices on her end. When she's back on the line, she grumbles. "I have to go. Mom doesn't want me on the phone. But let's pick this up later, okay? Please?"

I bite down hard on my lip. "Sure," I say, even though I'm not sure I'll be able to work up the nerve again. "Of course."

For the next hour, I drive around aimlessly, thinking that maybe I'll just run into a white Kia with a giant red A by happenstance. I think of where people my age might hang out on a Saturday: the mall, the nail salon, the gym. I spot a few white Kias, but none of them have even a hint of red paint on the door. I suppose she could have had the door fixed by now . . . but as Charlie said, the car was kind of a beater. Maybe her parents would think springing for that sort of repair wasn't worth it.

I look through Instagram and TikTok, too, searching for photos and videos of classmates and Kias. No luck there, either. I probably don't know the right places to look. I try calling Jake to see if he knows, but his call goes to voice-mail. Later, he sends me a text saying that he and his parents went to visit Finn in the hospital.

My heart lurches.

And?

No change. It's pretty devastating. And there's a cop outside his door. I guess they're waiting to see if he wakes up, maybe? To ask him questions? See what he knows?

I shiver. I start a text to Jake, ready to tell him everything—about Revenge's bargain and that all I have to do is identify who might have called for a prank on someone with a Kia. Maybe the guy who drives it is on the basketball team? But as I'm writing it, another text from Jake pops up again.

Phone dying. Talk to you tomorrow. Bring iPad, need to give to bio class for demo.

Something occurs to me. All these different departments. Always using the iPad. They can't always be changing the code. How could I not have thought of this? Could it be that simple? Could they all use the same code? How could I not have tried the one code that worked when I had to use it in physics lab: GWHIGH.

And I'm in.

I scroll through the different folders; there's pretty much one for every department. Finally, I locate the drama folder and scroll down. There are files for past audition scenes, cast lists, and schedules. Then my breath catches as my eyes land on an Excel file: *Concession Sales*.

I open it and scroll through the names. Lots of items, and EnergyFX is listed . . . but not many have sold. After careful counting, I only see four people who purchased a bottle. The first three are teachers. Older teachers, too—not to judge, but I have serious doubts that sixty-five-year-old Mr. Artinger, the shop teacher, knows how to use Instagram with any skill—same with Ms. Beverly, who teaches AP calculus. It amuses me that *they* would be buying EnergyFX and not students. I guess the beverage really isn't that popular.

The fourth name, however, is a surprise. I blink at the name. Could it *be*? *Parker Michaels*.

twenty

I'm still sitting in my car when I make this discovery, and it's growing dark. I need to get home, but home means facing my father. I don't get it. Why did Parker come to the school to buy EnergyFX?

That's got to be bad PR for EnergyFX. Kaye had jumped all over it. It seemed so obtuse at the time—beside the point—but she'd said it with almost . . . *giddiness.* Like she *hoped* this would take EnergyFX down. She also said Parker knew the two people who created the drink and that they stole the idea. But she'd acted strangely about that, too.

I grip my phone and google EnergyFX. I scroll down and click on some links to stories about the young entrepreneurs, Grace and Jason, developing the drink because of a mutual friend who had a hard time processing certain sugars. "Her mom had to wake her up every few hours to get food in her, otherwise her insulin would crash," the friends explain. She was on a special diet to keep her insulin steady, but they said she wished her life wouldn't be so interrupted all the time—if only she could just eat and feel sustained like a normal person.

Did Kaye send Parker to school that day? Or did Parker go on her own? And why? What did they have against the company?

As I read on, I learn that Grace and Jason used their chemistry backgrounds (both were Westinghouse scholars) to create their first prototype to see if they had discovered the type of nutrients this girl could digest. They tested it out on her, and it worked—she could drink EnergyFX, and her insulin level would remain stable. She didn't need to set alarms to wake up every few hours for food or insulin. It was a game changer. The next step was to turn the prototype into a formula with a longer shelf life. Naturally, sports-minded people found this beverage interesting, too—and so did beverage brands. Then there's the stuff I already knew: EnergyFX sold to a big brand last year, and now it's sold nationwide. There's a caveat at the bottom that says the drink hasn't caught on *quite* like everyone hoped— there's something artificial-tasting about the energy source they just can't figure out yet.

"But still, this is helping a lot of people," Grace is quoted as saying. "And we owe it all to our friend Parker."

Parker. I stare hard at the screen.

But it doesn't make sense. EnergyFX helped Kaye and Parker; it didn't hurt them. And there's certainly not anything in this article about Finn. I sit back in the seat and rub my eyes. There's no way I'm going to get answers just by reading articles. I have to actually ask some questions in person. And I'm dreading it.

. . .

I've never been to Kaye's condo across town. Let's just say I've been avoiding it in hopes things would fizzle out between her and my dad. I know the general area, though—a big, pretty community surrounded by a lake and a golf course. I pass condo after condo, wondering how I'm going to find the right one. When I finally spot Parker's Mini Cooper, I'm surprised to see a much shabbier-looking complex than I expected. I begin to rethink why I always thought Kaye was so rich. Maybe she's not as big of a lawyer as I thought. And who knows if her ex helps? Well, she's certainly not after my dad for his lack of money. Either way, Parker bought EnergyFX at our school. It might be the same EnergyFX bottle that made it to me, outside the locker room. *But how did it get there?*

I park a few condos away. As I walk up the drive, my anger grows. Jake is getting blamed. *I* am getting blamed. I *have* to do this, to save both of us. My mind flips back to the kiss from last night. I'm starting to fall for him. I mean, *really* fall for him. I have to kiss him again—and again and again . . . But if I don't fix this, we'll never get that chance.

Parker's Mini is parked in front of condo number 56, and when I get to the door, I hear a bubbly voice inside that sounds like Kaye's. Swallowing hard, I press the doorbell. I hear footsteps, but when the door swings open, I see a face I don't expect.

"Sabrina?" My father looks pleasantly surprised.

My stomach drops to my knees. *Ugh.* I hadn't noticed my dad's car on the street. I might not have continued if I had. Just as I'm about to leave, Kaye comes up behind him with a smug smile. "Sabrina! Come in! We're making pasta."

"Hey, Sabrina," Parker says, waving at me from inside.

As soon as I see Parker, all the fear, anger, and frustration I've been keeping inside these past few weeks explode.

"YOU bought the EnergyFX!" I spit out, barely making it through the door as the fragments from the bomb I just dropped hang in the air.

Parker blinks. "*What?*"

"You were at school. You purchased it at the drama concession!"

Parker looks at me as if I've gone mad. "When I picked you up at school? I didn't buy EnergyFX. I don't even drink it anymore."

"Don't lie!" I practically scream.

"Sabrina." My father crosses his arms. "What are you doing?" They all stare at me as if I've totally lost it. And who knows? Maybe I have.

"I bought it," Kaye stammers defensively. "I wanted to support my friend's daughter who is in *The Tempest*. I put it on Parker's account since they don't take cash."

"Who's your friend?" I counter, skeptical.

"What's going on?" My father intercedes, trying to diffuse the tension between the two women in his life.

"*Nothing,*" Kaye insists.

"I thought you swore never to give them another penny," Parker says, cocking her head. It's clear she's as clueless as my dad.

"So, why did you?" I ask, my heart pounding. "And why didn't you say anything to the police about Parker not just knowing Grace and Jason, but them being good friends—and creating the drink to *help* her?"

"The police?" My father looks at us. "Sabrina—you mean the other day? When they came to talk about . . . that *boy*?"

"This is ridiculous!" Kaye slams her palm down on the table a little too hard.

"Wait, the cops were asking about EnergyFX? Why?" Parker asks.

"They found traces of it in Finn's sports bottle," I say, clearing my throat. I realize I'm no saint either. I mean, I'm the one who *poisoned* Finn. Granted, I didn't know that at the time. I just thought it would make him break out in hives or something. But still, my actions landed him in the hospital, and now I have to find out who Revenge is to clear my own name—and Jake's!

I glare at Kaye as I press on. "The cops were asking about the drink when they came to the house, and you didn't say a word about Parker being friends with them."

"Why would I?" Kaye says breezily. "They didn't need to know anything about Parker's relationship with them. It's irrelevant."

"Sabrina, are you accusing *Kaye* of something?" My father is shocked. "That doesn't even make any sense."

"Don't you think it's strange that Kaye purchased a bottle from the school . . . and then a few days later, Finn collapsed? Do you really think it's just a coincidence?"

Everyone stares at me. Kaye bleats out a laugh.

"Oh, so you're the *detective* now?"

But by the caught expression on Kaye's face, I know I'm definitely on the right track.

And then, to my astonishment, Parker says in a near whisper, "What did you do now, Mom?"

Kaye whips around and glares at her. "I didn't hurt that boy."

"But . . . why did you buy a bottle of EnergyFX? You hate them, Mom."

"I . . ." Kaye breathes out raggedly. Then she turns around and storms into her living room. We all follow her. My heart is a rocket inside my chest.

Kaye walks to the fireplace and stands, back to us, for a good fifteen seconds. Her shoulders heave. I can't tell if she's crying or fuming. When she turns around, the tip of her nose is red, and her eyes are wild.

"This isn't what it looks like, okay? Someone asked me to buy it. They said it was just going to make the brand look bad, a little. Knock them down a peg." She points at Parker. "Doesn't it bother you that they used you like a guinea pig and never even gave you a cut? Doesn't it bother you that it was your idea, and they sold the brand for millions of dollars and you won't get one penny?"

Parker's mouth hangs open. So does my dad's.

"Kaye, what are you talking about?"

Kaye looks at my dad and then back at me. But it's Parker who speaks next.

"She's just mad because Grace and Jason didn't include me in the company. They are going to make a lot of money with the sale, but I honestly had *nothing* to do with creating EnergyFX. I was saying that I thought it would be a good idea if there was a drink people could take that helped balance their sugar highs and lows. The last thing I wanted was to be defined by that stupid illness."

"But you should have gotten something for it." Kaye shakes her head. "You were their guinea pig. And we could use that money. Your school and your programs are NOT cheap!"

I look around the condo. It's not fancy. It's not even *nice*. Maybe I was wrong about Parker—and Kaye's financial status.

My father is staring at Kaye with an expression on his face like someone has smacked him speechless. I start to feel a bolt of guilt—I hadn't exactly planned on *wrecking* things between them, not that I could have predicted Kaye felt this way. I thought it was Parker who bought the drink, not Kaye. But I can't back down now. I have to know what really happened that day.

Kaye stands with her lips puckered and her shoulders squared. She doesn't feel bad about her opinion, I realize. She still thinks she's right.

"Did you hurt that boy—to bring down the brand because your daughter didn't reap the profits?" my father starts. "That kid is in the hospital, Kaye."

"Of course, I didn't!" she spits out. "All I knew was that it was going to be used in some sort of harmless prank that, yes, was going to make the brand look bad. That's *it*."

"But who asked you to buy it?" I jump on this. It's got to be Revenge.

Kaye looks down. "I was contacted by email from a competitor brand. Given those specific instructions—to provide a bottle, to leave it next to this water fountain outside school . . . I didn't even go into the building. The drama sale was outside that day. EnergyFX is still hard to find . . . I didn't think this would be anything *dangerous*. I just . . ."

And then she trails off, her chin wobbling. It's like she's finally realizing the gravity of the situation.

"It's not my *fault*," she insists. "How do we even know that kid drank *that* bottle of EnergyFX?" But she looks like she doesn't believe what she just said. None of us do.

"Why didn't you report this?" my father whispers. "Kaye, you have an obligation. There's a crime involved. A *poisoning*."

Kaye's eyes widen as she watches him pull out his phone. "Please, Peter. I could lose my law license!"

"You should have thought about that before you did what you did, Mom," Parker says weakly.

Kaye's gaze darts to me, and her brow furrows. "I bet you're thrilled, aren't you? You've never liked me. It's so obvious. You were just waiting for an opportunity to take me down."

My mouth drops open, but no words come out. The worst thing is that it's true—kind of. But never did I imagine it would come to *this*.

twenty-one

I sleep restlessly that night, filled with dreams of beeping hospital monitors, broken school ID fobs, Charlie's outraged face, and bottles and bottles of EnergyFX. My house is quiet. I came home before my dad did, and I heard him let himself in a little after ten. I don't know the status between him and Kaye. I'm afraid he blames me, even though it really wasn't my intention to create a rift between them. Kaye's words keep gonging in my mind: *I bet you're thrilled about this.* Could Kaye be lying? Could she still be Revenge? Or could she have asked Revenge for the prank?

Who knew to contact her? Who knew her bitterness about EnergyFX was her weakness? Had Parker talked to someone about it? Surprisingly, Parker *had* reached out to me, in a text:

> Hey, I'm really sorry about everything that's going on. I'm beyond mad @ my mom. She's going to speak to the police. She promised ur dad.

I didn't know how to respond. In all honesty, I was surprised Parker was being so friendly and candid. I'd never texted with her before, and I thought she might be kind of snotty—and maybe not want to speak to me ever again.

I finally get it together and text Parker the next morning:

> Thanks, I'm sorry if I seemed like a total bitch

It's all I can think of to say. Seconds later she responds:

> Please there was only one person acting like a bitch last night and it wasn't you!

She punctuates this last part with a winking emoji. I'm relieved she isn't upset with me and respond with a hugging emoji. *Are we becoming friends?* I wonder. Irony of ironies—exactly what my father always wanted.

I drive to school, the theories swirling. I'm dying to talk to Emily about Kaye more or less losing it . . . but then I realize I *can't*, because Emily has no idea I'm seriously investigating what happened. Can I pretend it's purely for fun, like my *Criminal Minds* obsession? Except maybe she'll see through that right away. She'll question why I'm suddenly so interested in school gossip when it never mattered before.

I bite my lip hard. I hate leaving her out of this. I can tell how much it hurts her and how wildly her mind is swirling, second-guessing the way I'm behaving. With everything else Emily is dealing with, the last thing she needs is worrying about where we stand. I think, too, about talking to Charlie yesterday—and how some of what he said didn't quite make sense. It's like he assumed I knew something . . . or understood something . . . but I'm not sure quite *what*. Emily was so wrong about him being bullied; she's usually so attuned to people's feelings and motives. And if Finn *didn't* bully him, why did he abruptly go to boarding school?

I don't see Emily or Jake at school. Thursday is always my crazy day; I don't even have a free period for lunch. It's hard to fathom that school just keeps going on with all the insanity around it. Then, in the last period of the day, a note is passed from outside to my teacher who looks directly at me. I can feel the blood draining out of my face.

"Miss Richards, please go to the head office." Her tone is a mix of surprise and disappointment. I feel every eye in the room on me.

Oh God. They know.

. . .

I'm escorted down the corridor by the hall monitor. I'm so calm I surprise myself. But this can't be good. Why would they want to see me? Have they gotten into Revenge's account? Did someone see something? Did they catch Revenge?

The hall monitor indicates that I should take a seat. Gone are the usual happy exchanges with the ladies at the desk. No one will look at me, let alone talk to me.

This can't be good, I think again.

After a few minutes, I hear some voices coming toward the principal's door, but when it opens, I couldn't be more surprised to see Tess walking out.

Detective Carson nods toward me. It's not a friendly nod—more of an "I've got my eyes on you" look. Tess looks directly at me, and I see just a glimpse of a smile cross her face. But before anyone else can clock it, she is back to full-on maiden in distress, with the principal and detective fawning all over her.

"You did the right thing by coming forward, Tess," Principal Morgan says, patting her on the back.

"Yes," echoes Detective Carson, "And we're sorry for what happened to your car. We'll be in touch soon."

Her car? Wait. *Tess's car* had the red A on it? She was cheating on Jake? And why did Jake say that he didn't know it was her car? I try to search Tess's face for any indication of what's going on, but now she won't even glance in my direction.

After Tess exits the office, Detective Carson's body seems to take on more gravity. She barely acknowledges me when I see her. After she and Principal Morgan have gone back into his office, I wait for what feels like an eternity. Finally Principal Morgan opens the door and says, "Sabrina, please come in."

. . .

We sit in silence as Detective Carson continues to jot some notes in her pocket flip pad.

Is this how they do it? They say nothing, hoping you will crack? What do they know? What did Tess tell them? What should I tell them? Should I call Kaye? I can't call Kaye. She hates me now. My dad? I can't let him know my involvement; he's already disappointed enough in me. I can't call Jake or Emily. I'm alone. On my own. It's okay; I can handle this. I can figure this out.

"So, Sabrina," Detective Carson says slowly, flipping back through her notepad. "You're probably wondering why we asked you here."

I try to think of what to say, but I don't think I can even speak, so I just nod like a bobblehead and wait for her to continue.

"You told us that you were at the game." I nod. I did. Totally true. I'm a good person. Not a bad one. The detective continues, "But you didn't mention the New Year's Eve Party."

I'm trying to figure out what they are referring to. *Which part of the party?*

She barely lets me think before flipping to another page, "Or that you were outside of the party, alone, for fifteen to twenty minutes."

Was I? Had it been that long before Jake came out? I wait for her to continue.

"Do you know anything about Tess's car getting vandalized with paint?" she asks. It feels both rhetorical and like she wants me to answer. And I suddenly realize the implication of what she's saying.

"Yes!" I blurt out. "I mean, NO!"

The detective raises her brow.

"I saw it when I was outside. I mean, someone had already done it when I went outside!"

Detective Carson nods her head, as if I had just told her I had seen a unicorn outside instead.

"So, you went outside *alone*, and you *saw* the car painted, but no one had seen it like that before you were outside." This is said as a fact, not a question.

"The car was over on the side of the house," I offer. "You wouldn't see it if you weren't looking." Even I feel like it sounds lame.

"A big painted red A on a white car? In the snow?" She smirks. But before

I can respond, she quickly launches another strike. "You also didn't mention you were outside with her ex-boyfriend—your *new* boyfriend."

"He's not my boyfriend!" I know I sound a little too emphatic.

"Maybe not anymore." Detective Carson continues, "And you also failed to mention you and Finn had an argument that same night."

This is nuts. Somehow it seems like I had every reason to do something bad to Tess and to Finn. He took Brooke away from me, Tess hurt my "boyfriend," and clearly, I am a closet troublemaker. I have to say something in my own defense.

"I . . . I . . ." I hang my head in shame. "I was really drunk," I manage to eke out. I can see the disappointment in Principal Morgan's face, but I figure a drunk teenager is better than a murdering one. "That's all it was. I didn't paint her car!"

"Well," says Detective Carson, clearly not buying it as an excuse, "sometimes alcohol just brings out feelings we have . . ." she pauses, as if searching for the word, "buried."

Ugh. Why that *word?*

"Lots of people heard you screaming at Finn. Something about how he stole your best friend. That he was a cheater and a bully?"

My voice is barely audible. "Yes . . . I mean, I said that, but . . . but a lot of people felt that way."

"That may be true," The detective says sternly, "but not all of them were also seen outside the locker room before the game when Finn collapsed."

"Who said that?" I asked, hoping in the second it might take her to answer I could come up with a viable excuse for being there.

But the detective and Principal Morgan just stare at me. They think I did it. They think I am Revenge. And they're not entirely wrong.

I remember Kaye's telling me not to talk to the police without letting her know and to tell them I don't want to say anything else without my father. Thankfully, rather than calling him, they let me leave. They tell me to go home; they will be in touch.

I have no time. I have to figure out who Revenge is. I have to figure out what to do. I have to—

"Bri? Are you okay? Tell me what's going on!" Emily is standing in front of me. She looks so genuinely distraught for me that it only increases my feelings of guilt and shame. But it also makes me realize how stupid I've been to freeze out my best friend. She's the only person I can trust, the only one I can turn to. And since my body can't fight it any longer, I begin to feel like I am going to have a panic attack.

Emily steers me toward the front entrance of the school. Classes are just letting out, and while I appreciate that I can feel anonymous in the stream of exiting students, the push of the crowd only fuels my anxiety.

Once we get outside, the fresh air helps a little, and Emily tells me to take some deep breaths. She knows how to help me. She's the only one who gets me. She waits patiently as I calm down and the crowds disperse. The school buses pull out and the parking lot of senior cars starts thinning out.

Coming toward us is a white Kia, and though she's clearly tried to get rid of it, you can see a faint trace of a giant red A on the passenger side. Tess's Kia, and it's stopped at the light at the exit.

I drop my backpack on the ground and sprint toward it. I need to get some answers from her. Emily calls after me and starts running, too. Somehow, as I'm getting closer to the car, I can see there's someone else in the car. And by the time I get to the car and peer inside, somehow, I'm not surprised to see that next to her is Jake.

As the car pulls away and I can see Jake looking back in what looks like surprise, Emily finally catches up with me. She's winded, but manages to push out her words with frustration.

"Was that Jake *with Tess?*"

I don't answer. I don't even know what to say.

"Sabrina, *what* is going on? Why won't you tell me what's happening?"

I stare at my friend and realize I need to do what I should have done at the beginning. Because I feel like I've figured out a vital piece of information that maybe I wasn't supposed to stumble upon. And suddenly, heartbreakingly, it's turned everything upside down.

Tess was cheating with Finn. It's probably why Tess and Jake broke up. And then Tess's car was painted on—by Revenge. But maybe that wasn't enough. Maybe the revenge needed to be bigger.

Jake is Revenge, my mind whispers. *Jake painted that car as Revenge . . . Jake benefited when Finn couldn't play . . . Jake . . . hated . . . Finn. Jake is with Tess. Jake . . . is playing ME.*

Maybe everything Jake has told me is a lie. Maybe he's had me on a wild goose chase this whole time, withholding the iPad password from me, bringing over those screenshots—they're all things that point away from him . . . and at ME. I realize another thing, sickeningly: *Jake's mom knows Kaye.* He told me, outright, that they work in the same law firm. It's possible Kaye shared with his mom her frustration about Parker being left out of the EnergyFX deal. And Jake somehow knowingly used Kaye in the plot.

He also used me. As Revenge, he knew how pissed I was at Emily, *and* he set the wheels in motion to get Emily kicked out of Harvard. He set me up to feel guilty and be the perfect person to carry out his plan. And all that flirting with me, kissing me . . . it was all subterfuge. He framed me perfectly.

But why? And why did I let him in? I should have known better! And now I'm going down for his revenge!

"I will tell you everything," I finally say to Emily, not sure whether to burst with anger or fear, "just not here."

. . .

We drive silently to Emily's in her car. I leave mine at school; I'm too upset to drive. Emily indulges me by not asking any questions, and while she may have some suspicions, she clearly doesn't grasp the magnitude of the situation as she hums along happily to Taylor Swift.

I pray her mom isn't home. I don't know if I can hold it together enough to make polite conversation.

"Don't worry," Emily says, as she leads me toward her room, "Mom's at work until late, and Charlie went back to school this morning."

I breathe a sigh of relief. Per usual, it's like she can read my mind. What a fool I've been to freeze her out.

It's like when Emily, Brooke, and I would come home and have the house to ourselves. We would eat cookie dough, practice dance moves, and pretend we owned the place. How I wish that's what we were about to do.

I sit on Emily's bed and lean against the pillows. I stare around her messy and cluttered room. I see so many pictures of us, when we looked happier, younger. In Emily's room, life is normal—the life I remember, not the world of betrayal, near-death experiences, and revenge that have been plaguing me. Has it really been just a month since all this started?

Emily comes up and hands me some Annie's graham cracker bunnies and—ironically—a bottle of EnergyFX. I squint at it. Of course, how would she know it's the worst possible thing she could offer? I take the crackers, but I can barely look at the bottle and put it on the floor.

"I thought you could use the electrolytes," she says. Obviously, she wouldn't have realized how much that would trigger me. Why would she? She sits down on the bed, looking caught between being excited for the gossip while trying to be a sensitive friend.

"Why was Jake with Tess? Are they back together? Are you mad?"

Of course, that's what she thinks this about. A boy.

"Jake is Revenge." I say simply, as if I was telling her we had extra math homework.

"*What?*" Emily practically screams.

"And he's trying to frame me for everything." Again, I'm sorting it through as I speak. Emily stares wide-eyed at me.

I'm not sure where to even begin. The way I've betrayed Emily, or the heartbreak that Jake isn't who he says he is—and, oh right, the fact that I poisoned someone. It's all too much and too terrible. And will Emily even believe it?

"Jake . . . he's . . . he's been playing me the whole time."

The corners of Emily's mouth turn down. "He *has*?"

My thoughts feel so tangled. "And . . . and he *wanted* Finn to get hurt, I think." I try to explain that I'd figured out Finn was cheating with Tess behind Jake's back, and how by playing in the game, Jake got recruited to an amazing school. "I saw Tess's Kia the night of that party. Jake was with me. I *asked* him if he knew whose car it was. He said he didn't. He tried to steer me away from the car, and he was outside! And then later, Charlie said he saw Finn and Tess, too, by Tess's . . ." I trail off, realizing the mistake I've made.

Emily catches it, too. "Charlie? You talked to him about this?"

"I'm so sorry." I am a terrible person; I suspected my best friends' brother. "I thought maybe he had something to do with it. But when I came over on Saturday, we got to talking about Finn and the accident," I admit. "I guess he went to that party, the one at Sketch's house."

"Yeah, he tagged along . . . but then he ditched me." Emily looks scattered. "But I still don't understand. Why were you talking about *Finn*?"

My heart is pounding. Can she tell I'm hiding something?

"Charlie brought it up, I think. And he was saying that he thought Finn was a dick. I thought Finn bullied him, but he said that he didn't." I rub my jaw. "I figured that was one of the reasons you were crying the night of that party, all those years ago."

Emily laughs a little. "Yeah no, Finn didn't bully Charlie."

"Then why does Charlie hate Finn?" I ask.

"Well, you get what you give, right?" Emily laughs. "I mean Finn's a liar and a cheater."

The phrase jars me. And it seems awfully harsh about a guy lying in a coma.

"But Jake? I mean if he really IS Revenge, shouldn't you tell the police?" Emily continues.

I shut my eyes. It's all about to come crashing down. As soon as I report Jake, Jake—as Revenge—will report *me*. And then Emily will know. Everyone will. I need to tell Emily before that. I need to get it out. But it's so hard to find the words. I *ruined her life*. I ruined her chances at Harvard. And for what? It hardly seems to matter anymore.

I look around her room, The letter on her bulletin board. The Harvard pennant pinned up. The thick notebook with "Accepted Student's Day" printed across the binding. The neon green paper. And then I reach for the EnergyFX bottle by the bed. With a yellow star on top. I start to get up.

Emily grabs my arm, almost shoving me back down. "Sabrina. Focus. Shouldn't we tell the police about Jake??"

I turn and stare at her.

"Emily, did you and your mom go to a Harvard event this weekend?" I ask.

Emily's expression doesn't shift. Her eyes are dead. Her mouth is a straight line. And yet, she doesn't deny it, either.

"Does that mean you *did*?" My heart is rocketing. "So . . . they let you back in?"

Emily blinks hard. And then she smirks. "Yeah, Sabrina. That's right. They let me back in. Even though some awful, jealous person told on me."

But I know it isn't right. I know, but I don't want to know. And her tone of voice—she's being sarcastic. *Mocking*. She thinks, maybe, that this is funny. It's so *un*Emily that my throat is dry, and I feel afraid. Afraid because I'm not sure I know her. Afraid, too, because I realize I have to ask the follow-up question.

"You were never kicked out," I whisper.

Emily's creepy smirk stretches into a real smile, and then she lurches toward me, revealing something sharp and glistening she's hidden behind her back.

Is that . . . *a needle*? Aimed at . . . *me*?

"Emily!" I cry.

And then, the world goes dark.

twenty-two

The next time I open my eyes, my head isn't on a pillow but on a hard concrete floor. A harsh yellow light shines in my face. I try to move my hands, but they are pinned behind my back. I try to move my legs, but they're welded together, it seems, at the ankles.

I'm on a floor—a dusty, dirty floor. I wriggle around, trying to moan. But there's something covering my mouth. My heart starts to pound. As I look around, I realize I'm in the shed at the back of Emily's house. It's dark and damp. It's filled with broken pots and ancient, rotting bags of fertilizer. I only know the place because Emily and I sometimes came back here when her mom was being particularly annoying and we needed to escape. The shed is partially hidden at the edge of the property behind some tall azaleas that are in desperate need of trimming. It was our safe place. Or so I thought.

It all comes back to me. The memory hits me so hard I feel it, physically, in my body, zapping beneath my skin. The needle in Emily's hand. The warped look on her face. The facts that didn't add up. And then, her eerie, whispered "*Ding, ding, ding.* Joke's on you, Sabrina! Emily is Revenge."

A door bangs open, the bright light hurting my eyes.

"Oh, good!" Emily crows, as if I just woke up from a nap and we're going to learn a TikTok dance. "You're awake!"

She's hauling in equipment of some sort. Lights. A tripod. Something else with a long cord, maybe a microphone or camera? When she sets everything down, she approaches me.

"If you promise to be good, I'll take this off," pointing to the bandana across my mouth.

I nod quickly. Emily puts down a small knife she was carrying and unties the bandana, then quickly retrieves her knife before I can even think about trying to grab it. My mouth is so dry it's hard to speak at first.

"Emily." I struggle to move. "W-Why are you doing this?"

I keep waiting for the panic to set in. The sweat to start, but somehow, amazingly, I feel calm, almost as if every other panic attack had been preparing me for this.

"Sabrina, I don't need to answer that, silly!" Emily keeps up her light-hearted tone. "Surely you've figured it out by now!"

I lick my lips. "You're still going to Harvard. You faked getting kicked out."

Emily nods encouragingly. "Good . . ."

"Which means you must have seen my . . . request . . . to . . . Revenge." I look away.

"And . . ." Emily says soothingly, like a teacher encouraging a toddler to continue, "how do you think I saw that request?"

I gulp. "Revenge sent it to you?"

Please let it be this, I beg silently. But by the way Emily's brow furrows, I know it isn't. I clear my throat.

"Because . . . you *are* Revenge."

Emily claps her hands gleefully, "Good girl! A-plus-plus!"

"But Emily, why?" I gasp.

"Well," Emily crosses her arms. She struggles, as if searching for the right words. "I used to think how awful it was to be invisible. You know? That no one ever saw me? I mean, to most people, I'm just undistinguishable from the broken water fountain. I'm there, but no one cares that I exist."

I try to interrupt, but Emily shushes me. "Don't interrupt me, Sabrina—that's rude. I mean, I know you think I'm just your little lackey here to keep you company while you do 'important things.' But I am so. Much. More. Than that. So much more than YOU. And I realized there's great power in being invisible. When no one notices you, when they think you're just some wannabe weirdo who they'd rather avoid, you can do pretty much anything. You can convince security guards at a mall to give you the Wi-Fi password;

you can post something on the school board without anyone even seeing that it's you. You can put porn mags in your teacher's desk. You can even spray paint a red A without anyone even noticing you're there. It's almost like magic how much you can get away with when you don't exist."

"But you DO exist, Em. You're talented and funny and beautiful and . . . you're my best friend."

"Oh, please! Talented and funny maybe, but beautiful? Now I know you're lying. But I guess I should have known you'd be like all the other ones. A liar. A hypocrite. A selfish little bitch."

"Emily, I'm so, so sorry, but why . . . why Finn? Why did you make me do that to him?"

"You know, I'm beginning to understand why Harvard didn't let you in. For a smart girl, you're really pretty stupid."

I blink. The silence stretches. She's waiting for me to figure it out, but I don't see it yet. And then suddenly, I do.

"You," I whisper. "Finn hurt . . . *you.*"

Emily shuts her eyes and shakes her head. "We were *in love.* It started that summer, before ninth grade."

In love? I wrack my brain for any clue. I can only think of one.

"You said you hooked up with someone that summer. It was Finn? But why didn't you tell us?"

"I was *going* to tell you. At the party. I was going, and I would surprise him, and then everyone would see that we were this great couple! But then, he just . . . ignored me. He pretended he didn't even know me. He looked right at me like I was a joke. Like none of it mattered. And then, Brooke was flirting with him, and he was practically slobbering on her." She brushes her hands together. "It was awful."

"I can believe it," I whisper. Both because it's Emily, and this sort of thing would bulldoze her, but also if Finn were her first love. "But you should have told me," I add.

"How could I, Sabrina?" she says with an icy cold voice I've never heard before. "You left me. You ran *allll* the way home because all Sabrina cares about is Sabrina. It's all you've ever cared about."

"And what? You were plotting this for three years?" I ask. "Just because he didn't want to date you?"

"Of course not! I'm not a psycho!" She laughs. "I mean, yes, I hated him, and I hated Brooke. But once I had her out of our lives, I almost didn't care. I never imagined they would stay together this long."

I stare at the person I thought was my best friend. She looks like Emily. She sounds like Emily. And she's talking as if we were discussing an assignment she forgot to turn in, not holding me hostage in the back of her shed.

"But here's the thing, Sabrina. Finn *did* love me. I *know* he did. He just got confused by Brooke and her hair and her stupid little laugh and her perfect little life and . . ."

She begins scratching at her own hands so hard that I can see them beginning to bleed. But she doesn't notice. She just continues, "It was like she had him under some trance. And then, this summer when she was away, he was the same Finn who loved me again. He said he hadn't stopped thinking about me." She seems lost in the memory. And she looks thrilled. *Justified*. "I knew we were supposed to be together. Truth is, Brooke's a total prude and a major headache, according to Finn. We started hanging out again this summer."

I feel sick to my stomach. The person Finn was cheating with . . . *was Emily?*

"And . . . then what happened?" I dare to ask. Because, clearly, this doesn't have a happy ending.

"Oh, Sabrina we had the most magical summer," Emily says wistfully. "I would sneak out after my mom went to sleep and go to his house. We would be together, and he told me how much he cared about me and how important I was to him. And I *slept* with him, Sabrina. Remember our pact? Remember how we weren't going to do that sort of thing unless we were in *love*? I took that seriously. It was a perfect night. I was dying to tell you, but I didn't know how. I figured I'd wait until he broke up with Brooke. I was already imagining how the year would go. Finally, *finally*, people would *see* me. I would *be* someone."

Emily sounds almost giddy now, excited. "I was going to make sure people liked *you*, too, Sabrina. I mean, it wouldn't be easy. You have *no* idea what you're like. You're like this little robot with no feelings." She does a bizarre imitation of a robot.

I bite my lip, not sure I want to know. I have to do something. I start working the knot binding my hands. I was always a better Girl Scout than Emily, but it's tight.

"Then, little Miss Perfect came back from vacation. And it was like I didn't exist. Like I never existed. Like I was *nothing*. I gave him my virginity! I gave him my heart, my soul. And he *still* pretended he didn't even *know* me. I would go by his house late at night, but he had changed the gate code. I texted him and he blocked me. I even sent him pictures of me on Snap. And he . . . he . . . he showed them to all his friends and made me sound like some desperate stalker! He said if I told Brooke about us, he would post them *online*. It was humiliating!"

"So . . . that's when you started @Revenge?"

"I *had* to. Someone needed to teach him a lesson. Teach them *all* a lesson. The liars. The cheaters. The hypocrites! Revenge rights other people's wrongs! I'm *not* invisible. I'm a HERO!"

I can see the blood dripping from her palm to the floor.

"But, Emily," I say quietly, "I almost killed him."

"I know, right?" Emily rolls her eyes and smiles. "How did I mess that one up? Just a little more ricin would have done it. Oh, and don't worry. I thought you might back out, so you weren't actually the one who put the poison in."

"But . . . but why me?" I whisper. I'm making some headway with the knot, but I need to keep her calm. I need more time. "Why did I have to give Finn that drink?"

Emily stops and thinks for a moment.

"Karma?" She laughs. "I mean, I hadn't even planned on *you*. You, Sabrina, were the one person I loved and trusted. I had planned on framing Brooke. And then I would tell you, and you would be so proud of me! We would have gotten them *both* back. Everyone would love me! Love *us*!" Her eyes narrow. "But then, it turned out you are just as bad as all of them. Worse."

"I'm sorry, Emily. I'm so, so sorry." I had spent so much time focused on myself, focused on shutting people out, that I didn't realize the one person I thought I knew was nothing like what I thought. I'm beginning to sweat, and I can feel my heart starting to race. *No. NO!* I tell myself. *You will not lose it. You will NOT have a panic attack. Focus.*

"I mean, you know I was the one who applied to Harvard. It wasn't my mom. But I honestly thought you would get in, and *I'd* get deferred. But then once I revealed to the world that I was Revenge, well, *of course* they would let me in. And we could be together. Because I couldn't lose you. Not you. We *had* to be together."

I stare at her. I don't even know what to believe.

"But I guess we can thank the universe for intervening. I guess Harvard could see my genius and your true dark soul. Because when I saw that request to Revenge from you, of all people, I knew that *you* needed to be stopped, too."

"Emily, I can't imagine how horrible it must have been to see that request from me," I plead. "I was drunk. I didn't know what I was doing. It's not really how I felt."

"Please," Emily growls. "It's totally how you felt. I gave you so many chances to come clean. To tell me what you had done. But you didn't. Plus, you were so busy with your new, *popular* boyfriend. You would have dumped me any second."

"Emily, stop! You know that's not true!"

"Do I? I thought you were my one true friend. You betrayed me. You tried to ruin me!" She stops, regaining her composure as if she's recounting a book she'd read instead of a murder scheme. "So, I shifted. I made up the story about Harvard so you would feel bad. As bad as I felt when I got in! You would do anything *not* to have Revenge reveal your disgusting betrayal. And you fell for it. You're just like Brooke. You pretend you're not as mean and spiteful and selfish as she is—but you're *worse*."

You get what you give. I'd thought it was Charlie's phrase—but of course, Emily would have picked it up just from being around him.

"So, you knew who wanted Grant pranked. Was it because he was cheating? It wasn't with Brooke . . ."

"Of course, it wasn't with Brooke," Emily scoffs. "*I* started that rumor. I told Grace and Jason at the party. I figured it would get back to Parker. And you. But he was a cheat. They all are. And it was with your boy's girl. Tess! But I needed to keep you busy for a while."

"Emily . . ." I stare at my friend. "This isn't you."

"It isn't?" Emily cries. "I think it's *exactly* me. But maybe you don't even know who I am. It's always about *you*, Sabrina. You don't even see people around you half the time. Or if you do, it's in generalizations—*oh, she's the popular girl; oh, she's the nerd.*

"You're so wrapped up in your own problems you don't have time for me," Emily goes on, breathlessly. "You had *no idea* what I went through this summer. How heartbroken I was. Absolutely no idea."

"But you . . . you never told me about you and Finn. You never gave me a chance."

"Oh, like you would have supported it. You find so many reasons to judge people, Sabrina. It didn't feel like something I could tell either of you—and then Brooke had to go and hook up with him."

"Emily, I wasn't judging . . . I . . . I . . ." I moan.

"Please," Emily sneers. "Kissing Jeremy? The gummies? Even wanting to go to that stupid party the day Brooke ditched us? You get all high and mighty. You think you are *better* than everyone. More deserving? More special?"

I squeeze my eyes shut. "I'm sorry, Emily. I really am."

"Are you, though?" Emily asks, running her finger over the blade of the knife. "I mean, you said you were okay with me getting into Harvard. But you weren't. You said you and Jake weren't dating, but clearly you were. You TOLD REVENGE ON ME and LIED to my face. How do you think that felt? The ONE person I trusted. The ONE person who was supposed to always have my back."

Then I realize something. "Did you tell Brooke about Finn? The night of that party back in ninth grade?"

"NO! That would have been humiliating! But I told her he was an asshole. That he wouldn't be faithful to her." Emily rolls her eyes. "But she didn't listen to me. She went off with Finn anyway. So, she was dead to me from then on. Dead to *us*."

Another piece snaps into place. "It wasn't Brooke who dumped us, was it? *You* made that up."

"Please. It was going to happen anyway. I was just speeding up the process. So, I blocked her on your phone. You thought *she* blocked *you*. She thought *you* blocked *her*. Two idiots." Emily picks up the tripod. "Anyhoo, I need you to confess to poisoning Finn. That you're Revenge. That you wanted him dead."

I shake my head. "Emily, I can't do that."

"Yes, you can. It's easy. Just talk. A lie for a lie, remember?"

"But Finn isn't dead. The police will understand if we explain."

Emily crosses her arms. "I'm not explaining anything. *I'm* going to Harvard next year. I have a future. You? Well, no one will miss you."

My heart sinks like a stone, but somehow my nerves are icy steel. "Emily, no. You can't *make* me."

"Can't I?" And with that, Emily points the tip of the small knife right at the side of my neck.

twenty-three

The knife grazes my skin. I can feel the blade cutting into me. One quick swipe, and she'll sever my artery. Emily's hand is surprisingly steady. I have a terrible feeling she has no qualms about doing it.

"Start talking," Emily growls, nudging her chin toward the phone on her tripod. She presses record. "*Now.*"

"Okay, okay." I take a deep breath, but my mouth won't work; my brain won't work. I am solely focused on getting my hands free.

"Say your name," Emily whispers.

"Um, this is Sabrina Richards," I finally hear myself say. There's a long silence. Emily presses the knife in a little closer. I almost yelp.

"Finn!" I say. "I was the one." I pause for a moment, but I sense this isn't enough, because I feel the blade press even harder into my skin. I feel myself crumple inside.

"I . . . I hated him," I go on. "He took my best friend away. He was a bully. So . . . yeah. It was me."

Then I look at Emily with pleading eyes. "*Please,*" I mouth. "*Drop the knife.*"

"It's not good enough," Emily murmurs. "Your confession needs *more.*"

"More *what*?" I wiggle my bound wrists, wishing I were stronger, wishing I could break the knot. "Just tell me what to say. I'll say anything. Just let me live, Emily. We can start over. We can figure this out."

"Damn it, Sabrina!" Emily shrieks, losing it again. "You said my name! Now we have to start all over!"

It's at that moment that I finally free my hands. I roll off the seat with all my body weight, somehow knocking her to the ground. I start kicking. Hard. Finally my feet are free! Before I can gloat about being a better Girl Scout, I feel something slicing into me, eliciting the worst pain I've ever felt in my life.

We struggle—the camera on her phone still recording. It's almost comical. Neither of us really knows how to fight, but her swimming days give her more upper body weight and strength. Somehow I summon all my strength, all my might, and push her down to the ground, sending the knife careening across the shed. I make a break for the door, but she grabs me by my feet, and I trip. We struggle. She bites at my wrists. With what I think may be my final breath, I grab at the feet of the tripod and bring the camera careening down on her head.

Emily lets out a shout as a figure emerges through the door.

"Sabrina?" a voice screams desperately. A *familiar* voice. My eyelids flicker. Is that . . . *Jake?* I see a second pair of shoes, too. Beat-up sneakers. And then, I hear a voice. *Charlie!*

"Oh my God," Charlie says. He sounds sick. "Emily!" She's flailing at partial strength, but it still takes all of Charlie's strength to pin her to the ground.

Emily screeches like a wild animal. "Let go! You don't understand! *She's* the one you should be attacking! Not me! She's REVENGE!"

"Emily, *stop*!" Charlie screams. "The police are on their way."

"The police?" Emily screams.

As if on cue, I hear the sounds of sirens pulling up.

"You don't understand," she groans. "I'm the hero here. *Sabrina* is the one who hurt Finn. I have her confession!"

I hear shouts and footsteps, and the door to the shed bangs open. Two cops burst into the room and head for Emily.

"Get away from me!" Emily half-screams, half-cries.

It's hard to hear what anyone is saying. Emily is shouting for them not to touch her, Jake is yelling that Emily is dangerous, and the cops are looking at Charlie, probably wondering why he's got Emily pinned to the ground. I'm the only person not saying a word. I almost feel detached from my body, like maybe I've lost blood.

The police pull Emily up, get her on her feet, and put her hands behind her back. She isn't shouting anymore—now, silent tears spill down her cheeks. My blood has mixed with hers on her wrist.

They walk Emily from the shed to where I can't see them anymore. I hear more sirens; more officers have arrived, perhaps getting word of how serious the situation is. Meanwhile, I feel someone else's hands on my wrists, untying the knots.

"Oh, God," the third figure whispers. I feel fingers against my neck, putting pressure to stop the bleeding. "It's okay. You're going to be okay."

I look up and realize—it's Brooke. My old friend. Her panicked face swims before my eyes.

I feel another rush of lightheadedness. The room starts to spin.

"The cut doesn't seem that bad," Brooke says, looking at my neck. She glances into the yard, where the cops are dealing with Emily. I can hear Mrs. Simmons' screams but not the words she's saying. "I think you're in shock."

"Do you want to see if you can stand?" Jake asks me.

I nod as Brooke continues to put pressure on my neck. Jake finds one of the bandanas on the floor of the shed and hands it to Brooke who wraps it gently around my neck. As Jake helps me up, my knees buckle. He pulls me back up, and I find my footing.

"Sabrina, I'm so sorry," Charlie says as he approaches me. "I should have seen this coming. She's been acting so weird all break. I should have said something when you were over the other day."

"We all should have seen it," I said. And then I look at Jake, swallowing hard. "How did you know?"

"Brooke and I put the pieces together," Jake admits. "I was asking around to find out more about Revenge, and she mentioned the conversation you two had at the rink."

"Something was . . . off with you . . . but I had this weird feeling about the whole Harvard thing," Brooke said.

"You knew Emily was lying?" I gasp.

"I wasn't sure. But Jake and I went back to the school and asked Principal Morgan. He knew nothing about Emily's early admission being withdrawn. That's when we knew something was up and came over."

I bite my lip. That's all I would have had to do—check with Principal Morgan. But of course, I hadn't. I never thought Revenge would be Emily. I'd trusted Emily. Until today, there was no reason not to.

Jake says, "Then, when we got here, Charlie told us that Emily and Finn hooked up a bunch of times over the years."

"Which I thought *you* knew." Charlie looks at me. "I thought you guys told each other everything."

"I thought so, too," I say sadly.

"We all put the pieces together," Brooke goes on. "Tess had been with Grant, but I knew Finn had been with someone over the summer. Charlie told me Emily used to sneak out, and he would track her to Finn's house."

"That's why I hated him," Charlie says. "He didn't bully me. He was using my sister. I was going to say something the night of the party, and he told me he had pictures of her. Naked pictures that she sent. That she was a nutcase. I wanted to tell on him, but I didn't know who to tell. Emily swore me to secrecy."

That's who was in those pictures the night of the party. And it was Emily's picture Finn had in his locker.

"If she had told me she liked him back then," Brooke says ruefully, "I would never have dated him. Never." She pauses, then quietly adds, "Ovaries before brovaries, you know?"

I squeeze my eyes shut, thinking about all of this. Emily hiding that awful secret. Emily feeling shattered when Finn chose Brooke over her, not once but twice. And, worst of all, Emily thinking she couldn't talk to me about it. Twisting the narrative to make it seem like Brooke pushed *us* away, not the other way around. She would have hated admitting something so shameful and humiliating, thinking I would judge her.

"Anyway, we figured Emily knew you were getting too close to the truth," Jake says. "And we were right." His gaze falls to the blood on my sweater. His throat bobs as he swallows.

"There's something I need to tell you, though," he adds. "Something I think you know already. I reached out to Revenge, too. Because of Tess. That's when Revenge painted her car."

I nod, then peek at Jake. He looks wrecked.

"I shouldn't have," he says. "I should have known better. That account—it's toxic. It wasn't worth it."

"I thought Tess was cheating with Finn," I say in a small voice. "They were fighting at the party . . ."

"Yeah," Jake says. "He saw Tess flirting with me at Sketch's party. Even though we had broken up and she was with Grant. He told her to get her act together. Not to hurt me or Grant. He may have been a hypocrite, but he was trying to be a good friend to us."

"I was with her today because I was apologizing for her car," Jake says. "And because I wanted to tell her about you. But then you saw me, and I could tell by the look on your face, you thought it was me. I should have been honest with you, Sabrina. I should have told you that I'd used Revenge from the start. I just . . . I don't know. I felt ashamed."

That's a feeling I know all too well. And suddenly, I know I can't keep quiet about my own secrets. It's time.

"I used Revenge, too," I whisper. "On Emily. That's why she's so mad at me. She was right, what she was saying before. That . . . that maybe you wouldn't have wanted to rescue me if you knew."

Jake and Brooke glance at each other with barely a reaction. I realize—they already know. They figured this out.

"But that's not all," I sob.

And then the rest of it spills out of me. How Emily, as Revenge, tricked me. How I was the one who put the EnergyFX in the water bottle. Even if I wasn't the one who administered the poison. But then again, who did? Either way, I deserve to go down.

"So that's why you were looking into who Revenge was," Jake says slowly. "To save yourself?"

"Partly." I cover my face. "Probably. *Mostly.*"

"And you didn't tell me," Jake says.

"I didn't know how. I didn't know what to do." But then I realize how feeble those excuses are. I'm not taking ownership of this like I should. I still made the choice to go with Revenge's plan, all because I feared what would happen to me if I was exposed.

Brooke's shoulders are slumped. Jake's mouth is pressed into a straight line. Even Charlie seems shocked. They look disappointed. Regretful. Maybe they *are* second-guessing rescuing me or even getting involved. But weirdly, I also feel lighter than before. My secret is finally released. I did an awful, awful thing, but now it's out in the open, and I'm going to have to deal with it. At least I don't have to hide it anymore.

But then, Jake lets out a breath and exchanges a glance with Brooke I can't read. She nods faintly, and Jake walks to the camera that's still—as far as I can tell—recording every word we've said. Jake picks it up and studies the screen. There's no expression on his face as he taps the device; a little *ding* tells me he's stopped the recording. He will save it. Send it to himself. It's hard evidence. It clears up everything.

But then, he spins the phone around and shows me the screen. The tape has been erased. I blink at him, not sure I understand what he's doing.

"I'm not saying what you did was right," he says in a small voice. "And you lying to me . . . getting me involved without telling me the whole truth . . . it doesn't feel great. But I didn't tell you the whole truth either. And to be honest, I don't know what I would have done if Revenge put me in that position instead. You should have seen how Tess grilled me about her car. She knew it was a Revenge thing. She knew I was likely the one who requested it. She said she was going to turn me in—but she didn't have any real proof. Had Revenge come to *me* with blackmail like that?" He shakes his head. "I just don't know. I really don't."

I glance at Brooke. "He's your boyfriend," I say helplessly. "I would have never—if I had known—"

"I know," Brooke says, shrugging. "You couldn't have changed *that* much, Sabrina." She blows air out her cheeks. "Emily makes sense. The poison is in their backyard. It was her, Sabrina. It was her, for the most part. That's the story."

I stare at her. Then at Jake. They seem in agreement. I'm shocked, kind of. They're going to let me off. *Really?* I wonder what I've done to deserve that.

There are more footsteps outside. Jake spins around just in time to see my dad running toward the shed this time, a look of terror on his face.

"Dad?"

"Sabrina, oh my God." He rushes into the shed and grabs my wrists. His eyes widen at the gash on my neck. A hand flutters to his mouth. "I came as soon as I heard. What *happened?*"

"I'm okay," I assure him. "I'm going to be all right."

He gathers me in his arms and hugs me tight. "If I would have lost you . . . I don't know what I'd do."

I look up at my dad, realizing something. He and I are kind of in the same situation. For a while now, I've been too afraid to tell him much of anything going on in my life. I figured he was too busy dating Kaye, and that he'd rather I be a perfect daughter like Parker. I'd concealed my rejection from Harvard and my struggle to apply to the other schools—not to mention the pain of Emily getting in instead, or the temptation to use Revenge, and certainly the mess I got into with Finn. If I'd just talked to him from the start, would I be in this mess? But I knew why I hadn't—it felt like I'd failed him. And my mom. Emily won out over me, and I was so embarrassed, so *ashamed*, that I'd shoved it all under the rug and tried to handle it myself. What was I *thinking?*

Jake and Brooke duck their heads and leave the shed. Outside, I can hear the police talking to them, probably getting their side of the story. I hear Charlie's voice, too. And I hear Emily's name uttered over and over again.

"I'm sorry, Dad," I whisper. "I'm so sorry."

I feel his grip loosen on me. "You have nothing to be sorry for."

But I shake my head. I do—and he does, too. We lost each other. Mom was the glue that held us together, but we should have worked harder to be close. I hadn't let him in, but he hadn't really let me in, either. Not the way we should have.

I have to tell him, I realize. I have to tell him about Finn and Revenge and all of it just like I told Jake and Brooke. There are probably ways around it.

The cops won't believe Emily about setting me up to kill Finn. It's her word against mine, and Charlie's, and even Finn and Brooke's. Everyone is gunning for Revenge these days. I could keep my mouth shut, pretend I had no part in it, act like I'd stumbled upon information I shouldn't have, and that was that. But it wouldn't solve anything with my dad. We wouldn't grow. There would still be huge secrets between us.

I have to tell him.

I wriggle from his grip and look up at him, my body suddenly filling with fear. He frowns. "What is it, Sabrina? What?"

I swallow hard. But I know I can do it.

I have to set it all free. And for the first time in so many years, I cry. I cry like a baby. And somehow, I've never felt better.

twenty-four

The morning of graduation is sticky and hot. The weather is so sweltering that the staff decides to hold the ceremony indoors in the huge gym with the state-of-the-art basketball court. There's some pause with this decision. After all, the gym is where *it* happened—not even that long ago. Some calls were made. Some hoops were jumped through. In the end, Finn's family gave permission. Apparently, his mom didn't want to, but it was Finn who finally voted yes. He kind of made fun of the situation, saying he had absolutely no memory of the basketball game at all—so he had no trauma from it.

"It's the rest of you that're all messed up from that night," he said. "I'm all good."

Finn isn't good, though. I mean, he's alive, and he's out of the hospital—but his life is changed. There's no basketball in his future. The poison messed with some of his organs, and he has to take medication. Rumor has it he has memory problems and some neurological damage, and his poor parents are a total mess. But there are some improvements, too. Finn seems kinder now. Gentler. I don't forgive a lot of his actions, but I don't think he knew the pain he caused so many people. He's taken some amusing and vulnerable pictures of himself at the hospital—getting help from nurses, struggling to walk, goofing around in a wheelchair. I don't want to say the experience has been good for him, but it's definitely been humbling.

Brooke isn't surprised, though. She says she's pretty sure that deep down, Finn wasn't that crazy about basketball by senior year, so it came as almost a blessing.

"Like, he was doing it because he was good at it, and his parents were thrilled by the idea that it would get him a full ride to college, but he didn't love it like he used to," she told me.

It was one of those things he begged her not to tell anyone, though. Especially not his parents or his coaches—they had so much hope for him. Everyone just expected him to keep playing basketball, so that's what he did. Funny how we sometimes just fit ourselves neatly into the boxes our parents and teachers and coaches have created for us. Funny to think that *Finn*, of all people, was going through the same sort of pressure that I was.

Not that Brooke knows for *sure*, of course. She and Finn haven't talked in a while. About a week after Finn woke up—which was a few days after Emily was arrested—Brooke broke it off with him. She had to tell him at his hospital bed. Finn wasn't surprised. He knew, by then, that Emily was Revenge—and why Emily wanted to hurt him. He knew Brooke knew he and Emily fooled around. He knew he needed some time to sort himself out.

It wasn't easy for Brooke to break up with him, though. Not because, as I used to assume, Finn was Brooke's ticket to popularity, and she was a nobody without him—Brooke genuinely cared about Finn. They were, she told me, best friends, as unlikely as that seemed. She hated going her separate way, but at the same time, everything that happened seemed kind of insurmountable. Not just that he'd cheated, but that he'd cheated with Brooke's old friend. Over. And over.

I asked Brooke if Finn had an excuse for why he'd fooled around with Emily in the first place. She shrugged. "I think she was good for his ego. I was hard on him sometimes. I kept him in line. And . . . I stuck to our pact . . . No sex till prom . . . and I think he was . . . a little frustrated. From what Grant told me, Emily was always throwing herself at him."

"I didn't realize Finn needed an ego boost," I said.

Brooke gave me a level look. "Finn's deeply insecure. He just hides it better than most people."

Brooke and I have been hanging out more. And after a little bit of time licking our own wounds over the lies we told each other, Jake and I have gotten closer, too.

On the morning of graduation, I get a FaceTime from Brooke, bright and early. I groan and pick up the phone on the fourth ring.

"I was sleeping."

"Which dress should I wear?" Brooke chirps. "I'm sending photos."

"You need *my* opinion? I'm not exactly an OG fashion icon."

"Will you shut up? I'm sending them now."

A few moments later, photos of Brooke in two different dresses appear. I choose a pale-yellow midi dress with thick straps.

Good, Brooke writes. *That's the one I liked better, too.*

I smile. It's nice to be talking to Brooke again. What we both went through with Emily brought us closer. Most days, we'd find each other at school, chat between classes. It's never about anything that deep, but it's been nice to have the company, especially in the past few months. I think Brooke takes pity on me. I know a lot of people don't understand why she talks to me at all. Even though no one really knows I was involved, being known as "the Psycho's" best friend made me even more of a weirdo. I had wanted to come totally clean, but Charlie, Brooke, and Jake all felt it would just confuse things. Especially since we no longer had Emily on tape saying my bottle only had EnergyFX and not the ricin poison.

And hanging between us, in every conversation, is Emily's ghost. I mean, not literally—Emily is still alive, in a mental health facility attached to a juvenile correctional facility—but still. It's obvious we're both always thinking about her and what happened.

It's strange to think Emily drove a wedge between Brooke and me *and*, in a weird way, brought us back together. We don't talk about that day in Emily's shed. Brooke cared enough to drop what she was doing and save me. *Me*. We weren't even friends anymore, and she did that anyway. She's a way better person than I give her credit.

There's also that I confessed something huge to her and she didn't turn around and tell on me. She could have. Maybe she *should* have. It was her boyfriend I'd hurt. But she didn't. Deep down, I think she wanted Emily to be the one who was fully blamed for what happened to Finn. It was her own little Revenge plot, kind of. Maybe because of how Emily had cheated with

Finn. And maybe because her heart was broken . . . and she wanted Emily to pay.

But we definitely *don't* talk about Emily. Like I said, she looms large between us, but neither of us know how to talk about her. I think we're both also afraid of what happened to her. Me, because it happened while we were friends, and I didn't see it. Brooke, because it was her boyfriend who'd hurt her. And that Emily deliberately drove a wedge between us. It's hard to wrap our minds around that. We both also carry the memory around of how unhinged Emily was on that last day—and that's too scary to talk about, too. A few times, Brooke has asked me if I've seen Emily in the psychiatric hospital. I've thought about it, but I'm not sure Emily would want me to come.

I roll out of bed and look at my own choice of dress for today's graduation: a simple white dress with cap sleeves. My dad and I bought it together. Months ago, he would have just sent me to the mall with his credit card, but I can tell he's doing his best to be more involved. When I think back, it wasn't all his fault. After my mom died, I never let him in. I never let anyone in. I was so set on guarding myself against being hurt that I hurt myself even more. Even Emily. We were best friends, but we never really knew each other.

There's a knock on my door, and my dad pokes his head in—as if on cue.

"Oh good, you're up," he says, smiling. His gaze drifts to the dress on the hanger. Next to it is a hanger with my cap and gown. His mouth flickers. "You ready?"

I turn away so I don't meet his gaze. "I still don't know if I deserve to do this."

My dad gives me a level look as if to say *no more of that.* Then he remembers something and reaches for his pocket. "This came."

He hands me a letter. It's thin and has my name on the front. My stomach flips over, and I can't help comparing this moment to the last time a letter came for me—my rejection from Harvard. It's a peculiar full circle, not one I would have ever expected. And when I tear it open, it's an acceptance instead. Though not from Harvard. Far, *far* from Harvard.

I show him the letter from the Golden Horizons, a charity program in town that works with at-risk teens, especially those with mental health issues.

We are pleased to tell you that you have been accepted into the counselor-in-training program, it reads.

My smile broadens. "They want me! This was my first choice!"

"Of course, they do," my dad says, pulling me into his arms. "Congratulations."

A year ago, I would have been confused—mortified, even—that this was going to be my future for the next year. Interning at a support group *here in town*? See, even though Brooke didn't sell me out, and even though my dad didn't know what to do with my confession about Finn, I decided I needed to take some time to put some good in the world. And I needed to make sure that I was going to the right school for the right reasons. Not because of a name or someone else's dream.

Maybe someday this will make a great college essay, but not for a little while. I need to untangle my toxic thinking about college first. I need to disassociate where I'm accepted from my sense of self-worth. I need to do something for me. Not my mom. It's okay I didn't get into Harvard, and I need to keep telling myself that. Being rejected doesn't make me any less smart or special. It's just college. It's just one school. It's just one opinion.

My mom's life was her own. And so is mine. After a lot of work, I've come to realize my mother's death was not my fault. And trying to control everything in your life doesn't create good things or prevent bad ones from happening.

I read through the details of my letter for the counseling program again. I'm grateful they want me. I'm hopeful what I've gone through will help someone else. I hope I can learn counseling skills—maybe it'll even be a springboard for a career. Mostly, it'll be nice to have something to do with my time. Without the stress of academics and college admissions, I've been making up for lost time, making some new friends, hanging out, even going to parties. But I'm definitely not drinking.

Then, to my surprise, my dad hands me a second envelope.

"And, um, this is for you too."

This envelope has no return address, just my name on the front in familiar printing. *Really* familiar. I look up at him, a lump suddenly in my throat.

"Is this . . . from *Mom*?"

My dad's eyes turn down at the corners. He nods. "Yup. We both wrote you some letters when you were born in case, we weren't there for the import- ant times. This is the first one. We meant to write others—one for every year of your birthday, I think—but . . ." he trails off.

The envelope is pristine, like it's been kept well-preserved in the seven years since Mom left us. The day of my graduation. It meant so much to her. I bite my lip, once again feeling that I've failed her, but then I swish the thought from my mind.

I slice the envelope open with my nail. When I see my mother's hand- writing on the paper inside, my heart clenches. It's like she's with me again. Then I start to read.

> **My dearest Sabrina,**
>
> *Congratulations on graduating high school. If you're reading this, it means I'm not there to share it with you, and just saying that breaks my heart.*
>
> *Please know that whatever you decide to do in your life, it is enough. I spent so much of my life mourning that I was not able to attend a silly school. But if I had, I might not have met your father, or had you—the two greatest loves and joys of my life. I had everything I needed to make my life happy and fulfilling. I know that fully with 100 percent of my heart. Sometimes achievement isn't everything. It's not about what you think others want or prize. Sometimes trying to be the best comes at too great a cost. You are a shining star just as you are, no matter how well you do, no matter what your future plans are. You don't have to know everything right now. You don't even have to know anything right now!*
>
> *All I ask is that you try to put kindness into the world. Help others. Try to leave the world a little better than you found it.*
>
> *Listen to your heart, not all the noise that will swirl around you in life. Take joy in the good moments. Know that you have the strength to get through the bad. That is truly the greatest definition of success.*

And remember I love you so much, my baby. Always know that. I am always here, with you.

Forever,
Mom

I can't get through the letter without crying. I've become a veritable fountain these days. And with a laugh, I shove it toward my dad so he can read it next. Tears come to his eyes, too, and he grips my hand hard.

"I miss her so much," he says.

"Same," I sigh.

We look at each other, but I don't know what to say. I resort to the fail-safe reaction I've been using lately—to make a joke. I hold up the precious letter.

"Wish I'd read this *before* I got rejected from Harvard."

And just like that, we're both laughing—or crying—or maybe both.

• • •

Graduation doesn't give me the thrill everyone always talks about. We're crowded in the gym, sitting on uncomfortable folding chairs, looking kind of stupid in our caps and gowns. Our parents are crammed into the bleachers. And the sound from the microphone echoes in strange ways. The valedictorian is Ryan Farber, who was always neck-and-neck with me in terms of grades. I feel some of my peers turn to me when he goes up to speak, their eyes saying—*that could have been you.* I also notice some people looking shocked that I'm here at graduation at all. I just keep my head down. Neither opinion is wrong.

The speeches are boring, the gym is airless and sweltering, and I can feel sweat gathering at the small of my back, but it's not a panic attack. In fact, I haven't had one since everything happened in the shed.

Our names are called in a rush, like the teachers are just trying to get through it as fast as possible. It feels like I'm the only one who notices where Emily's name is supposed to be—and that it isn't called. Brooke's name gets a lot of cheers, and she waves to the audience as she collects her diploma. I hear my father clapping for me, but I rush to grab my diploma before everyone can register I'm even on the stage. Finn gets a huge round of applause. He walks slowly to the podium, wincing as he climbs the steps, but then gives the crowd a grandiose wave of his arms.

And then, it's over. Out on the lawn, kids are smooshing together for photos they'll surely Instagram in minutes. It makes me feel lonely. Without Emily, I don't really have anyone to celebrate with—sure, the inroads I've made with Brooke are nice, but she has her own group of friends. So, I put my head down and search for my dad. It's better just to get out of here. Go home, hide, regroup. I've graduated, which is a gift. Now I need to forget this year happened. Start over . . . eventually.

But then, I feel a hand on my arm and an arm go around me. When I turn, I see Jake. He's in a light-pink button-down shirt, fitted khakis, and Vans. "Congratulations," he murmurs, kissing me on the cheek.

"Thanks."

I feel my cheeks redden. It's still weird for me to have a sort of boyfriend. I was embarrassed that I suspected him. And when he was willing to trust me again, I had to take the leap and do the same.

As much as you might think all of this had pushed me deeper into my shell, it's had the opposite effect. I've realized that as much as you try to color code, organize, clean, or shut yourself off, life will bring on the unexpected. And leaning on others can soften whatever blows might happen. I've become friendly with some of Jake's friends, and Jake also has befriended Charlie, who stayed home for the rest of the semester to lend support to his mom and Emily. Charlie, Brooke, Jake, and I have been hanging out a lot. Sometimes including others, sometimes on our own. There's no OGs versus losers, nothing more than trying to know individuals for who they are.

Next to me, another graduate sweeps past, her gown billowing. I catch sight of Finn across the lawn, too. He's sitting on a bench while his parents gather around him. He isn't able to stand for long periods of time, I've been told. Not that I know firsthand. Finn and I haven't spoken. But we're all so mixed up together, after all—him, me, Emily, Brooke. Finn has to know that. Sometimes, I'll see him glancing my way in the school halls, that sort of thing. I sent him a note before he came back to school. It wasn't a confession, but it was my own version of an apology. At the end of the day, I really am to blame. I would love to know how he's doing, *really*. But it's not my place to ask.

As I look at him, I catch his eye. I wonder if the panic will come back; this is the time it would. But it doesn't. My heart is sad but more at peace these days, and my body seems to know that.

Finn looks at me and gives the faintest smile. It's not exactly warm, but it's a far cry from the steely gaze I would have expected. Holding my gaze, he tilts his head as if to say, "It's okay, we both screwed up, and we'll both get through this." At least, that's how I'm reading it.

"What now?" I ask Jake; it's unlike me not to have a plan.

"I think my mom and your dad said something about lunch," he offers.

"Perfect," I say softly. My dad and Kaye are taking a break. He says he wants to focus on me.

Jake smiles. "Great, I'll go grab my mom."

Just as Jake turns to walk away, I hear his phone ping. And mine. There is an echo of pings all around us. I watch in slow motion as smiling graduates and students pull out their phones. As I do, I feel a strange sense of dread. And as my phone illuminates, I see why.

> **@Revenge** has made a new post.

I click on the button taking me to the screen. There, in a black square . . . the number *1*.

reading group guide

1. Sabrina's relationship to her late mother is complex. How did that relationship affect her connections with others, such as her father, Kaye, and Emily? How did her view of her mother change by the end of the story?

2. Milford High has a common social hierarchy in which the OGs reign at the top. How are the narratives of high school stereotypes shown to be inadequate depictions of the characters in *A Lie for a Lie*?

3. An unreliable narrator is a storyteller who either deliberately or unintentionally misrepresents the depiction of events. Are Sabrina and Emily unreliable narrators? How do their perceptions of issues in their lives, like college admissions or relationships, cloud their judgment and cause them to seek their own justice? If any, which of their actions are justified?

4. Teenagers face a lot of stress these days. College admissions have been a point of motivation, stress, identity, and pride for generations. For each character in the novel, what does getting into the college of their choice mean for them? Why do you think Sabrina made the decision not to go to college yet? Do you think it was the right choice, and why?

5. Project into the future. What options does Sabrina have after the counselor-in-training program? She has different goals now; do you think she will need to go to college to reach them? Does it matter which college?

6. A red herring in mystery is defined as a misleading clue or detail that diverts attention from the real culprit. What were the red herrings in this novel? Did any of them mislead you as the reader?

7. When the truth of who Revenge was came to light, were you surprised? Why?

8. How did Revenge evade Sabrina, the school, and officials? What advantages did Sabrina have in her investigation that allowed her to discover the truth before anyone else?

9. Discuss the use of social media to enact and publicize Revenge's actions. Do you think social media encourages negative mindsets and behaviors that result in real-life consequences? Does social media contribute to or alleviate the pressures placed on teenagers? Could you see an @Revenge existing?

10. The resulting consequences of Revenge's pranks increase in severity over the course of the book. Do you think any of Revenge's actions were beneficial or justifiable? When did the pranks start to change for the worse and for what reason?

11. Shame and guilt are big themes that are explored in this book. They are what rope Sabrina into helping Revenge in the plot against Finn and then are what stop her from going to the police. Do you think you would have confessed to your best friend for betraying them rather than go along with Revenge's scheme? Once Sabrina found out that she had a hand in Revenge's murder attempt, do you think she should have confessed to the police? Would you have?

12. How does the concept of revenge differ from that of justice? Why do you think the Revenge account was so popular at Milford High School and so many people turned to Revenge for help? Were they wrong to do so?

13. Sabrina experienced a trauma at a young age. How does that event and the subsequent coping mechanisms she developed affect her choices and actions as a teenager?

14. In her investigation, Sabrina discovers that many of the people she trusts the most are hiding secrets. How well do you think we can actually know the people we're close to?

15. Who do you think could be behind the @Revenge post at the end of the novel?

author q&a

What inspired you to write a young adult mystery? Are there any books or writers in particular that you took inspiration from?

Well, when I was twenty-one, I was in the middle of writing a YA novel that was actually going to be published when my mom died very suddenly. It was a really difficult time for me for a lot of reasons. I found it hard to sit and write and be alone with my thoughts, so I stopped and never finished it.

I've had a lot of ups and downs in the last few years, and one of the silver linings was that it made me reflect on myself and my life and resolve a lot of undealt with issues. In doing that (it's an ongoing process), I found I was better able to sit alone with my thoughts at a computer. So, I started with a new story, one based (loosely) on a real incident at a school near me.

I love reading YAs. I find they don't try very hard to be something they are not. I was also a huge fan of Pretty Little Liars and all of Sara Shephard's books. Her books make even the most hateable characters likeable, and I personally think that no one is all good or all bad. I wanted to write a book that showed that it is hard to be a young adult but offered a great fun ride along the way.

Did you have to do any research to write the novel? Did you interview anyone to portray realistic twenty-first century teens?

In my "day" job as a trend forecaster and researcher, I am lucky to get to spend a lot of time with young people. I also have a twenty-two-year-old son and a twenty-year-old daughter, and their friends are always around. I never think that I truly "know" young people, but I do try very hard to present them in an authentic way. I think people too often stereotype teens and typically in a negative way, and I really don't want to do that.

What gave you the idea to write a story about an anonymous figure who seeks revenge for others?
I think, sadly, we've all seen how easy it is to say awful things when it's anonymous online and how much anger there is among people today. And that just keeps escalating. I think so many people think about "getting even," but most people don't do anything. But when you have the opportunity to have someone else decide if a revenge is worthy, maybe you don't feel as culpable. Our Revenge starts off harmless and embarrasses the offenders, but then as the acts of Revenge get darker, it goes from pranks to a real problem.

Why did you choose to have social media play such a big role in this story? Do you think social media exaggerates the pressures that teenagers already deal with?
I think it's hard to ignore the huge role social media plays in everyone's lives today and especially among young people. I think there are some great things about social media. It allows you to stay in touch with people you might not otherwise. It exposes us to lots of information and people and places we may never have known.

I *do*, however, think that social media amplifies some of the hardest things about being a teenager. Being a teen, even without social media, is challenging. It's a time when you are physically and emotionally changing, trying to figure out who you are and who you want to be, and attempting to navigate pressures around you. Social media amplifies all of that. It gives the voices, opinions, and perceived lives of others a much bigger role than they might have without social media. It presents a view of life that isn't real. It's everyone's best moments, not everyone's daily ups and downs. It allows people to feel extremely loved but also extremely torn down. It's hard enough to not feel left out, inferior, or pressured to present a "positive" view of one's life as an "adult." For a teen, it's particularly challenging.

Sabrina's response to trauma is very realistic. Is her fixation on order, control, and self-reliance something you can relate to or something you've seen someone else use as a coping mechanism?

There is certainly some of me in Sabrina. When my mother died very suddenly, I was shocked, sad, angry, scared. I felt like I had no control over anything and that at any moment something horrible and unexpected could happen again. I think trying to create order and gain a sense of control were ways that I dealt with it. I needed to believe I could control life around me so that I could avoid that pain again. I think becoming self-reliant is another way we deal with loss, whether it's death or the end of an important relationship in our lives. Being self-reliant means other people can't let you down or disappear. But it also means you close yourself off to letting other people in.

And while my reaction was caused by death, I think a lot of people—especially young people—use these mechanisms to deal with all of the stress and pressure they are under today. Yet it's a lot for a young person to expect of themselves. And as we learn, control is an illusion.

Events in *A Lie for a Lie* are (hopefully) a dramatized version of a high schooler's life. What were you like in high school, and what similar things did you experience to the characters in the novel?

While I think the acts of Revenge are a very dramatized version, I think much of the rest is kind of accurate. It really is stressful being a teenager today. There is so much pressure, stress, exposure to things you shouldn't have to experience at a young age, and more.

As for me, I was a bit like Sabrina in that I worked very hard and getting good grades was very important to me. But my best friend was NOT like Emily, and we did go out and have a pretty big social life. My parents were divorced, and my mom was nothing like Emily's mom or Sabrina's dad. Plus, I grew up in New York City, which is, in my opinion, a really different way to grow up.

Do you have a favorite character in the story? If so, what aspect of that character do you most admire?

Picking a favorite character is like picking a favorite child! I genuinely love them all the same amount but in different ways! I really tried to make the characters more than the typical teen stereotype. I think people are far more multidimensional than we like to think, and I believe, especially with teens, we like to try to "define" them. Without giving it away, I will say I like writing villains. I want us to see that no one is all good and no one is all evil. I am also really excited about some of the characters who were more minor in this book but take on a bigger role in the next!

Are any characters in the story based on a real-life people?

Yes and no. There are traits in each character that started with real people, but no character is really one real person. It's more like a real person—or what I think I know about that real person—is a launching pad for a character. Other times, characters are just a glimmer of someone I knew.

How long did it take you to write the novel, and what was your process like?

I knew writing fiction would be a lot harder than my experiences writing nonfiction. My previous books (The Modern Girl's Guide series) were like doing a really long research report. I could take a section and write it in thirty minutes because it was more "fact based." But with fiction, you can just sit there staring at your computer and find you have hit a wall and have nothing to write. Because I had a full-time job while I was writing, I had to write mostly at nights and on the weekends. And sometimes I wouldn't write for a few weeks. But I found I was always thinking about the book and the characters and trying to come up with plot ideas that people would really like.

I didn't tell anyone I was writing it because I wasn't sure if I COULD finish it, or whether it would be any good.

For me it was like trying to run a marathon but without actually training to do it! But in the end, I did it!

How do you get in the mood to write? Is there anything in particular that helps you stay focused? Do you have any writing rituals, for example?

Well, as someone who likes to be organized and in control, I would literally clean the entire house, organize every closet and cupboard to avoid writing. The best-selling author Kate White gave me the best advice, which was to set a timer for twenty-five minutes and promise myself not to do anything for that time period (no texts, no playing with the dog, no re-alphabetizing the spice rack) until it rang. Then take a ten-minute break. That allowed me not to feel as much pressure or feel like I would spend hours sitting at a blank screen. And I found with that freedom sometimes the timer would go off and I wouldn't want to stop! But when I did, I would take a ten-minute break and then start again.

If someone came to you for advice on how to get started writing, what would you tell them? What is the best—and the worst—advice you've ever gotten about writing?

The best advice I got was to write an outline of my story from beginning to end. Which I didn't do. And so, I wound up writing pages and pages that I eventually had to cut because they weren't going anywhere. When I finally DID write an outline, I found the process of writing so much easier because I knew where I was trying to go.

The worst advice I got was to "just write." Because when you have writer's block or you don't know where your story is going or you are working, you feel like you should be able to "just write." But that's a little like saying "just fly a plane." You have to start smaller. You have to learn and make some mistakes before you "fly."

Did you already know who Revenge would be when you started writing the story? Why did you choose that character specifically?

In fact, I *changed* who Revenge was about halfway through writing the book. (Like I said, probably should have taken the advice of writing an outline!) But as I wrote my original idea, I realized I had a more complex and interesting one. I had to then change SO much to make it work, but I was so glad I did. Now I can't imagine Revenge having been anyone else!

What were some challenges you faced in setting up the story to keep building the suspense, leave clues, and not give away who Revenge is?

It's hard when YOU know who did it and you know what the clues mean, not to feel like you are making things too obvious! I hate it in books when I figure things out early because it's so much more fun to be taken on a ride where you don't know! On the other hand, I really hate it when at the end the person who did it comes out of nowhere so you could NEVER have figured it out. So, I had several people whom I trust and who would give me real criticism, read the book to see what they found too obvious and to make sure the payoff was satisfying.

What was your favorite part about writing this book? Were there any particular chapters or scenes that were the most fun to write? The most difficult?

Once I really knew my story and how I wanted to get there, it was a lot of fun trying to make it happen. It was like putting together a model airplane; I knew I had to take my time to make it stay together, but I was also super impatient to see what the end result would look like.

I found writing the romance parts kind of challenging because this certainly wasn't a rom-com and I didn't want to make it seem like one. I also really wanted to make sure I didn't make the characters feel cliché.

Did any part of writing this book surprise you? Did you learn anything about the process or about yourself?

I think what I learned most about myself was that I could finally be at peace with myself. I could sit and stare at the screen and not have thoughts and feelings that I couldn't handle run through my mind and make me feel like I needed to escape them.

I hoped that the book would get to have an audience, but I was really writing to see if I could do it. In the same way people train for a marathon but aren't trying to "win," I was writing but not trying to make a bestseller. I had given up on myself and the belief that I could write a novel for so long. And for many of the past years I felt vulnerable, unworthy, scared, and small. I didn't trust my own judgment. I was afraid. Writing helped me remember that I wasn't my own worst thoughts about myself. I was able to accomplish something . . .

Photo by Sean Scheidt

about the author

Jane Buckingham is the founder and CEO of Trendera, a marketing and trend forecasting company, and is one of the world's leading experts on Generations X, Y, and Z.

Prior to starting Trendera, Buckingham helped pioneer the trend forecasting field by creating the youth marketing and consulting firm Youth Intelligence and *The Cassandra Report* in 1996, both of which she sold to Creative Artists Agency in 2003.

At seventeen, Buckingham wrote the book *Teens Speak Out* to help explain her generation. She was featured on *The Oprah Winfrey Show*, the *Today* show, and many others.

Jane is the bestselling author of the Modern Girl's Guide book series and starred in the TV show of the same name. Buckingham has been a contributing editor to *Glamour* and *Cosmopolitan*.

Though this is her first piece of fiction, writing a YA thriller has been a lifelong goal. Jane lives in Los Angeles with her son, Jack, and daughter, Lilia, as well as their dog, Ghost, and cat, Mable, and has no interest in revenge.